Counter Identity

By

Karl Braungart

Book 2

The Remmich/Miller Series

ISBN 13: 9780985219383

Dedication

This novel is dedicated to the US Army for teaching me to use the values instilled in me, including a belief in education and the need to plan to accomplish my goals. Although I was in just one branch of the US Armed Forces, I learned it is because of group efforts that we are and will remain a nation that epitomizes a thriving democracy.

2

The Offer

It was the last encryption seminar at Patch Barracks, in Stuttgart. The V Corps' headquarters instructors finished the advanced military intelligence workshop covering coding, decoding, and vocabulary translation. Lieutenant General Ed Sutherland, the CO, arrived with his entourage to shake hands and award certificates. At the end of the meeting, a G-1 administrative sergeant walked into the room. He read off names and departure times for those flying back to North Africa and the Middle East. The Army scheduled the attendees to leave by troop bus to the airport after lunch.

The MP guard station was busy at noon. Cars were in line to enter the Army post. A green van stopped at the station; the Russians used a different vehicle this time. The contractor's papers weren't registered for work that day. The MP told the driver, Nikulin, to go to the guard shack to fill out papers before he could be approved to enter. After what happened to the two CID soldiers, V Corps ordered strict inspection of non-registered vehicles and people. Irritated, Nikulin parked the van next to a troop bus. He and his partner had disguised themselves again. This time, Nikulin's natural dark blond hair was dyed black. They waited in line. When their turn arrived, the MP gruffly asked for identification and the purpose of their visit. Nikulin explained they needed to examine electrical work done at a circuit box installed by their company.

In reality, the chair rails in 205 and 207 were what they wanted to look at.

The MP's obnoxious manner didn't sit well. Nikulin's passenger bristled when the soldier ridiculed them for thinking they could enter the base without proper papers. Leaning over to appear to read a page pinned to the bottom of a bulletin board, the Russian reached into his satchel and dropped a small package into the trash

Dedication

This novel is dedicated to the US Army for teaching me to use the values instilled in me, including a belief in education and the need to plan to accomplish my goals. Although I was in just one branch of the US Armed Forces, I learned it is because of group efforts that we are and will remain a nation that epitomizes a thriving democracy.

Books by Karl Braungart

For maximum enjoyment, read the series in the following order:

Lost Identity

Counter Identity

Fatal Identity

Principal Characters & Locations

Paul Stanley Remmich – American citizen, grew up in England. West Point graduate. Stationed at 32nd Security Intelligence (S-2), Hindenburg Kaserne, Würzburg, Germany

Eric Miller – West Point graduate. Works in U.S. Army military intelligence. Stationed at 32nd Security Intelligence (S-2), Hindenburg Kaserne, Würzburg, Germany

Lilly Remmich – Paul Remmich's wife. Manages Schiller Hotel in Amsterdam, which is owned by her parents

Candice Harper – Graduated from USAF Academy '97. Employed by Delta Airlines. Eric Miller's girlfriend

Lieutenant General Ed Sutherland – Graduated from Citadel Academy. Commander, V Corps at USAREUR (United States European Command), Patch Barracks, Stuttgart

Major General Gerald Elliott – West Point graduate. Stationed at Patch Barracks, Stuttgart, Germany (G-2)

Colonel Joseph Collins – Commanding officer at 32nd Security Intelligence, Hindenburg Kaserne, Würzburg, Germany

Major Tom McKinsey – Second in command at CIC (Army Counter-intelligence Corps)

First Sergeant Ed Randolph – Head of non-commissioned force at 32nd Security Intelligence (S-2), Hindenburg Kaserne

Master Sergeant Terry McClain – Security office assistant at 32nd Security Intelligence (S-2), Hindenburg Kaserne

Diane Elliott – General Elliott's wife. Lives in Stuttgart with him

Oskars Linkov – Russian ambassador in Washington, DC

Yury Nikulin – Russian spy

Arif Yildiz – Major, Iraqi Tariq'Allah, and chargé d'affaires in the city of Istanbul, Turkey

Adnaw Alzuhari – Captain in Iraqi Secret Service. Works for Major Yildiz

Tara Yako – Iraqi Secret Service, works with Alzuhari

Faisal Mustafa, DDS – Iraqi chief of dental surgery at Leighton Barracks

Iyad Aboona – Iraqi Secret Service, works for Major Yildiz

Pedro Sola – Field officer in Cuba

Colonel Victor Hatch – Psychiatrist

General Phillip Thomson, MD – head of the hospital at V Corps

Leighton Barracks – CIC (Army Counterintelligence Corps) offices, Würzburg, Germany (S-2)

CID—*Criminal Investigative Division*

Patch Barracks – V Corps, USAREUR, Stuttgart, Germany (G-2)

INSCOM – (U.S. Army Intelligence Security Command), Ft. Belvoir, Virginia

Hindenburg Kaserne – 32nd Security Intelligence offices (S-2), Würzburg, Germany

Table of Contents

1
Murders

Two Russian SVR agents rode in a van marked *Schmidt Sanitärfirma*, identifying it as a plumbing business. They'd stopped behind two vehicles at the US Army MI (military intelligence) V Corps base at Patch Barracks, in Stuttgart. One of the cars in front belonged to Paul Remmich, an American former military intelligence officer raised in England, now a civilian. The MPs noted his BMW's Army license plate and the US government sticker inside at the upper left of the windshield. Remmich didn't return their salute before he drove on base.

Captain Paul Remmich was in his early 30s, with short blond hair he kept neatly parted. At 6'1", he maintained a trim physique, and his sky blue eyes reflected intelligence, as well as a sometimes-cheeky British sense of humor.

Right now, however, those eyes were focused on his mission. He'd resigned from the US Army months ago because he didn't approve of the UN withdrawal. It was during a time when the United States agreed with the UN to reduce aid to Third World countries. It was a coincidence a spy associated with the underground organization known as Tariq'Allah ("the Shining Star of God"), found him at the height of his dissatisfaction with his country's policies. He wasn't the Iraqis' original target. His Army friend was the one they initially sought. Remmich inadvertently drank a beer laced with Rohypnol, a sedating drug. Fortunately for the beautiful spy who set the trap, he equaled his friend in military intelligence information. He was not only qualified to do the job, but in the right place at the right time. He was drugged and hypnotized into becoming their tool.

The Foreign Intelligence Service agents were on duty to verify he was carrying out his assigned task. The senior agent had followed Remmich for months after finding out what the Iraqis planned. The Russians wanted to be sure they got access to any information Remmich acquired for the Iraqis, like the first top-secret document Remmich confiscated dealing with solar energy production.

They pulled up to the gate and stopped. Looking stern, an MP used an electronic scanner to verify the van's windshield ID sticker. The MP compared the number to a list of companies permitted to work on base. Although it was a weekend, the gate guard stood at attention and motioned for them to go ahead. The order sheet said it was an emergency. Luckily for the Russians, neither had to speak to the MP. Their accents might have made him suspicious.

The men smiled and sighed with relief, then drove on at the posted speed, watching Remmich walk into the building. Yury Nikulin parked the van. He lifted a wheeled tool bag out of the van's rear cargo section, and his assistant closed the doors. After extending the handle, they walked into the building housing the headquarters. Remmich finished speaking to a charge of quarters (CQ) security guard and walked up the stairs, carrying a rolled-up blueprint. Several sections of the headquarters building weren't renovated entirely. He needed to verify the receiver-transmitter devices he'd placed were still intact

and the antennas were secured under the chair rail.

The Russians also walked up to the CQ, and Nikulin explained they had a work order to inspect the finished plumbing work in the upstairs latrines. This guard wasn't concerned about his accent, thinking he was just another of the many foreigners working in Germany. Nikulin handed the CQ the clipboard with an order form showing specific plumbing areas needing inspection. They cringed as the CQ opened their tool bag and lifted out some tools, but he didn't search thoroughly. The spy asked if they could use the elevator to the second floor because the bag was so heavy. The guard's face puckered as he dropped the heavy tools back into the bag and gave permission to use the elevator. The doors opened, and they went up to the next level.

Outside, two Criminal Investigative Division (CID) soldiers noticed the van in the parking lot. The higher-ranked officer said, "I didn't know they worked on weekends." Since the vehicle was in the headquarters lot, they assumed the plumbers were inside. The front windshield had a legitimate sticker.

Somewhat suspicious, they entered the building. The CQ told them the plumbers were on the second floor. They walked upstairs and noticed the workmen watching someone in the corridor. When the Russians saw the CID guys, they quickly went into the men's latrine. The officers ignored them and focused on the person in conference room 205. He appeared to be examining the wall. As they walked in, Remmich was bent over while moving his hand under the chair rail. Sounds of footsteps distracted him. When he stood up to face them, they noticed the Army ID card with his photograph attached to a lanyard. He tried not to act defensive, but he knew Saturday construction work was forbidden.

Remmich smiled and said politely, "Good morning, gentlemen. I'm here to examine the status of this renovation." He pointed toward the studded walls. "As you can see, it's almost finished." The higher-ranked soldier asked to look at the plans. They walked over to the table and looked at the drawing. They saw the words "US Army Corps of Engineers" on the blueprint. Satisfied, they said goodbye and walked out. Remmich went to the door and watched them go into the latrine. He heard muffled voices after the door closed.

The CID official said to the Russians, "I didn't know contractors worked on weekends. Why are you two here today?"

"The work in here is finished," said the other official. "What are you going to do?"

Nikulin's grey eyes grew sharp, but he recovered control of himself and said, "We have to inspect these new connecting pipes to the sinks and the toilets." He pointed to the drain lines under the sinks.

The accent made these officers curious. The lower-ranked officer said, "Show me your worksheets." He expected to see their names on the approved contract, indicating their authorization to be there.

Meanwhile, the other Russian rummaged through the tool bag, pretending to ignore the officers. He removed tools to show he was preparing to work. The next item he put his hand on was a 9mm pistol with a silencer. The officer looked at the paperwork again, but it wasn't dated. He got indignant and demanded to see identification. Nikulin's heavy eyebrows knitted as he pretended to search for his wallet, giving his partner the opportunity to pull the trigger twice. Both CID agents fell to the floor.

Remmich heard two pops, then the muffled talking resumed. He didn't want to go into the latrine, so he stood alongside the wall. He listened to faint sounds; tools dropped into the bag.

Nikulin said, "We will walk out and talk about finishing earlier than expected." When Remmich noticed the door opening, he moved back to hide and watched them get on the elevator.

With his mind back to focusing on his mission, he didn't consider anything was wrong. He walked to conference room 207 to examine the other chair rail.

When they got off the elevator, Nikulin casually told the CQ they finished inspecting. They said goodbye and walked out. The CQ didn't think to ask for a copy of the finished work order.

The Russians got into the van and drove off base. A block away, Nikulin parked the van, got out, and climbed into his rented Mercedes E-Class 350. The partner drove off in the van.

A short time after finishing his inspection, Remmich wondered why the CID guys hadn't come out of the restroom. When he pushed the door open to check, he saw the officers on the floor with blood pooled around their skulls and upper torsos. Rushing downstairs, he told the CQ, who called the police. MPs ran into the building ten minutes later. Four sprinted up the stairway. Two questioned Remmich and asked to see his ID. He handed over the lanyard.

An Army ambulance parked at the curb and two medics pushed gurneys into the building. More CID officials arrived, and they interrogated Remmich more thoroughly. The MP handed his ID to one of them and indicated it was authentic. During the questioning, they learned he was a security intelligence official. Although a civilian, his presence was authorized. He answered their questions, and they released him.

A day later, the CID examined security camera footage to identify the plumbers. The investigators were unsuccessful; Nikulin and his partner had disguised themselves.

2

The Offer

It was the last encryption seminar at Patch Barracks, in Stuttgart. The V Corps' headquarters instructors finished the advanced military intelligence workshop covering coding, decoding, and vocabulary translation. Lieutenant General Ed Sutherland, the CO, arrived with his entourage to shake hands and award certificates. At the end of the meeting, a G-1 administrative sergeant walked into the room. He read off names and departure times for those flying back to North Africa and the Middle East. The Army scheduled the attendees to leave by troop bus to the airport after lunch.

The MP guard station was busy at noon. Cars were in line to enter the Army post. A green van stopped at the station; the Russians used a different vehicle this time. The contractor's papers weren't registered for work that day. The MP told the driver, Nikulin, to go to the guard shack to fill out papers before he could be approved to enter. After what happened to the two CID soldiers, V Corps ordered strict inspection of non-registered vehicles and people. Irritated, Nikulin parked the van next to a troop bus. He and his partner had disguised themselves again. This time, Nikulin's natural dark blond hair was dyed black. They waited in line. When their turn arrived, the MP gruffly asked for identification and the purpose of their visit. Nikulin explained they needed to examine electrical work done at a circuit box installed by their company.

In reality, the chair rails in 205 and 207 were what they wanted to look at.

The MP's obnoxious manner didn't sit well. Nikulin's passenger bristled when the soldier ridiculed them for thinking they could enter the base without proper papers. Leaning over to appear to read a page pinned to the bottom of a bulletin board, the Russian reached into his satchel and dropped a small package into the trash can. Meanwhile, the desk sergeant handed Nikulin forms to have his company registered to work on base. Moments later, the two walked out, disgruntled and angry. Before they left, the partner placed a black object under the parked bus's luggage compartment section.

The Counterintelligence Corps (CIC) hosted a luncheon briefing for the seminar attendees. They needed officers and NCOs (non-commissioned officers) to become familiar with potential threats directed against the US. It included directives for tracking spy activity and AWOL soldiers. The Army hoped to get volunteers. One of the attendees' interest increased; Captain Eric Miller liked challenges. The captain recalled his advanced training taken stateside and at UNIMI (United Nations International Military Institute) in Stockholm, but he felt it was nothing like this.

Miller was an attractive, clean-cut Black man. In his early 30s, he retained his West Point muscular physique on a 6' frame. With short dark hair, coffee-colored eyes, and an easy smile, he was well-liked by his friends and co-workers.

He didn't leave after lunch. The quiet dining room atmosphere gave him time to consider joining. He wondered if it meant a transfer from the 32nd military intelligence (MI) office. A mess sergeant interrupted his daydreaming, telling him he had to leave the dining hall. The kitchen helpers, better known as KPs, needed to clean up and get ready for dinner.

Miller was a dedicated active-duty soldier. After graduating from West Point as a second lieutenant, he spent eighteen months being schooled in military intelligence, including covert military operations, encryption and decryption, and seminars provided by the CIA and FBI. It gave him a good foundation for this military specialty.

He got up and rolled his suitcase to the car. While opening the trunk, he noticed soldiers who were stationed in the Middle East and Asia entering the troop bus taking them to the airport. Moments later, it drove off base while he placed the luggage into the trunk. Getting in the driver's seat, he checked his email before starting the car. He erased the junk but saved a message from his girlfriend, Candice. She was an Air Force Academy graduate who'd served as an officer in the US and Turkey. He pictured her beautiful features and thought of her sophisticated charm. His personal motto emphasized wine, women, and a good life. He could fall in love with her.

The message read, "I'm flying into Amsterdam and will be there next weekend. Delta has me piloting back stateside Monday afternoon. Can we spend the weekend together?" Months before, she'd signed a lease for a small flat in Amsterdam they shared when both were in town. This news triggered a thought to call his British-born buddy, Paul Remmich.

Remmich served as a former MI officer. He and Miller had been friends from the time they graduated from the West Point Military Academy. They'd attended the same graduate courses but got stationed at different Army bases. They hooked up again in Germany under V Corps. For a while, they worked together at the 32nd Security Intelligence office. Remmich had resigned from the Army, but Miller didn't know it was done without Remmich's conscious cooperation. He'd been drugged and hypnotized and was now acting under post-hypnotic suggestions. He worked in Amsterdam as a wine buyer for his wife's family business, the Hotel Schiller, as well as a civilian specialist for the Army. As a clandestine spy for Tariq'Allah, his work let him do espionage duties undetected.

Miller smiled and, as he replied to her message, heard a loud explosion. It sounded like it came from the direction of the street outside the base. Then another blast rocked the MP guard shack. The shock waves vibrated Miller's vehicle, and his ears rang. He got out and ran through the dust toward the rubble. He saw dismembered bodies all around the wreckage of the guard shack and troop bus. Some who were still alive moaned; others farther away had less severe injuries. Shattered window glass was everywhere.

An on-base fire truck raced to the scene, along with two Army ambulances. Soldiers ran out of buildings to help. Local ambulances and police vehicles arrived at the street bombing. The scene shocked everyone; the bus was obliterated. Locals watched from the sidewalk, horrified the only thing left of many people were body parts. More police vehicles arrived.

Investigators showed up as the Army troops stood around, sickened by what they saw. The police tied yellow caution tape to poles to prevent people from getting too close. They let the soldiers begin their arduous and grisly task, searching for dog tags. Seventeen GIs and one driver got identified only by their tags. Sometimes they had to turn away because of the smell of dead men and their body parts. Miller worked with them for two hours before leaving town.

He drove north to Leighton Barracks in Würzburg, where he lived. The news traveled fast; six MPs at the guard gate thoroughly searched cars without US tags for explosives.

"Hurry, damnit," he mumbled. He needed to make a pit stop.

An MP lined up the tagged Army and civilian cars and waved them through another security gate. Miller returned the salute. He parked and hurried into the PX sub shop to find the bathroom. After finishing and washing up, he got into the food line. There were two people ahead of him. It gave him time to figure out what to order; an Italian cold cut with everything, a Diet Coke, and a bag of chips.

Dinner in hand, he arrived at his apartment building. After unloading the car, he got the mail and unlocked the new deadbolt system on the apartment's door. Most of the flats on the Army base didn't have those locks. His did because a prior break-in by an Iraqi spy almost cost him his life. The accumulated mail landed on the table. He put the sub and drink into the fridge and went to empty the suitcase. That done, he took off the combat boots and fatigues. He lay down on the bed, planning to rest for a while. His eyes closed.

When he opened his eyes, he heard the Frankfurt Armed Forces radio station broadcasting the news. He stretched and focused on the digital clock radio. It was 5:30 a.m.; he'd slept through the night.

"Damn!" he whispered to himself.

Walking into the bathroom, his grumbling stomach reminded him the sub was in the fridge.

***

Colonel Arif Yildiz checked into the Hotel Schiller late Sunday morning. A valet took his suitcase to the room, while the medium build, thinly mustached Tariq'Allah chargé d'affaires for Istanbul walked to the restaurant. Tariq'Allah is a branch of the Iraqi National Intelligence Service (INIS). This Baghdad group had to hide their international campaign; the United Nations Internal Oversight division limited Iraq's trade. But the Tariq'Allah did what it wanted, even though it had no intention of openly breaking the law. Yildiz finished lunch and went to his hotel room.

The front page of the London *Times* had a story about Syrian cities devastated and the thousands killed from bombings. It said many thousands of refugees had turned up in Turkey and Europe. The unique patterns of Russian attacks in the cities caused the US to consider it a well-planned scheme; they won because the attacks wreaked havoc on civilians. Al-Assad's Syrian government ignored the needs of the fleeing people. Another article related to the problems of infiltrating ISIS spies. The report associated their combat strength with illegal artillery sold to them by the Russian Mafia. It turned out to be a 3-way holocaust, including Syria, ISIS, and Russia. A final sentence from the US ambassador at the UN read, "Their war maneuvers excluded shame." Aside from the atrocities, he found another article amusing. It speculated about Iraq's reason for leaving the oil cartel and dropping out of the UN. The next caption surprised him the most. It described the explosions at Patch Barracks and the troop bus. ISIS got blamed for it.

The telephone rang.

It was Alzuhari. A captain in the Iraqi Secret Service, he spoke several languages and often found himself the go-to person for General Yildiz. His level head and even-tempered personality brought order to Tariq'Allah's projects. Like his boss, he sported a mustache but added a neatly trimmed goatee to his confident face.

He talked to his boss about the routine business trips Remmich made to buy wine for the Schiller Hotel. "And I told him to come to the eight o'clock meeting tomorrow morning."

"When he returns at the end of the week, let him attend the computer training for his company." Yildiz frowned, believing Remmich's learning new computer skills was a waste of time.

Captain Adnaw Alzuhari joined Tariq'Allah two years before. Their goal centered on establishing international relations with Third World nations. Part of the first effort was conscripting a US Army officer. Although they offered financial gain to someone to heist a scientific discovery, that method failed. The US officer, Eric Miller, saved his own life by killing the Iraqi emissary in Stockholm. The second try by another spy team targeted Miller again but planned to drug and hypnotize rather than coerce him. With their subconscious control, he would do whatever they wanted. As it turned out, Remmich got caught in the net instead of Miller. Remmich's task was to get them classified information. Yildiz, then a major, selected Alzuhari for his present position. They'd worked together off-and-on for a few years. This man now served in a civilian capacity.

***

The Monday morning meeting at Tara Yako's flat started on time. The Tariq'Allah security intelligence group was quietly drinking their coffee and waiting to hear their next move.

Yildiz focused on their spy and said, "Paul, I want to talk about your career with Tariq'Allah. Do you still want to help Third World nations advance economically?" Remmich nodded stiffly.

"Good. I am assigning you to a foreign country for a short time." He stirred his coffee, expecting their man to respond.

He answered, "Yes, sir," showing his hypnotized mind accepted the command.

"You will investigate the area first." He leaned toward him and added, "A few days later, you will return." Remmich sat silent. "Inform your wife the transfer is critical. Explain how you want her to go. Tell her it's for a six-month stay. You will receive a salary, and there will not be any living expenses. Your money will arrive electronically to your Dutch bank from Baghdad twice monthly. It is a wonderful offer." He stared into Remmich's eyes and asked, "You want to know where you are going, don't you?"

"Where am I going?"

Yildiz said, "Havana, Cuba."

Remmich's level of awareness was unlike the deepest level of hypnotism. His post-hypnotic state had conditioned him to agree to anything they told him to do; it commanded obedience and attention to detail. His conscious state-of-mind didn't exist anymore. But he continued to have cognizance of his normal activities and the ability to respond.

He said, "I want to follow your orders, but I…I still work for military intelligence, and I need permission to travel out of my stationed area."

Yildiz countered with, "I'm sure you can get permission."

He couldn't disagree. "Yes, I will go, but I don't know if I can go now. My father-in-law is not going to like it."

Yildiz overlooked the statement and said, "Paul, tell him you need to talk to international security advisors. Briefly explain the Army asked you to act as a temporary diplomat. You don't have to give the details. Now, what are your calendar plans?"

Remmich looked at his datebook and saw he had a dental appointment. He said, "I have to go to Würzburg for my dental exam."

"When is that?"

"Next Monday at ten."

Yildiz stared at him, thinking, *That's the day Tariq'Allah instructed me to have you travel to Havana.* "You need to change the dental appointment, Paul. Tell them you have to go this week because of your military responsibilities."

Remmich dialed. The receptionist put him on hold. She returned and said the scheduled time could not be changed. His mental state rebutted, and he said aggressively, "Surely, you can change an appointment time. I have military responsibilities to do."

"Please hold on," she said. The colonel told him to switch to the speaker mode. He did and moved his mobile phone closer to his superior.

Moments later, they heard a "click," and the dentist, Dr. Faisal Mustafa, came on the line. Yildiz spoke in Arabic and told the dentist Remmich had to go out of the country.

Mustafa argued, "I need to examine the tooth that has the receiver implant to see if it's loose. He might not feel the vibration if the chip isn't secure. I can change my work schedule so he can come in this Wednesday instead."

Frustrated, Yildiz told the dentist he'd get back to him. They hung up, and he asked Remmich, "What else is in your schedule?"

"V Corps G-2 instructed me to call their office in Stuttgart next week about an upcoming meeting. The Army is unsure when the renovations are going to be finished."

Yildiz stroked his mustache while he thought, then said, "We are under a work schedule to begin construction of a building, an energy cylinder, and its battery storage units. This construction is in Havana. You must get your work schedule changed for this week. Tell your father-in-law how the Army instructed you to be present at an OAS meeting. Don't tell them anything else."

The colonel texted the dentist, saying Remmich would keep the dental appointment for Wednesday. The dentist's text confirmed the day.

"Paul, now we want to teach you how to disguise yourself for your own safety." Yildiz handed him a box. "These disguises will help you evade foreign intelligence squads."

Remmich examined makeup pencils, jars of facial makeup, stick-on beards, mustaches, and eyebrows, and a collapsible walking cane. Curious, he extended and retracted it. The last two items were a pair of trousers and dress shirt.

For the next hour, Yildiz watched Yako instruct Remmich. Tara Yako was a dark-haired, olive-skinned beauty. Being multilingual and with a Harvard education, the Tariq'Allah was pleased with her abilities and ambition. She'd been the bait when the Iraqis were seeking a mole, so Remmich had already been the target of her hypnotism skills.

She held up three jars of makeup and selected the one closest to his skin tone. Using her fingers, she applied the cosmetic to his face on one side, then told him to do the other cheek and his forehead. Next, she compared the eyebrows and mustaches to find which one best matched his own, then added a beard. When he looked into the mirror on the table, he didn't recognize the face staring back. Adding a pair of steel-rimmed clear-glass spectacles, his handlers were pleased. Alzuhari excused himself to place a lunch order.

Yildiz said, "Replace these clothes with your own. Always change clothes and groom yourself in a man's lavatory behind the water closet door." He removed a flat object. "This kit contains a mirror. When you pull off the paper liner, like this, it exposes these adhesive sections." He pressed the mirror to the marble table and then had Remmich pull it off. The colonel put back the covers.

Twenty minutes later, the food delivery arrived. During lunch, they talked in their native tongue. Remmich didn't join in because he didn't understand. When they finished eating, Yildiz said, "I want to talk with you about someone." Remmich looked at him in silence. "You will work with this person in Havana. Do you understand?"

Remmich blinked slowly and answered, “Yes.”

“I also want you to study Cuba on your computer so you’re familiar with the area and culture.”

Yildiz dialed the Istanbul office. Luma answered, “Yes, Colonel, I am finishing up with the passport and visas. They include the countries you selected.”

Luma Samir was bilingual in Arabic and English. She learned English in school, along with business administration and computer skills. Those proficiencies got her promoted. Unfortunately, being a woman, she had to work in Istanbul as an office manager. At least that’s what they called her. She hoped it would lead to a further promotion.

***

Months before, the Russians found out Iraq’s plan to steal a scientific discovery developed in the US. The research showed a new way to convert solar energy into electricity. The SVR office in Moscow assigned Yury Nikulin to Amsterdam. The ambassador in Washington, DC, managed him. His job? To watch the Iraqis in Istanbul and find the document. Before this mission, he’d worked at the Russian embassy in DC.

He’d rented a flat in Amsterdam and monitored the whereabouts and dealings of Alzuhari, Yako, and sometimes Remmich. One evening when the Iraqis met Remmich at the Blue’s Alley Bar and Restaurant, he took a taxi to Yako’s building. There was no security system on the outer doors, so he entered and took the elevator to her floor. He used a unique tool to jimmy the door lock and go into her flat, where he hid a transmitter-receiver in an inconspicuous place. He then did the same thing in Alzuhari’s lodgings.

During Remmich’s disguise lessons, Nikulin listened to them talk from his own flat. When the meeting adjourned, he removed the

3

Various Adjustments

Lilly, Paul Remmich's wife, sat at a table with her father in the central dining area of the Schiller Hotel. They concentrated on reviewing personnel schedules. The room's wood floor echoed with footsteps. The noise stopped, and she looked up.

In an alarmed tone, she said to her husband, "Where have you been?"

"I needed to get together with you, too," exclaimed Franz Van Horn, her father. Irritated, he said, "Now I have to revise your work calendar, Paul. We have to maintain a regular schedule."

Remmich turned his attention to his wife. Sensing her frustration, he composed himself. "V Corps has assigned me to attend an OAS meeting in Cuba. It shouldn't be longer than a few days, and I'm scheduled to leave next Monday."

"What is OAS?" demanded Franz.

"It stands for Organization of American States."

The name did not mean anything to either of them, and his father-in-law groused, "That means I have to do the traveling again!"

He sensed an argument and sighed regretfully to appease. "I know, I just found out a little while ago." He repeated the trip was for a few days, although he didn't give a specific number.

Lilly's jaw was tight with resentment when she said, "I thought your military business was only from Stuttgart?"

Lying had become second nature to him since his hypnosis. "Not all the time. However, it is a special meeting."

She really didn't know what he did in his job, because it was something he never discussed. He was less reticent when telling personal stories, like the weekend trips to different German cities with Eric before he resigned. He also liked to discuss current global events with her.

He softened his voice and laid on his British charm. "I'm sorry I can't tell you more, but I'm not supposed to discuss it with anyone." He gave them both the departure and return dates. Their frustration didn't matter. He looked at her and repeated, "I will come back in a few days, my dear."

"Where is this meeting in Cuba?"

"Lilly, my supervisor at Patch Barracks, said I'll be staying in Havana. Discussions will be with the Central American Free Trade Agreement countries." Remmich knew he was telling another outright lie, but he thought he could appease her by fibbing. Cleverly, he added, "Oh, I shouldn't have said that. Anyway, like I said, it's classified."

She retorted, "Humph! You're visiting a resort without me?"

At that, her husband and father struggled not to laugh. Remmich thought, *You don't give up, do you?*

He answered, "Yes, I want you to come with me. Perhaps I can take you with me on the next trip." She smiled, somewhat soothed.

He focused on his father-in-law and said, "I'll be busy this week with other Army obligations." He then turned and left abruptly, without saying goodbye.

On the way to the condo, he felt a vibration in his molar. When this happened, he automatically slipped into a deeper hypnotic state of mind that controlled all actions. He pressed the autodial button on his phone that would connect him to the Amsterdam headquarters.

Two rings later, he said, "Hello, this is RSP." Alzuhari said, "The Iraqi passport and visa paperwork will arrive today by express mail."

They hung up before he could respond. In less than two minutes, his subconscious reverted to its normal hypnotized state.

He notified the front desk to expect the package and call him when it arrived.

Remmich telephoned his friend. Getting the voice mailbox, he told him, “Hello, Eric. This is to confirm our get-together on Wednesday. I have a dentist’s appointment tomorrow. I will contact the officers’ club to make a dinner reservation for us at five-thirty. Call me only if you can’t make it. Bye.”

***

A couple hours later, Yildiz contacted his cohorts in Amsterdam. He wanted a conference call with Remmich. Alzuhari activated the satellite relay to the mole’s tooth. Yako waited to hear the connection on her phone. Moments passed, and the vibration in Remmich’s molar eased him into the more profound subliminal state.

He made the call and said woodenly, “Hello, this is PSR.”

Yildiz said, “Paul, when you are at the Havana airport, a driver will hold a sign with your name printed on it. Go to him. He will drive you to the hotel. After you register, find out if there is a message for you.”

“Yes. I’ll look for it.”

Yildiz then told him, “You’re to meet a man there. The message you get will have the man’s hotel room number. After you meet him, he will review the construction work with you. And remember to take the disguise case with your own clothes.”

After they hung up, Alzuhari asked the colonel, “Is it safe to think he will stay in the subliminal state while he is away?”

Yildiz said, “Remmich’s subconscious mind is controlled by us. He will get what we want.”

***

It surprised the CIC head officer, Colonel Kirby, to have a volunteer so fast. He presented a covert operations outline to Miller. “As I explained at the luncheon, CIC has several avenues to travel. The upcoming mission is to search for AWOL soldiers who confiscated classified information for money. You need to find these soldiers and bring them back for military JAG trials.”

***

Remmich arrived at Leighton Barracks on Wednesday morning. He registered at the base hotel at 9:30, rode the elevator upstairs, and entered his room. He needed cigarettes and walked to the PX, buying two cartons. Back in the place, he watched TV for a while. He relaxed a while before heading to the dentist’s office.

At 5:20 p.m., Eric Miller walked into the officers’ club in civilian clothes. He saw Remmich and joined him at the bar. He noticed his buddy had an empty glass and signaled for two beers.

The civilian offered him a cigarette and lit it for him. Miller blew out the smoke and teased him. “Hey man, why don’t you use a lighter and stop murdering matchbooks?”

Remmich snickered, while the bartender set the beers on the bar. “Do I have to listen to your lecture again? I guess it’s become a habit.”

“So, what happened at the dentist’s office?”

“It was a routine examination on my filling, but I have to revisit tomorrow. Apparently, the filling is loose, and the dental office doesn’t have the right adhesive to reset it. The receptionist told me the supplies come before the place opens. I’m staying overnight again.” He took a puff and blew the smoke upward and asked, “How are you doing with Candice?”

“She’s flying into Amsterdam this weekend.” He leaned over and flicked his ash into the ashtray before saying, “Unfortunately, I won’t be able to see her.”

as the hypnotic state was triggered. He picked up the cell phone the aide had placed on a table beside him. Alzuhari expected the call.

Remmich identified himself, then heard, "Goodbye."

Mustafa looked into his patient's face and said, "The...sun...is...shining...outside." He waited.

Remmich remained seated for a few minutes as the deeper hypnotized state-of-mind wore off. Two assistants removed instruments and left. He had no recollection of what had happened, except he'd had dental work.

He heard, "Everything is fine, Paul. You are free to go home to Amsterdam. We will contact you in a few months for another examination."

Remmich got back to Amsterdam late in the afternoon, finding a note his wife left. She was on a business trip, and he didn't feel like sitting by himself. Instead, he went to the bar and chatted with his bartender friend, Kirk Felders, and others. At 9:00, he left; his body told him it was time for bed.

***

Friday began well; it was 6:45 when he got a kiss goodbye. Lilly left to go to a meeting with hotel-restaurant owners in Amsterdam at 8:00. He got out of bed after she was gone; he couldn't sleep any longer. After a shower and shave, he went down the stairs for breakfast. There was no need to rush. There weren't any vineyard visits for a while. Relaxed, he remembered Yildiz's command to read about Cuba. The Internet provided a vast amount of information. The Caribbean climate data advised visitors on how to dress for comfort. The island's history interested him, and he read for over an hour. He also had thoughts of the mystery man in Havana.

Lilly entered the condo at 1:00 p.m. She placed her purse on a chair and walked into the bedroom. After removing her shoes and running her fingers through her chin-length brown hair, she walked

It surprised the CIC head officer, Colonel Kirby, to have a volunteer so fast. He presented a covert operations outline to Miller. “As I explained at the luncheon, CIC has several avenues to travel. The upcoming mission is to search for AWOL soldiers who confiscated classified information for money. You need to find these soldiers and bring them back for military JAG trials.”

***

Remmich arrived at Leighton Barracks on Wednesday morning. He registered at the base hotel at 9:30, rode the elevator upstairs, and entered his room. He needed cigarettes and walked to the PX, buying two cartons. Back in the place, he watched TV for a while. He relaxed a while before heading to the dentist’s office.

At 5:20 p.m., Eric Miller walked into the officers’ club in civilian clothes. He saw Remmich and joined him at the bar. He noticed his buddy had an empty glass and signaled for two beers.

The civilian offered him a cigarette and lit it for him. Miller blew out the smoke and teased him. “Hey man, why don’t you use a lighter and stop murdering matchbooks?”

Remmich snickered, while the bartender set the beers on the bar. “Do I have to listen to your lecture again? I guess it’s become a habit.”

“So, what happened at the dentist’s office?”

“It was a routine examination on my filling, but I have to revisit tomorrow. Apparently, the filling is loose, and the dental office doesn’t have the right adhesive to reset it. The receptionist told me the supplies come before the place opens. I’m staying overnight again.” He took a puff and blew the smoke upward and asked, “How are you doing with Candice?”

“She’s flying into Amsterdam this weekend.” He leaned over and flicked his ash into the ashtray before saying, “Unfortunately, I won’t be able to see her.”

"Why not? I thought that's why you wanted us to get together?"

"Let's not forget, civilian, I have military obligations," he said, smiling. "I'm supposed to—" He stopped talking and pretended to cough and clear his throat. He swallowed and sipped some beer. He belched and said, "That's better." The pause gave Miller more time to consider changing the subject instead of telling the truth.

He said, "I have a Stuttgart meeting. The group of us will focus on immigrants getting work with the Army here in Germany."

Remmich's head bobbed in agreement as he wrapped the matchbook cover around its striking section and then bent the entire thing back and forth with one hand.

"There goes another mangled matchbook."

He looked into his friend's eyes, grinned, and said, "Yes. It's a foregone conclusion I'm headed for the loony bin. It's not clear why I do this." He held the mutilated matchbook and just looked at it.

"What's on your mind?" asked Miller.

Remmich had his story prepared. "Actually, I wanted to talk to you tonight. I have to postpone this weekend, too. My father-in-law wants me to visit several vineyards operating in the Baden-Baden area of southwestern Germany."

"Well, it seems to be working out to be a draw." Relieved, he asked, "Hungry?"

"I am indeed."

They finished their beers, and Miller placed a ten dollar bill on the bar.

***

Remmich walked into the dentist's office on Thursday. The receptionist greeted him and notified a dental assistant. He accompanied her to the treatment center and sat in the patient chair.

Dr. Mustafa entered, and they exchanged greetings. The assistant lowered the backrest.

"Now open wide, please." He positioned the light and used a tool to remove the loose filling. "Did you feel aching?"

"No."

The day before, Mustafa found the old filling had loosened. He was unable to separate the old microchip from the composite resin. A new chip had to be inserted. The assistant mixed a two-part composite resin to secure the filling. It was placed into the tooth opening, and air was blown through a tube into the drilled-out area to speed the curing process. The doctor pressed a new microchip into the resin and filled the remaining space with more of the material. He told Remmich to bite down gently to ensure the surfaces meshed. The chief surgeon temporarily wrapped the molar with a non-metallic barrier, which prevented Remmich from biting down hard. Extreme pressure from the tooth above might dislodge the chip and filling before the adhesive hardened. It was uncomfortable. Remmich was sent to the waiting room and read to pass the time.

A half-hour later, a technician walked him back to the room. The doctor said, "We have to take an X-ray to make sure there are no air pockets."

The woman placed the mouthpiece between the upper and lower molars. "Bite down," she said before pushing the button on the hand-held remote control. She removed the mouthpiece and walked away to transfer the picture to the computer.

Mustafa walked into the area. The screen displayed the picture. "The new filling is in place." The dentist pressed the floor button, moving the chair to a more upright position. He needed to test the vibration levels of the new microchip.

The doctor ran the test twice. Remmich flinched uncomfortably from the first one. The doctor didn't want that to happen…it was too obvious. After lowering the level, Remmich's face remained passive when the tooth vibrated but became serious as the hypnotic state was triggered. He picked up the cell phone the aide had placed on a table beside him. Alzuhari expected the call.

Remmich identified himself, then heard, “Goodbye.”

Mustafa looked into his patient’s face and said, “The...sun...is...shining...outside.” He waited.

Remmich remained seated for a few minutes as the deeper hypnotized state-of-mind wore off. Two assistants removed instruments and left. He had no recollection of what had happened, except he’d had dental work.

He heard, “Everything is fine, Paul. You are free to go home to Amsterdam. We will contact you in a few months for another examination.”

Remmich got back to Amsterdam late in the afternoon, finding a note his wife left. She was on a business trip, and he didn’t feel like sitting by himself. Instead, he went to the bar and chatted with his bartender friend, Kirk Felders, and others. At 9:00, he left; his body told him it was time for bed.

***

Friday began well; it was 6:45 when he got a kiss goodbye. Lilly left to go to a meeting with hotel-restaurant owners in Amsterdam at 8:00. He got out of bed after she was gone; he couldn’t sleep any longer. After a shower and shave, he went down the stairs for breakfast. There was no need to rush. There weren’t any vineyard visits for a while. Relaxed, he remembered Yildiz’s command to read about Cuba. The Internet provided a vast amount of information. The Caribbean climate data advised visitors on how to dress for comfort. The island’s history interested him, and he read for over an hour. He also had thoughts of the mystery man in Havana.

Lilly entered the condo at 1:00 p.m. She placed her purse on a chair and walked into the bedroom. After removing her shoes and running her fingers through her chin-length brown hair, she walked to her husband's office. He felt her arms wrap around him. She leaned around to kiss him. Without revealing his intentions, he got up and unbuttoned her blouse. After it fell to the floor, he unzipped her skirt and lowered her underwear enough for her to wiggle them off while she unhooked her bra. Her green eyes sparkled as she helped to unbutton his shirt. He let it fall behind him and removed the T-shirt, loosened the belt and undid his trousers, then lowered the zipper. He stepped out of his pants, and she pulled off his underwear. Breathing heavily, they held hands while he led her into the bedroom. They both enjoyed afternoon lovemaking.

They lay side by side while their bodies cooled and heart rate slowed. Satisfied and relaxed, they fell asleep for a few hours. When they woke up, he ran his fingers down her arm and suggested they shower and go out for an early dinner. She took his hand and softly kissed his fingers, then his lips. They had two days remaining before his trip.

4

Guantánamo Promotion

It was late Friday afternoon when Eric Miller drove along the Autobahn on Frankfurt's south side. The loud roar of a descending jet told him the airport was nearby, while the traffic jams reminded him of the Washington Beltway at Connecticut Avenue on Friday afternoons. He drove onto the ramp, where double overhead signs directed drivers into the commercial entrance of the Frankfurt International Airport; the access paralleled the Air Force base entrance. The ramp split, separated by high fencing; Rhein-Main US Air Force Base was on the right.

Many buildings came into view. Locating the sign for headquarters, Miller parked and went inside, carrying his travel bag. The clock on the wall told him it had taken twenty minutes to get there from the Autobahn. It was 5:45. After checking in with the reception desk, a sergeant approached him.

"Excuse me, sir. Are you Captain Eric Miller?"

"Yes."

"Please follow me."

They walked down the corridor to a closed door. The sergeant swiped an ID card through a sensor.

They walked into the room, and he said, "You can place your bags over there with the other officers' things."

Miller followed him down another corridor, and they stopped at a conference room. The sergeant said, "I believe you'll find three other CIC officers in there, sir." The NCO looked at the daily record book. "Please initial here, sir."

Miller recognized Colonel Kirby and Major McKinsey, but there was another, lower-ranked officer there he didn't know. All eyes were on him as he walked to them.

McKinsey walked up and said, "Good to see you, Eric."

They shook hands. Miller also shook hands with Kirby and was introduced to Captain Carroll.

Kirby said, "We have to talk about the plans for this weekend and a little beyond. The CIC meeting at INSCOM begins tomorrow morning at Fort Belvoir. We'll get more info there."

Miller said, "I take it we're not staying here on base this evening?"

"Correct," answered Kirby. "There's another reason for this evening's meeting, but I'll let General Baldwin handle it. He'll be here soon. Anyway, we are leaving late tonight and will land at Andrews Air Force Base tomorrow morning. We're staying at Fort Belvoir for two nights. Depending on our timing, we will stay one night after returning for debriefing, if required."

The colonel looked at McKinsey. "It's all yours, Tom."

McKinsey sat up and looked at Miller. "Eric, you and I will work together for a week. Colonel Kirby will work at the Pentagon with the top brass. Captain Carroll will be with him."

Miller asked, "Where are we going?"

Kirby answered, "I'm under strict orders to let both of you, and only you, know you will search for AWOL soldiers." He asked McKinsey if there was anything more and got a "No, sir."

Just then the door opened, and a major entered, followed by another person. All four men stood up when they saw a man in Class As with a silver star on his shoulder pad. He was an Army brigadier general.

The major said, "At ease," and the foursome remained standing, while he handed a satchel to the general.

General Baldwin greeted them, then directed his full attention to Eric Miller. "Come forward, Captain, and stand at attention."

The general was a tall man. His gray, parted hair added to the neatness of his charisma. He looked into the captain's face while getting in front of the junior officer.

A dozen thoughts ran through Miller's head. There had been no announcement of what was to happen.

He obeyed the order and stood upright. “Yes, sir. Is there something wrong, sir?”

The general smiled. “No. Everything’s right.” The major removed a box from the satchel and handed it to the general. He cleared his throat and said, “Captain Eric James Miller, by the authority vested in me by the United States Congress and the United States Army, you are at this moment promoted to Major Eric James Miller.” Since he was in civilian clothes, the general handed the box to him instead of pinning bronze leaves onto civilian attire. “Go ahead, open it,” said the general.

It contained two sets of bronze leaves for Class A attire and four fatigue rank insignias. The general shook his hand while the major took several snapshots. He included one with the other three officers standing with Miller. The general and others present saluted Major Miller.

Smiling, he said, “These pictures will be sent to your MI office.” The general wished him luck, then departed with his attaché.

Eric just stood there, overwhelmed, his promotion entirely unexpected. Colonel Kirby said, “Incidentally, Major, this was the other part of the meeting.” A rash of laughter followed, then each of them shook his hand again, greeting him as “Major.”

“Well, shall we get back to work?” suggested Kirby.

The evening discussion continued for another two tedious hours. The talking stopped when Kirby’s phone jingled.

“Yes, we’ll leave right away. That was the control tower, gentlemen. We have to be at the main loading dock ASAP. A bus will take us to the transport. We’re scheduled to take off for Andrews at twenty-one hundred hours. It’s an eight-and-a-half-hour flight. Don’t forget to reset your watch time to US Eastern.”

The group headed to the locked room to get their baggage, but the desk sergeant stopped them and said, “Gentlemen, your bags are already at the loading dock. Please, follow me.”

A bus drove them to the jet. After boarding, a sergeant directed them to their seats and told them to buckle up. Another flight NCO secured the entrance door. The rear loading dock pneumatically lifted into place.

The engines got louder, and a little exhaust stink entered the cabin. A tractor pushed the jet transport backward and to the right. It disengaged itself from the jet's front wheel assembly and backed up. A cloud of black diesel smoke puffed upward out of the tractor's vertical exhaust, and the operator drove off.

The four large jet engines got louder, and the plane vibrated as it moved to a takeoff ramp. The acceleration from a dead stop pushed their bodies into the seats' backrests. Soon, they felt a thump as the wheels lifted off the runway. The jet began a straight course, then turned starboard. Below them, the city of Frankfurt looked like garlands of holiday lights. The scene captivated Miller for a few seconds, then the jet turned westward, gaining elevation every second. The illuminated ground disappeared beneath the clouds.

Two US Air Force attendants served boxed fast food dinners to them: bottled iced tea, a tortilla roll-up, a bag of chips, and a red apple.

Miller commented, "Looks good!" The tension and mystery about the trip dissipated.

There was little discussion while they ate. After the sergeant collected empty boxes and plastic drink bottles, the group talked with the crew and exchanged stories about their duty tours. Hours later, they lowered their backrests to relax. The engines' smooth hum soothed them, and they fell asleep. It was approaching 0100 hours.

***

The jet landed, and the tower assigned it to a designated area. Eric Miller woke up and wondered if he was still dreaming. Then he realized they were no longer flying. He looked around as the other three awoke. Sunlight shone through the jet's windows. A loud noise came from the rear as the cargo ramp lowered. The men looked out and saw familiar looking red brick buildings. The time was 5:40; they'd slept right through the landing. Looking out another window, they saw a tractor forklift coming toward the transport. The men got up and took turns in the bathrooms.

An Air Force sergeant walked up the ramp into the plane. He verified the count of transported items to a sheet on a clipboard. Miller returned to the group, and the sergeant said a vehicle was waiting and their baggage had been loaded in the van.

They walked out of the transport at the rear to a minivan. The sergeant gave a packet to Kirby, who snickered and said, "Like I need another bag of papers."

As the van drove off, the colonel opened the packet and read the first page. He stated, "I think all of you need to hear this while we're on our way to Fort Belvoir. The subject we'll be discussing is the espionage tactics of US military moles and AWOLs." He read in silence for a couple moments, then added, "Representatives from the FBI, CIA, and our own DIA will be attending. The Defense Department thinks it's a good idea for us to get a complete update."

No one noticed time's passing on Saturday. The briefings were intriguing; each person spoke about the branch of security that employed them. Some explained their organization's view of spy infiltration within the government at home. One person talked about the same problem occurring at military bases abroad, while another spoke about espionage in US embassies. When the meeting ended at 1500 hours, they were told to return Sunday morning at 1000 hours.

When they got back to the hotel, Kirby suggested they meet in the lobby at 1700 for dinner. While they ate at the officers' club, they all complained of jet lag and needed an early night.

On Sunday morning, the foursome attended a meeting hosted by INSCOM-based Colonel Fromm. The meeting focused on the work orders of the four visitors. The colonel said, "Colonel Kirby, you and Captain Carroll will be at the Pentagon. You will be in direct contact with V Corps at Patch Barracks in Stuttgart and with the two majors. It may be a hit-or-miss situation for us." He told them Sutherland needed to know everything. No one commented.

Fromm sat up straighter, eyeing the majors, and said, "Your job will be challenging, because it's the first time we're taking a bounty hunter approach."

McKinsey asked, "How do we go about carrying it out? I mean, where are we being transferred?"

"First, let me say we're beginning by investigating the countries where we know defectors go. We are laying the groundwork, so to speak."

"Why don't they use stateside military?" asked McKinsey.

The INSCOM colonel sat closer to the table, smiled, and said, "Good question, Major. We selected both of you because you two work under the direct command of V Corps. The handful of soldiers who have defected from your command have caused problems." He noticed the time. "Let's take a break."

It was a little past 1300 when they returned to the conference room. Colonel Fromm said, "To answer your earlier question, Major McKinsey, your temporary duty station is Cuba. It's close and will allow our US Marines to provide backup if we have a problem with locals or the AWOLs. Since it's our first assignment, we want to keep it safe."

McKinsey said he knew about the increasing number of Army defectors. What he didn't understand was why they'd wind up in Cuba from Germany. He thought it far fetched when the island was a quarter of the way around the world from Europe.

Fromm said, "Some of the Army people couldn't live on pennies a day. They turned themselves in at the Guantánamo Naval Base. During interrogation, they admitted they flew on commercial jets out of Frankfurt to Madrid, then to Havana. An unknown source gave them money to pay for the trips." He focused on the bounty hunters and said, "We're not sure of anything, but we have to begin somewhere."

The majors got flight information to Miami International Airport for the next morning. The sergeant instructed them to go to the Army recruiting station at the airport, where they'd take a military vehicle to the helicopter bunker. Their next stop would be the US Navy base at Guantánamo Bay.

"Be sure to take your nine-millimeter pistols and ammo, just in case. You'll never know how an AWOL soldier will react. Safety first. If you need more ammunition, inform the Navy. This concludes our meeting, gentlemen," said Colonel Fromm.

***

KLM Royal Dutch Airlines flew out of Amsterdam at 7:15 a.m. on Monday. The flight leveled off at thirty thousand feet, then the flight attendants served a European continental breakfast. While he ate, Remmich listened to the co-pilot announce the flight path to the passengers in English. The jet flew over the west coast of France toward Spain. Two-and-a-half hours later, it landed at the Barajas International Airport in Madrid and taxied up to the jetway.

Remmich felt like he was in a zoo with the variety of characters on the plane. He wasn't in a hurry, but the people crowding into the jet's aisles were. Inside the terminal, the overhead departure/arrival boards weren't showing flights to Havana. He wondered about that, so he looked for a passenger information booth. A woman spoke English, and she directed him to another building.

"It's within walking distance." She pointed to a map and added, "Your bags will be taken there, I'm sure."

***

Miller and McKinsey walked off the twin-blade helicopter at Guantánamo Bay Naval Base. A Navy escort carried their bags and placed them into the back of a Humvee. After being logged in at the headquarters building, a man approached them. He introduced himself as Pedro Sola and verified his employment with his CIA ID. He signed a release form saying he was taking full responsibility for them while they were in Cuba. They followed him into the conference for a briefing.

5

Havana Discovery

The jet funneled through dense clouds. The safety belt signal dinged, and the indicator lit up. The city's outskirts became visible. The plane leaned toward the port side and began its descent against strong winds. Remmich squeezed the armrest, while the aircraft descended. The serving carts shook, soda cans banged against each other, and cups fell into the aisle. He clenched his stomach muscles as the jet landed. He hated flying on windy days. The tires skidded, the fuselage leveled off, the engines reversed and roared, and the brakes were applied.

"Jesus!" he mumbled. It was 11 o'clock.

Portable pneumatic jetway tunnels were being built, but most gates still used old methods. The passengers exited onto a platform with stairs. Remmich strolled out last, enjoying the warm, humid breeze. He and the other passengers walked to a section in the main terminal to retrieve their baggage.

People held signs with names. Remmich saw his on one of them. He approached the driver wearing a dark green shirt with a colorful "Hotel Ritz" inscription on the pocket.

"I am Paul Remmich," he said.

"I am supposed to drive you to the hotel, señor. Please, follow me." The escort rolled the suitcase, while Remmich followed him outside with his small carry-on.

Further down the sidewalk, the escort pointed out a four-door Cadillac Seville in the pick-up zone. The shiny, dark green car had the hotel's insignia on the front door. The rear one had a smaller emblem of Cuba's flag. Remmich sat in the air-conditioned vehicle, while the driver put his luggage in the trunk. Out on the highway, they passed many trucks carrying full loads of green stalks shaped like bamboo.

"What's in these trucks?"

The driver explained they were transporting sugarcane to the processing factory. He also said it was Cuba's primary industry, and tobacco for cigars was also a large trade item.

"And we grow coffee, too." He hesitated for a moment, then added, "Tourism in Cuba is increasingly profitable as well."

The vehicle stopped at the classy Hotel Ritz entrance. Attendants approached. One opened the Cadillac's back door, while another removed the suitcase from the trunk. The hotel's automatic door opened, and they walked into the lobby.

Remmich signed in, and the desk clerk gave him a note that read, "After unpacking, visit room 318. We will have a talk with our boss."

The bellhop held the elevator door open for him.

Just visit a room, without giving someone's name?

Yildiz had neglected to clue him in about this.

They entered his hotel room, and the bellboy placed his bag onto a luggage rack. He turned and waited. Remmich realized why and reached into his pocket for the tip. All he had were euros. He handed a five euro note to him, which the kid looked at curiously. He expected Cuban pesos or US dollars but pocketed the cash anyway, then thanked him and walked out.

Intrigued about the individual he was to contact, Remmich called the room first, but the line was busy. He unpacked the suitcase, pulling out a holster with a nine-millimeter pistol. He put it aside for the moment and called again.

Still busy!

Just in case, he attached the holster to his belt. A loose, casual shirt covered over it, but there was a bulge. He changed his mind and left the gun.

No one was in the corridor. The doors on this floor were farther apart, indicating suites rather than just bedrooms and baths. Room 318's entry was ajar. Before knocking, he paused to listen to someone inside speaking Spanish. He didn't understand the language and hoped the person also spoke English. He pushed the door a little to see if the people were visible, which caused a screeching sound. Giving up on secrecy, he knocked.

A man appeared, with a cell phone in his hand. He studied the stranger for a few seconds before saying, "Señor Paul Remmich?"

"Yes."

The person spoke a few more words into the phone and pressed the off button.

Remmich stepped into the studio apartment. The man who let him in was in his 40s and fit, with combed jet-black hair, a loose shirt, a gold necklace, a gold watch, and a diamond ring. Large dark eyebrows highlighted his face.

The man smiled. "Buenos dias, señor. I am glad to meet you. I am Miguel Gonzales." They shook hands. "We've been waiting for you."

He followed Gonzales into the well-appointed condominium with a balcony overlooking the Gulf of Mexico. Seagulls rode the winds above the breaking whitecaps.

"Beautiful, isn't it, señor?"

"It certainly is."

"Please come into our dining area. We use it as an office because it has a table to do our work."

Remmich lifted the message out of his shirt pocket and handed it to him. "This note didn't say who I am supposed to contact. Is it you?"

"I left it at the front desk, but Señor Jerry is the man you will talk to. He is coming back in a few minutes. Right now, he is picking up a package at the main desk. Please, try to relax. You've been on a tiring trip. Can I bring you a drink, Señor?"

"It depends on what you are serving, Miguel."

Gonzales smiled broadly. "How about a Mexican Corona?" He got a favorable nod.

The door screeched as it opened again and shut. Remmich glanced up as a person walked toward them, and his eyes widened. He jumped out of his chair and gasped, "General Elliott!"

"From the look on your face, Paul, you're surprised I'm here."

He chuckled at Remmich's astonishment as he looked at Miguel and said, "Bring me a Corona, too, Miguel, and get one for yourself. Please, gentlemen, have a seat. I need to glance over our duties for the next few days. Drink and relax, while I read a bit."

While Remmich continued to process his confusion at seeing the general, Elliott placed a brown envelope on the table and took the end seat. He took a small keychain penknife from his pants pocket to open the packet. Gonzales put a beer in front of him and sat down, facing the new contact. Elliott glanced over the drawing and read the printed information.

After a few minutes, Elliott opened a map of Havana on the table and invited the other two to study the areas. Gonzales pointed to the layout of streets and building figures. The general glanced at the now calm mole, satisfied.

"Paul, we're going to become familiar with the city beginning tomorrow. Today, relax and get used to the time change." He sipped some beer and continued. "I guess you're wondering why I'm here." Remmich nodded vigorously, his eyebrows raised. "First, I'd like you to know my interests parallel yours. We plan to increase the social and economic well-being of Third World nations. Iraq wants to expand Cuba's foreign trade by acting as an advisor. Please keep this confidential."

"With our new technology, Cuba won't have to buy oil to use for power. In other words, Iraq is using an underdeveloped Western country to influence poorer nations."

Remmich's subconscious had the same information.

"Currently, contractors are constructing the photosynthesis building. Like me, you're here to be a diplomat advisor. You are to visit this place often, so the Cubans see you at the job site. I'll be with you this first trip only." He stopped talking and took out a cigar from a three-section case. "Do either of you want a cigar?"

They declined. Elliott snipped off the end. While lighting it, he rolled the cigar around to let the flame burn it evenly. Remmich and Gonzales took out their cigarette packs, and the Mexican lit both their smokes.

"We'll use the first couple of days to speak to the engineers and government workers." He described the information in the notes, one by one. Finishing, he told them, "I am attending a meeting with the Iraqi representatives." He stopped to sip and puff the cigar. After blowing the smoke upward, his mouth curved roguishly. "So I'll let Miguel take you out into the nightlife."

He put the drawing between them, sat back, and reiterated how the plan was more than a political goal. He talked about improving the economy with jobs, education, and hospital expansion.

"Someday, Iraq's influence will help to improve the situation of some of the four billion impoverished people in the world. It's an alarming percentage of the overall population. Strange, isn't it, when we think of this republic as impoverished, we know other countries are in even poorer condition."

It was just about 5 p.m. "I want to stop now. Let's meet here tomorrow morning at oh-nine-hundred." While they walked out, Elliott said, "Oh, before I forget, Miguel, get someone to oil the door hinges."

Walking to the elevator, Remmich's stomach grumbled. "I am more hungry than tired. Any suggestions for dinner?"

"The general gave me strict instructions. While you're here, I'm paying for your expenses. Whatever you want, whether it's for yourself or a gift for your wife. I'll be reimbursed. And to answer your question, we have many restaurants offering different cuisines. However, there's a place I think you'll particularly like."

They got into Gonzales's car, and Remmich asked, "So what type of restaurant do you have in mind?"

After fastening his seatbelt, Gonzales grinned teasingly. “I will surprise you, Señor.” He drove a peppy five-gear white Jaguar. It made Remmich think of his sporty BMW. He enjoyed the Jag’s nimbleness and acceleration.

Gonzales reached the destination and parallel parked next to a curb. “Across the street, Señor, is where we are eating. If you look up, you’ll see the head of the long-horned bull, the El Toro. It’s also the restaurant’s name.”

“I take it the food is good?”

“It’s excellent. You’ll see.”

“Like what, for example?” He was salivating.

“This place specializes in beef. But they have seafood, too.”

The place was packed. The maître d’ informed Gonzales he had to wait for an hour for a table. He suggested they sit at the bar instead. They followed the headwaiter.

A bartender approached them. “Dos Coronas, por favor.” The guy nodded and left.

Remmich lit a cigarette, while his host pulled one out of his own pack. They exhaled as the barman placed beers before them.

“I’m surprised this is on tap. I thought your country was still undeveloped.”

“Amigo, you have been out of the States too long. My country is on its way out of economic problems. We have come far from the days of Fulgencio Batista.” They talked about Castro’s death and the development of Cuba.

Minutes later, a barman interrupted them. “Are you interested in an appetizer?”

Gonzales said they just wanted to order dinner. The man wrote down the orders for filet mignon steaks, with two side dishes.

He stopped writing and said, “Señor, your order will take fifteen to twenty minutes. We are busy.”

They sipped, and Gonzales boasted about the beautiful things Cuba offered, despite its reputation.

“How did you get this job, Miguel?”

No one had ever asked Gonzales that question. "Iraqi diplomats visited the island a year ago. I met them here. They heard me speaking English. The person I talked to was an American who defected from the Army. He does odd jobs for me now, and I pay him a decent salary. After that, I was contacted by a man who introduced himself in English as Arif Yildiz. We met for dinner, and when we were almost finished, he shocked me by offering a job. Before we left, he gave me a hotel card and asked me to meet him there.

"On Tuesday morning, I met Yildiz and his associates, Iyad Aboona and Ramzi Hamdi, at the Ritz. They explained Iraq's desires in more detail. It intrigued me. The following day, we went to the office of Cuba's secretary of affairs. Since I speak Spanish, I acted as their interpreter. I guess I'm lucky because I was in the right place at the right time."

"How did you become involved with General Elliott, Miguel? Where did you get together?"

The Cuban explained Yildiz wanted him to fly to Frankfurt to meet someone. "The guy couldn't get away to come to Cuba, so they sent me to him. Months later, the general was able to come here for a few days." Gonzalez believed the Iraqi told the truth about helping undeveloped countries.

They placed their cigarettes between their lips, but Gonzales's lighter wouldn't work. After several more unsuccessful tries, his guest struck a match and lit their cigarettes.

"Muchas gracias."

Remmich dropped the burning match into the ashtray. Gonzales noticed him playing with the empty matchbook, wrapping the cover around the striker section and bending the whole thing in half. Then he forced it back and forth, using his thumb, forefinger, and middle fingers.

"You get your rocks off doing that, Señor Paul?"

Remmich smiled, ready to give a wisecrack answer, when a delicious aroma distracted him. The waiters placed the trays with their dinners on folding tray stands. Another server locked wooden bar saddle-trays in front of them. The mole stopped fooling around with the matchbook. He took one last drag and put out the cigarette.

***

The briefing at Guantánamo Bay Naval Base finished at 3:30. Now the Army majors were on their way north to Havana. Miller and McKinsey needed to explore the Havana area for a military defector. They realized defectors wouldn't maintain their Army-style clean cut looks. They'd be difficult to distinguish. Yet they knew a way to find them; listening to a person's speech and inflections would identify Americans.

They boarded a troop helicopter at Leeward Point Field and fastened their seatbelts. The aircraft stopped for refueling on a carrier at a halfway point. The final landing was at the José Marti International Airport. Pedro Sola, the driver, walked away to get his car, a beige Ford. Forty-five minutes later, they arrived at the Hotel Havana. After they checked-in, the agent tipped the bellboy before he pushed the luggage carrier up to the rooms.

"Meet me back here in fifteen minutes."

They took the elevator up to their rooms to freshen up.

Sola decided to drive them through a different section of the city to show its picturesque shops and restaurants. The weather paralleled Miami, warm and humid.

"Are you both hungry?"

"I'm starving," replied Miller.

"Me, too," answered McKinsey.

Sola smiled. "Bueno. When was the last time you guys ate a good steak?" Miller turned around and stared at his buddy, then they burst out laughing. Sola's sense of humor tuned in with theirs. Smiling, he commented, "That long, huh?"

He turned right and parked at the curb. The white Jaguar was two cars in front. Sola stepped out and stretched; it had been a time-consuming day for him, too. His pointing made the officers take notice of the restaurant's logo. They strolled ahead, stopping to admire the Jaguar.

Sola mentioned, "This is the best restaurant in Havana, Señors." He explained the quality of the food and draft beer.

They crossed the street. People blocked the entrance. "Wait here," said Pedro.

He nudged forward, saying he was the policia and waved his opened wallet, displaying his CIA badge. The agent closed it so fast, the people in line couldn't see the ID. He motioned for the officers to follow.

A manager stood behind a marble reception podium. He wrote Sola's cell phone number on a list and stated, "You have to wait for a half-hour, maybe longer. And you can't stay inside." The man turned halfway and pointed. "As you can see, Señor, we are jam-packed. You must wait outside or cancel your reservation."

Pedro told his companions, "We have to go back out. They will call me when a table is ready."

Outside, the waiting line of guests frowned at him. They were irritated about him using his influence to get ahead of them. Sola leaned against the car, disgruntled. Fifteen minutes passed, and he went into the foyer again. People still crowded the access, so he gave up and returned to the men.

Miller and McKinsey passed the time talking about their days at West Point and the duty stations where they'd served. Four men moseyed out of the restaurant and walked by them. They clowned around, speaking Arabic. Sola's countenance changed to a stern stare. Since he understood their language, he was curious. It was unusual to see people from the Middle East in Cuba. McKinsey and Miller, noticing Sola's look, stopped talking and watched. The group passed them, got into a van, and drove away.

Their host's phone vibrated, and he answered. "Good news, Majors! We can go in."

They walked inside, and the reservations manager told him bar seats would be ready within minutes. They waited inside the foyer. It was half-past 8 o'clock.

***

Remmich swallowed the last bite of steak, put his utensils on the plate, and reached for a cigarette. Finding his matchbook empty, he waved his arm back and forth to get the barman's attention. Gonzales tried his lighter again. Finally, another barman dropped off three packs of matches. The matchbooks had El Toro's bull head symbol.

Seeing they'd finished, a busboy removed their plates, while a barman unlocked the saddles and carried them away. Gonzales accepted the check, studied it, and paid, including a generous tip. They started to walk out, but the dense crowd changed their minds.

Gonzales tapped Remmich on the arm. "This way. We can leave at the side door."

The bouncer held it open for them.

***

The Americanos followed their driver. Lucky for them, five empty seats were in the smoking section. Sola hurried up to three vacant chairs. He stretched his arms out to stop anyone from trying to sit in them first.

Once they were all seated, he suggested, "Drinks, Señors?" He waved for a bartender and ordered Coronas.

Miller's stomach did a quick flip when he noticed the glass ashtray contained a matchbook bent up and twisted the same way Paul habitually tortured his. How likely was it there was someone else with that strange habit? A barman came to take it. Miller grabbed and held on to it, raising his voice to stop its removal.

"No, Señor. Leave it here."

Sola asked the barman to bring three menus as McKinsey looked at Miller's stunned expression.

"What is it, Eric?" he asked.

6

The Find

Miller was oblivious to the noise in El Toro. He sat stone silent, as if in another world.

It's the end of our first day on the job in Cuba. I know I'm exhausted. But this?

An idea twirled around in his head. Looking at the matchbook, the cover folded around the striker section and bent; could it be a coincidence? And if it wasn't Paul Remmich's, who else did this zany thing?

McKinsey shook Miller's arm and said, "Hey, Earth to Major Miller. Earth to Major Miller."

Miller picked up the bent-up matchbook. His continued lack of response prompted McKinsey to grab his friend's cigarette pack. He lit two cigarettes, holding one out to Miller. He took the cigarette but remained mute.

They watched him unfold the matchbook. Miller read the inscription and dropped the mangled cover out of his hands.

His face twisted with anger, he blurted out, "You sonofabitch!"

McKinsey asked, "What's wrong?"

"This matchbook has the name of the Hotel Schiller in Amsterdam on the front." He turned to look at Sola, then into his associate's eyes. "My ex-Army buddy, Paul Remmich, was here tonight."

"So what?" said McKinsey.

Miller took a puff to calm down. As he exhaled, he said, "It's complicated. Since his transfer to Germany, his military life has been with V Corps at the Thirty-second. He was the primary security intelligence agent doing the encryption deciphering. Many officers, like us, have learned cyber offensive and defensive logistics. Most of them don't want to work in this military occupational specialty. The Army noticed Remmich liked the challenge. But he recently surprised everybody in G-2, including me, by resigning. Generals Sutherland and Elliott asked him at his debriefing to stay on as a civilian government worker. He's paid a bimonthly salary, and things are working out fine. Only, he's a civilian now."

"I don't get it," said McKinsey. "Why have a civilian doing this work? Isn't that why you got transferred there?"

"That's one reason, but you know the Army never tells us what they have in store for us. Anyway, Remmich helped to broaden the present encryption satellite coding and decoding message system with INSCOM. Part of his success is due to the help he got while working with NSA's division in North Yorkshire, England."

"What do you mean?"

"The connection with these people greatly assisted him in writing the basis for the classwork I took before joining your group, Tom. INSCOM put together encryption code classes for this seminar, based on some of what he did, to prevent cyber infiltration. Paul is valuable, and INSCOM wouldn't want to lose him to the private sector or a foreign government."

"He'd surely get more money," interjected McKinsey.

Miller pointedly ignored that comment. "Anyway, he told me at dinner the other night he had to go into an area called Baden-Baden this week. Supposedly, he'd be traveling for a few days. I told him I couldn't get together with him either over the weekend." He held up the bent matchbook. "But after looking at this, especially with the Hotel Schiller name on it, he was obviously lying!"

Sola and McKinsey sat motionlessly, with their eyes fixed on each other. Their judgments were on Paul Remmich, who apparently had turned spy.

Miller hesitated a few seconds before saying, "I don't want to accept it as true yet. As long as he's an active worker for V Corps, we have to respect what he's doing. He's innocent until proven guilty. Right?"

McKinsey picked up the matchbook and said, "Yeah. I suppose so." He rolled the matchbook up and tried to bend it as Remmich had.

"Here, let me show you what he does with this thing." Using his middle finger and thumb to hold it, Miller bent it back and forth with his forefinger. "This is the crazy shit he always does when we're smoking and talking."

McKinsey chuckled. "I guess it shows some form of intelligence. Where's he from? I mean, which zoo?"

Finally, the three of them laughed. McKinsey blurted out, "Well, I see you still have your sense of humor."

"We need to find him and ask what in the hell he was doing a couple thousand miles from the Baden-Baden business trip."

Pedro slipped in a question. "Amigos, are you still hungry? If so, let me order now. I'm starving." He signaled the bartender, calling out, "Podría ver la menú?"

A barman placed one on the bar in front of Sola. "You guys still want steaks?" He got favorable responses and placed the order for three thick ones, cooked medium rare, with baked potatoes and salads. They ordered three more beers.

"I want mine rare," said McKinsey.

"Oh, you understand Spanish?"

"Very little, but I understand the word 'raro.'"

"I wouldn't order just rare. The beef in this place is so fresh, it's almost just cut out of the steer and waved over the coals if ordered rare. Trust me, mediano raro will still give us a nice piece of meat."

The officers nodded in agreement, and McKinsey asked, "So what else is on your mind, Eric?"

"I don't know, Tom. I don't want to be critical and condemn the guy without any evidence. But I sure as hell can't ignore the matter. I don't want to say he's one of those moles we talked about at the INSCOM meetings, but why did he lie to me?"

McKinsey took a drag, exhaled, and said, "This has to be reported."

Hesitantly, Miller replied, "Yes, I agree. If he is an undercover agent, we'll find out. But give me a few days. If he's still on this island, we may find him. After all, our job is to find an AWOL person, maybe a spy. Right?"

McKinsey nodded in agreement, while three more beers replaced the empty ones. He said, "Look. If you don't want to report him, say for a couple weeks, I'll keep my mouth shut. But he has to be questioned."

For the next 20 minutes, the three men debated Paul Remmich's motives. Was he really involved in espionage? And if it was true, what had influenced him to become a spy?

Sola cleared his throat. "This is where the CIA might come into this full force, amigos." The majors nodded their heads in agreement.

It was close to 25 minutes after he'd placed their meal order. Sola motioned for the bartender, but the guy read his mind and said, "They are bringing them to you right now, Señor."

It was already 9:15 p.m. A man interrupted them to secure wooden bar saddle trays in front of them. Two apprentice waiters carried a large serving tray filled with three oval platters. Baked potatoes sat beside the steaks. Another serving tray had three smaller bowls of salad with lots of chunky, fresh blue cheese dressing. One assistant split the potatoes and placed a large piece of butter on each. The barman put salt and pepper shakers in front of them.

While he seasoned the steak, Sola asked, "Excuse me for asking now, but are you guys going to begin to work on a plan this evening?"

Miller swallowed his first bite and sipped beer. "Cuba is a small island, five hundred miles by forty miles. That's a hell of a lot of areas to cover in five or six days. Since we believe he's on the island, we must narrow down departure points. The only one I'd consider is the airport."

"I agree. Let me check with Navy staff at Guantánamo. They can pull up computer listings of commercial flights out of Havana." They took another bite of steak, then some salad. He gestured with his fork to get attention. "I don't think he's going to return directly to Amsterdam. Many NATO alliance airlines will still not fly directly to or from Cuba. It probably won't happen until the United States negotiates to change the communistic system with a democratic structure. Spain is a NATO member. They are friendly with Cuba. I think this is the country we'll look for flights." He took a sip of beer and added, "I wonder if he's got a fake name, too?"

Eric smiled. "You know, Pedro, Spain is a good idea."

"I believe he'll fly into Barajas Airport in Madrid," said Sola. "Spain wants to maintain a good face with its NATO affiliates. They also want to look good in the eyes of their Spanish and Portuguese friends in Central and South America."

"You seem to be familiar with Spain. Have you ever lived there?" asked McKinsey.

"I *am* Spanish. My father is from Spain, but my mother is Algerian, although she is a Christian. I grew up in Barcelona and attended Madrid University before coming to the United States. I earned a master's degree in foreign relations from American University in Washington, DC."

"You're multilingual: Spanish, English, and, I guess, Arabic?"

"Yes, Eric, I understand and speak Arabic. When we were outside and those four men passed us, they mentioned a new construction job. I wondered what they were doing in Cuba. I realize this sounds strange, but this was the first time I've heard people here speaking Arabic."

For the moment, his comments didn't trouble them, and McKinsey said, "I wondered how you learned to speak English so well. I mean, the slang you use in sentences makes it seem so natural."

"Gracias, Tom."

"Did the CIA hire you because you speak three languages?" inquired Miller.

"Sí, but I never had any military training. The interviewer wanted to know if I'd be interested in learning how to shoot a gun to defend myself. Naturally, I expressed my interests. It took fifteen months of training at The Farm in Virginia. It was a lot of work, but it was exciting. They often told us, 'Reveal nothing, learn everything.'"

When they finished eating, he motioned for the bartender to remove their plates and bar saddles. Then he asked if a table was available. Within minutes, the maître d' approached and told him a booth was vacant.

He excused himself, while the majors followed the maître d' to the booth. When the agent returned, more beers were on the table. He dropped a writing tablet onto the table and sat down.

"It's wise to record our ideas."

Miller sipped his beer and followed up with, "Who's taking notes?"

"I will," answered Pedro.

"I agree with the first strategy you mentioned, Pedro," said McKinsey, "to see if Remmich is leaving from this airport."

While he wrote, Miller said, "Let's consider travel in and out of Miami?"

The agent replied, "It's convenient if the right vessel is available. For example, those thirty-five-foot fiberglass crafts used by the drug cartel and illegal tobacco dealers. They can reach various shorelines along either coast of Florida within an hour-and-a-half or less. But the same boat could easily reach the northern countries of South America, too."

"Yes. I see your point, Pedro," said Miller, his brow furrowed in thought. "But getting back to airline travel, do small planes frequent the island?"

"Sí. I know because the FBI worked on a project with us. I was one of several people transported to my new job by a small plane landing in the field of a tobacco farm. The Cuban government is concerned about illegal drugs entering their country. They asked the FBI for help because they don't have the manpower. But the FBI never got the money approved by Congress. Simply put, Cuba can't provide the funds."

"It's interesting. We didn't have this information at the INSCOM gatherings before coming here," said McKinsey.

"Maybe the V Corps was not informed. It was a political move, not military. But in the meantime, we need to begin tomorrow in Guantánamo. Agreed?"

They concurred, and he said, "Bueno," while he wrote.

"Let's share other possible ways to leave Cuba," added Miller. He took a sip of his Corona and lit a cigarette. "Our man is not a fugitive. He's not running away. I'm sure he's not avoiding the authorities. Personally, I believe he came here on a commercial flight. Let's start there."

Sola stopped a passing waiter and said, "Camarero, la cuenta, por favor." Next, he quickly wrote Eric's comments. The waiter brought the bill and waited. The agent took US dollars out of his wallet.

He parked in the lot at the hotel. "This is it, Señors." They all got out, and Sola locked the doors. "This is where I live. I feel it is a good idea for us to be close together while you're here.

***

They flew back to Guantánamo Bay Naval Base on Tuesday at 0800 hours. US Marine military police guards stood at attention on either side of the helicopter door and saluted.

McKinsey asked, "Are you an officer, Pedro, even though you aren't in the Army?"

"Sí. My payroll and rank are equal to an Army captain. Although I am not allowed to show any rank insignia, I am a US government employee like you guys."

They walked into a one-story brick building. A seaman first class led the group to the office of Marine Brigadier General Stanton. Sola introduced the two officers. The general told them to sit in the chairs across from him.

"General, these are the CIC, V Corps gentlemen working with me. We need to find out when commercial flights are coming in and out of Havana from the Barajas airport." He explained the circumstances.

Stanton made a telephone call to his secretary and explained they needed a computer line open to check on commercial airline flights. He looked at each man and said, "Gentlemen, you will find Master Sergeant Arnold waiting for you upstairs in room two-oh-seven."

The computer screen displayed international flights. Agent Sola cracked his knuckles before he brought up Iberia International Airlines' flight times. The next page included the names of passengers. After a couple of minutes, he found Paul Remmich's name listed on the flight two days earlier.

"I found him."

They didn't find Remmich's name for a return flight. Each got a printed copy of the flight schedules.

"We're going to have to schedule someone to wait at the airport to see when Mr. Remmich leaves," said Miller, his face grim.

"You sound determined, Major," said Sola.

"I am. This is one of the biggest blows I've ever had to my sense of trust. It was totally unexpected, Pedro. Totally!"

"Well, are we going to return to Havana this evening, or stay overnight and leave in the morning?" asked McKinsey.

Miller looked at his watch. “Let’s stay here overnight. We’ve had a busy day.”

“Sí. I think you have a good idea, Eric.”

7

Seen

They met in the lobby and walked to the mess hall on base. It was already 90 degrees in Cuba, humid, and the temperature continued to rise. The sea breeze floated breakfast aromas in their direction.

"Smells good," said McKinsey.

They entered the officer section and got in line, which moved at a decent pace. Sola paid, and they found a table. A couple swallows of food and coffee later, McKinsey focused on both of them.

"Are we taking turns at the Havana airport? I don't know if that's the best use of our time. Can we schedule MP patrols to find out if our man gets on the jet to Spain?"

"I don't want to wait around the airport any more than you do," said Miller. "For now, we should let the MPs do their job."

They spent 15 minutes talking over specifics, then the agent asked, "Do we have a photo of this guy, so the military police in Havana know who to look for?"

Miller took out his cell phone and said, "No, so I'll call Stuttgart now. They'll fax a color photo of him and a physical description to the MP office."

"Have your office fax two of each; one to Havana, and one to Guantánamo Bay Naval Base," said Pedro. "And while you're doing that, Eric, I'm going to call General Stanton's office and tell him what's happening. And I'll call the MP office in Havana."

***

By midmorning, they boarded another Chinook helicopter. This time, other military passengers were on the trip back to Havana. Their pilot landed to refuel on an aircraft carrier on the Atlantic side.

They arrived at the airport and returned to the hotel to freshen up and change clothes. Sola suggested going into Havana and getting something to eat and drink. He also reminded them to wear loose shirts to hide their pistols.

He drove toward a section of Havana the officers were unfamiliar with. "There's a place on the southwest outskirts. We passed it last night. It's called Fiesta, and it has delicious sandwiches and good salads." He made a left turn onto Santiago Street and parked.

As they walked to the restaurant, McKinsey said, "Hey, this looks like the white Jaguar we saw at the steak place the other night." The agent made a mental note of the license number.

The restaurant was a corner building with big windows. They were among others entering the place. The air conditioning felt good. The second floor was as crowded as the downstairs.

The Spaniard talked to a waiter, who led them to a table in the back on the first floor. While they got settled, the majors took note of the other customers and waiters. No one was speaking English except them. He answered a call and wrote down the information on a pad before hanging up.

"So, what's going on?" asked McKinsey.

"It was the Havana military police headquarters," said Sola. "They received Paul Remmich's ID paperwork and a photograph. The captain said Guantánamo got their copies, so we don't have to call them. They're faxing the information to the city police and will assign two Marines to go to the airport with the same information. Oh, and a city policeman will be working with them. He'll translate."

"Boy, that response was fast," remarked McKinsey.

They finished lunch, then Sola requested the bill. Miller excused himself and got up to use the men's room. While walking past the central stairwell to the second floor, he smelled a familiar cologne scent, Remmich's favorite brand.

Just a coincidence, he thought.

When he came out and reentered the dining room, the odor was most noticeable by the stairs. His curiosity aroused, he walked slowly up the stairs.

Standing on the top step and holding on to the banister, he peered between seated guests and passing waiters. A waiter came over and asked in broken English if he needed assistance. He shook his head. Two waiters carrying full serving trays walked up the stairs. Miller had to turn sideways to let them pass.

The movements of the servers around Miller caught the attention of the general's attaché, Gonzales. He sat at a table about fifteen feet from the stairs, with Elliott and Remmich. He asked the general if he expected Americanos for lunch.

Elliott laughed derisively and said, "No, why would I invite anyone, especially an American? Why do you ask?"

Gonzales explained the activity at the stairway, and the man standing there. When Remmich heard he was a tall, clean-cut, military-looking Black man, chills ran up his back. He slowly turned around, then quickly turned back after seeing his friend's profile.

Meanwhile, Miller, frustrated by the crowd, and assuming he was mistaken, gave up and returned to his table. Sola was on the phone again. When he finished the call, the agent looked up at them.

"I was just informed Cubans are doing some construction work with Iraqi help." He held up the note and added, "It's in the northwest part of the city. I don't have an address, but it's not far from the hospital, and across the street there's a power plant. It supplies electricity. I know the area."

"Are we going to go look?" McKinsey asked.

The waiter returned with the bill attached to a clipboard. The agent handed a credit card to him. When the server returned with the credit card and bill, the agent signed it. They then walked to the Ford across the street.

***

The afternoon sun wasn't shining through the front windows of the restaurant. Remmich sat, facing an open view of the outside. Looking toward the street, he watched three men open the doors, Eric Miller clearly visible. The other man also looked military, with his stance and crewcut. The third guy looked Hispanic. Paul nudged Elliott with his elbow and told him to look out the window and across the street.

"General, are you aware of a search team? And do you recognize the Black man with those two other men? It's Captain Eric Miller."

Elliott's eyes widened. "Where?" he asked.

"Look across the street, before they get into the tan Ford."

"Oh, my God. You're right." He turned and added, "You didn't hear about this at the last security meeting you attended in Stuttgart, did you?"

"No, sir, I didn't. I can't imagine why the officers are here. Do you think they know we're here, General?"

"Possibly. It is more likely they know there are Iraqis on the island, but I doubt they know the reason. The photosynthesis project is still so deeply secret that many higher-rank officers are unaware. I only found out because I worked from INSCOM in Fort Belvoir during my last tour of duty. Few knew the discovery existed. During some of the meetings I attended a couple years ago, there was information about this scientific discovery. Nothing technical; just to inform us. Anyway, we didn't understand much of it."

Gonzales asked for the bill.

"Paul, one other thing," said Elliott. "You referred to Miller as a captain. Our office received data saying he got promoted to major last week. He's also now a member of the CIC division."

Shrugging off a momentary flash of envy, Remmich still asked anxiously, "Why is he here in Havana? Do you believe he's looking for me?"

"Actually, Paul, I believe you're getting upset over nothing. Now that he's with CIC, I think he's here to find defectors, nothing more. I'm not worried," explained Elliott. He took his last sip of iced tea, backed up his chair, and said, "Are you guys ready to go back to the job site?"

***

Sola carefully drove by the construction area and parked on the other side of the street. When they got out, they had to yell to be heard over the din from the dozer and backhoe. They walked closer to watch the construction. Two cranes worked in unison to lower and hold a twenty-foot-by-ten-foot aluminum cover onto a large cylinder frame assembly. They got close enough to see both the outside and inside of the horizontal tube construction. The interior was really an anodized chrome metal surface mechanically fastened to the covers.

McKinsey said, "I wonder what's being built?"

No one said anything. They just watched.

Spot welders made temporary bonds to the outside steel plate butt joints to fit around the half-moon tube frame. Two metal workers followed the spot welders to weld the outer aluminum joints to protect the chrome interior. A superintendent on the inside used a walkie-talkie to guide the workers while he measured to ensure the sections were in place and even. Iraqi engineers examined blueprints to ensure the work met specifications.

The Spaniard noticed a group of men just standing around talking, not following the job's progress. As they watched, one man left the group and walked in their direction.

Before he got to them, Pedro said, "I remember seeing those four men walk out of the restaurant the other night. They spoke Arabic. I wonder if they're the Iraqis I've been warned about?"

There was no time to respond, because the stranger interrupted them. He wanted to see identification. Sola turned to him, and they exchanged a few words. Miller and McKinsey stood mute, unable to understand.

Frustrated, Pedro turned to them and said, "He asked if we have construction passes to be at this job. When I told him we didn't, he said we have to leave, or he'll call the police."

As they walked away, Miller saw Remmich come out of the construction trailer wearing a white hard hat. He walked up to the workers with his back to Miller. They crossed the street and noticed the Jaguar. From the license plate number, they noted it was the same vehicle.

8

Conference Call

Their discussion during the ride back from the construction site was tense.

As Sola parked the car at the Hotel Havana, McKinsey asked, "What are we going to do?"

Miller's attitude toward Remmich was a combination of betrayal, anxiety, and worry. It was also emotionally tiring.

Resigned to continue the analysis, he said, "Why don't we freshen up and you guys come back to my room? We need to talk." He focused on the agent and said, "And Pedro, bring those notes from the other night."

In his hotel room, Miller splashed his face with cold water to remove the sandy, salty crud around his eyes, relieved himself, and called the front desk. He ordered six cold beers. Ten minutes later, the other two arrived, along with the waiter carrying the bottles. Miller tipped him, and he left.

"Help yourselves to a beer and let's go out on the balcony."

When he opened the door, the air conditioning drifted out, while a warm breeze came in. Another building blocked the afternoon sun, so the breeze felt good. A waist-high wall separated the deck and next room balcony. They sat down.

Miller leaned forward, with his arms resting on his knees. "I want to have a conference call in a few minutes with Colonel Kirby. We need to report the fact that Paul Remmich is not only on this island, he's somehow connected with the Cuban and Middle Eastern officials."

Sola said, "Yes, the Arabic-speaking men at the construction site were the same ones who passed us outside the restaurant. Now I have a better understanding of what they talked about. I overheard them mention photosynthesis energy and that this job was the starting point. Several of these structures will be built for the Cubans."

McKinsey tightened his lips and showed a sorrowful look. "So we have to say he's working with the Iraqis and Cubans." They came to an agreement.

McKinsey pressed the autodial. When the ringing started, he put it on speakerphone.

Kirby answered, and Miller said, "Good afternoon, Colonel."

Before he spoke another word, they heard, "How are things going? I haven't heard anything from you and assumed all was going well."

"Sir, I have some bad news. I believe we found a spy, not an AWOL."

Miller briefly related the specifics of Remmich's story, the same details he'd told to McKinsey and Sola.

Kirby didn't speak for a few seconds.

"You're sure it's Paul Remmich?"

"Yes, sir, I'm afraid so."

"Wow, this is unbelievable."

"Colonel, I haven't had a chance to put too much thought into this situation. I'm just as flabbergasted as you are. It's like I've lost my best friend." He stopped to catch his breath. "Major McKinsey and I discussed the matter the other night, when I suspected he was on the island."

"What do you mean you suspected he was on the island?"

Miller explained the details about the matchbook cover. "Sir, I was curious because I don't know anyone else who has that habit. When I unrolled the cover and saw the Hotel Schiller name, where Remmich lives in Amsterdam, I was certain." The colonel didn't speak.

Sola mentioned their visit to the construction area. He told Kirby about the four Arabic-speaking men and seeing the work in progress. He frowned as he explained how the superintendent had told them to leave or else.

Miller told the superior officer about seeing Paul Remmich come out of the construction trailer.

"Isn't Paul Remmich the guy who works with the V Corps security encryption program?"

"Yes, sir. Um, I may be jumping the gun, but we should try to bring him in ourselves."

They waited for a response. No one moved until Kirby said, "I'm not sure you can legally detain or arrest him. He's no longer an active military officer, even though he does encryption work for V Corps. He's got civilian status, and we could get into serious trouble." He stopped talking again for a few seconds, then added, "I was just thinking. He's in Cuba and seems to be involved in a construction project. So what? But why is he working with Arabic-speaking people, and what are they doing there? Listen, we'd have a better chance of grabbing him when he returns to Amsterdam. He'd be within our military property area, so to speak. If you try to apprehend him in Cuba, he might demand authorization. He's within his legal rights to travel anywhere, associate with anyone, and work for any company. He can also refuse to talk to us without a subpoena."

Miller breathed easier; the colonel's decisions took the matter out of his hands. "I'm sure he'll go back to Amsterdam because his wife is there. But we don't know when."

"We'll find out, I'm sure. Keep a low profile. In the meantime, I want you two to prepare a summary about your knowledge of Remmich's actions since his resignation. I'm going to make arrangements for your flights back to DC. I'll notify Guantánamo and get you stateside as soon as possible. We'll go back to Germany whenever a flight is available at Andrews. I'll contact you when I get more information."

McKinsey ended the call. "That was simple."

He looked at his watch, then at them. "I have an idea," said Pedro. "It's four-thirty. Are you hungry?"

"I'm getting there," said McKinsey.

Miller leaned back in the chair, rubbing his stomach. "Yeah, I can use some food."

"Well, since this may be your last night in Havana, I think we should return to the El Toro. If we get there early, we should be able to get seats without waiting." Miller wanted to know if they could make reservations. "I tried once, but they wouldn't accept phone reservations." They grabbed another beer and left.

During the ride, McKinsey said, "I have a feeling Kirby's going to contact General Sutherland. We know how our V Corps lieutenant general wants to be prepared ahead of any attack."

Miller remarked, "Yeah, I agree. So, let's develop that list of Remmich's actions. At least we know most of what he's done since he resigned."

Twenty minutes later, the agent parked outside the restaurant. The maître d' welcomed them at the door and walked them to a table. Sola asked in Spanish if they could sit at a booth. Once they were seated, a waiter greeted them, and he ordered three beers. The server wrote the order and walked away.

Miller sat back, his face glum. While the other two talked, he remembered finding the folded matchbook.

The waiter broke his attention by placing the beers on the table. He spoke to Sola for a moment.

"He wants to know if we want to order dinner now."

"I do," said McKinsey. "And you, Eric?"

Trying to snap out of his melancholy, he shook his head and answered, "Yes."

When the waiter walked away with the order, Sola placed the notepad in front of him. "How about I write the ideas?" He held up the glass of Corona and said, "Cheers!"

All eyes were on Miller. "I want to list everything I explained to Colonel Kirby, but I want to back up to when I transferred to the Thirty-second. During my initial briefing with Colonel Collins, I found out Paul was stationed there, too. He'd been there close to five years."

The other two men sipped and listened.

"Anyway, while we were in the snack bar, Colonel Collins told me Paul wanted to resign. It was a surprise; one I didn't want to believe. Paul happened to be there then, and I joined him at a table. Seeing each other after so long was gratifying at first. But he quickly turned the subject around to his disagreement with the UN's reducing its support of Third World nations. He was more irritated with the US government for going along with the decision. Physically, he was the same guy I hung around with at West Point and during our MI training. After that chat, we went to Amsterdam for Memorial Day weekend. Since that weekend, he's changed. He's not the same guy. I believe something else happened to make him defect. It's got to be more than just his dispute with the UN's policy with Third World nations."

The waiters interrupted them, carrying their food trays. It then became a race to see who could cut their steak first and take a bite.

Miller realized he forgot to tell the colonel about another incident involving Remmich's behavior. He shocked his cohorts when he told them about Remmich carrying around a flash drive containing decoded encryption information. Miller related his friend's defensiveness when confronted about its possession.

"Could it be related to the construction we saw today for the photosynthesis business?" asked Sola.

Miller answered. "I have to assume, if they mentioned the word 'photosynthesis,' it probably is."

"So I pointed out the matter to Generals Elliott and Sutherland during the special meeting we had at Patch Barracks. That meeting excluded Paul Remmich, if you recall, Tom. But Elliott didn't seem to be too concerned, and Sutherland followed suit, so I dropped the issue."

Sola asked, "I know who this Sutherland guy is, but who is Elliott?"

McKinsey told him the general's background.

Miller repeated grimly, "Something's happened to this man, and we need to find out what. It's eating my guts out, because he's so drastically changed from the person I used to know."

McKinsey asked, "When did he resign?"

"June thirtieth."

McKinsey kept eye contact with his cohort and used his fingers to count out loud. "July, August, September, October, November, and December. We have until December twelfth, which is the allowed six months to be away. We must get him back full-time or do something legally to prevent losing him."

The agent interrupted. "I've copied everything you talked about, but can you tell me any other things that make you suspicious, Eric?"

Miller related a day they sat in the snack bar for breakfast. Paul suddenly got up and walked away, never excusing himself. "A few minutes later, I saw him talking on his cell phone. When he returned to the table, he acted as if nothing had happened. I noticed he acted disoriented, like he was thinking and regaining his thoughts. He couldn't even answer me right away."

"I wonder if his calls were recorded on his cell phone."

Miller finished eating, looked up, and said, "I never thought about that, Pedro. Good idea."

"So when we get to Guantánamo tomorrow, I'll copy and print this out for you and Tom."

***

Thursday morning, they flew back to the naval base. An MP drove them to the administration building, where Sola showed the reception sergeant his ID.

"These men are scheduled for transport back to the States," he said, giving their names.

The sergeant looked at the day's events on the computer and saw the majors' names. Their scheduled flight was at 7:00 p.m. He made a call to confirm the CH-47 Chinook helicopter flight.

"I need to use a computer." Agent Sola removed six handwritten pages from a yellow pad.

It took more than one hour to type up a chronological summary of Miller's experiences with Remmich, including making changes and refining the wording. Sola printed out four pages. He pulled out the USB drive and turned off the computer.

***

They arrived at Miami International Airport and checked in at the US Army recruiting station. The NCO recruiter gave them tickets to fly to Reagan National Airport at 11 o'clock. When they arrived in Washington, DC, an airman held a sign with their last names. They were driven to Andrews Air Force Base and given a room at the base hotel.

They didn't get up until 0900. Colonel Kirby thought they could use some extra rest while he and Captain Carroll arranged for a flight back to Germany. They met up with the majors in the hotel's lobby.

"We're scheduled to leave Andrews at nineteen-hundred tonight," said Kirby, "and will arrive in Frankfurt tomorrow morning around oh-one-hundred. We're flying back with the same crew we came here with."

Nothing more was said as the officers in pursuit wondered what was next.

9
Unexpected

It was midmorning and the second day of visiting the job site. Gonzales and Remmich met the Havana officials. The Cuban interpreted. They walked and talked while looking at the construction's progress. The discussion got more detailed as the bureaucrats learned the new energy source would also supply electricity to their government buildings. They didn't understand how to harness energy from photosynthesis.

The finance guy wanted to know how the system worked. Remmich had already memorized his talk. He explained how natural or artificial light processes food sugar in a green plant.

He said, "Sugar molecules break down into chemical properties known as atoms. When an enclosed gas comes into contact with the particles, it creates electric waves. The waves magnify after meeting the vapor. The waves then pass through rubberized conduits surrounding bare copper wiring. The association causes an imbalance and sends an electrical charge through the wire. The resulting energy transfers to storage receptors to power any electrical device." He finished with, "The large storage batteries will store great amounts of energy. The percentage of energy is greater than what's needed. You'll never run out of electrical energy. And the production process provides an energy source without harmful exhaust."

The men left him and wandered around the site. They were still somewhat mystified about the process.

Gonzales met with Remmich and told him it was time to leave. The Jaguar's air conditioning felt good when they got on the road. His cell phone showed a voicemail message.

He listened to General Elliott's recording and told Remmich, "The general wants us to return to his quarters for lunch."

***

The Ritz Hotel elevator door opened, and they stepped on. It reached the 3rd floor, and they went to their separate rooms to freshen up.

Paul left his room and headed for suite 318. When he got there, the door was ajar. Remmich heard Elliott and Gonzales talking. He knocked on the opened door and walked to the kitchen.

"Gentlemen," he said.

"Come in, Paul," said Elliott, who sat at the bar, puffing a cigar and holding a tall glass of iced tea. "Care for a glass?"

"Yes. Thank you."

The table was set for three people. Gonzales poured their iced teas, then both men sat at the table. Everyone served themselves grilled tuna and fresh salad. Gonzales reached over the bar for a crusty loaf of sourdough bread.

"There's butter in the refrigerator if you don't mind getting it for us, Miguel."

He sat straight and wiped his mouth with the napkin. "I didn't accompany you to the construction site this morning because of a meeting. I've got bad news. An Iraqi intelligence agent stationed here informed me the men we saw at the Fiesta restaurant are CIC agents. And we know one of them was Eric Miller." He took a sip of iced tea and added, "Their mission here is to look for Army defectors. The Iraqi agents said they were at the construction site. It's unknown if they saw either of you there. Anyway, the three didn't have any job site IDs, so they were ordered to leave."

"Was that this morning?"

"Yes."

Elliott took a sip of iced tea, then added, "I spoke with Colonel Yildiz before you arrived." The general watched Remmich to see if he understood. "He thinks it's a good idea for both of us to leave Cuba on separate planes and fly to Caracas. He thinks the US Army might place military police at the Havana airport. It's obvious the Iraqi Foreign Service doesn't want them to find out anything, especially why we're here."

"So we're leaving today," said Remmich.

"Yes. My wife's visiting with our daughter in Atlanta because she thinks I'm attending Pentagon meetings. She expects me to get together with her when I'm finished. I'll fly to Miami, then to Atlanta. I'll spend my remaining leave days with her and my daughter's family."

After lunch, they shook hands and bid each other farewell. Remmich walked to his room to pack. He met Gonzales outside the main entrance, and they drove out of the city and took a dirt road adjoining an open tobacco field. The Jag parked under a tree. They saw a two-prop plane in the distance and watched it descend. A cloud of dust followed. They waited a few minutes for the dust to dissipate so they could see. The pilot stepped out and shook hands with Gonzales, who introduced Remmich. The man took Remmich's bags and put them into the plane.

One hour and fifty minutes later, the Caracas airport became visible. The pilot radioed the tower. Gusts of wind forced the plane to land hard, but the slow taxiing to the parking section relieved Remmich's tension. The pilot took his suitcase, and they entered the terminal.

The pilot led him to the Iberia Airlines ticket counter, extended his hand, and said, "Adiós, señor. They speak English here. Have a good flight."

"Adiós. Thank you." Remmich handed him a twenty euro note.

When he got to the attendant, she asked for his name in broken English. She pushed a few computer keys, and the printer produced two sets of tickets; one for Madrid, and one for Amsterdam. She placed the travel documents into an envelope and taped an identification tag around the suitcase's handle. A helper set it on the conveyer belt, where it disappeared beyond two swinging doors. She wished him a good flight. He thanked her and left for the B7 terminal.

There was no delay at the security checkpoint. Remmich walked to the departing gate and joined the others entering the jetway.

Meanwhile, Elliott also arrived at the Caracas airport. The pilot carried his bag to Delta Air Lines. They shook hands, and Elliott gave him a twenty-dollar tip.

***

The Pentagon was busy as usual; lower-rank human "runners" took packets of classified information, and robots delivered government scripts and industry contracts assigned to individual offices. In the midst of the usual scene, however, there was a problem. Elliott had someone looking for him.

Mrs. Elliott had called the Pentagon's security intelligence department on Wednesday morning. She explained to the officer that her husband, a major general, was there for a meeting. Diane made clear she'd called him and left a message on his second day away, but he hadn't returned her call. She wanted to know if he was all right. Her concern was legitimate, but Brigadier General Aaron Morris's attaché was puzzled.

How in the hell did she get a direct number to MI, G-2?

He called his CO right away. Morris didn't know Elliott's whereabouts at the Pentagon either, so why did he get a message that the general's wife wanted to talk to him? He decided to investigate and had his attaché make the return call to Atlanta.

The phone rang, and Diane answered. The attaché introduced himself and wasted no time asking how Mrs. Elliott had reached the security division.

"Oh, I just telephoned the information center. When I told them who I was, they gave me the number."

This security breach was mind-boggling and needed to be brought to the attention of General Morris. "Please let me check on this, and I'll call you back, Mrs. Elliott."

When Morris's assistant told him what she said, the general told him to follow up with security. He also decided he might as well find out what she wanted.

He dialed her on the office phone and said, "This is General Morris. Can I help you?"

She recognized his voice. "Yes. Good morning, Aaron. I hope you remember me. You transferred to Fort Carson in Colorado when Jerry and I lived there. It's been a few years since we've talked."

Morris figured since she'd addressed him on a first-name basis, he'd do the same. "Yes, Diane, I remember. It's good to talk to you again." They exchanged pleasantries for a minute, then he asked, "I understand you called earlier. Is there something wrong with Jerry?" The sound of his voice suggested aggravation.

She hesitated, then said, "I don't know, Aaron. I haven't heard from Jerry since I left Stuttgart last weekend to visit with our daughter here in Atlanta. He's attending a week of conferences. I realize the full week isn't over yet, but he usually calls me within a couple days. I was just checking to be sure he was okay."

"I haven't seen him, Diane. Of course, it doesn't mean he isn't here. There are many daily meetings and seminars at the Pentagon, and I'm not familiar with them all. Unless I'm working with him, I wouldn't know where he might be. I'm sure you understand."

She didn't want to admit she was unfamiliar with Pentagon ins and outs. "I guess so, but I'm beginning to worry."

"Diane, let me see what I can do. But I want you to know, some Army security intelligence officers don't have to sign in for security reasons. I'll have my secretary find the list of visiting Army personnel, and I'll call you back." He hesitated before saying, "Wait a minute. Are you sure he said he was coming here? Maybe he went to the NSA at Fort Meade or INSCOM at Fort Belvoir."

"No. Jerry said the Pentagon." She hesitated, then added, "Well, wait a minute. He did say something else, and it could have been INSCOM. I'm sorry if I'm a pest. I just wondered if there was a reason he didn't call."

The conversation ended, and Morris telephoned his secretary. He gave him instructions to check listings of all Army personnel attending meetings and those staying at the Fort Belvoir hotel. Within one hour, a sergeant returned with the information.

"Sir, there's no one here by the name of Major General Gerald Elliott."

"Thank you, Sergeant."

He watched the NCO walk out of the office. He knew Elliott was a guy who always stuck his head in an office for a brief hello. So, Morris assumed he wasn't there.

So what? His wife got her wires crossed.

The matter was becoming a pain in the ass; it would take too much military time to look for Elliott at NSA and Fort Belvoir. He also knew people attending classified meetings couldn't be contacted until they adjourned. Unless the president called.

Morris decided to wait until he was ready to leave for the day before he called Diane Elliott back. After all, her husband had helped him get his last promotion. But he didn't feel like looking for the man and knew Elliott could take care of himself. If the guy involved himself in something he didn't want his wife to find out, Morris didn't want to know either.

***

Remmich boarded the Iberia 767 and sat first class next to a window. He saw the drink cart and ordered a Corona Familiar, a liter size not sold in the United States. It felt good to be comfortable. He looked at his watch; 2:38 p.m.

Major General Elliott boarded his Delta jet early in the evening. An attendant asked to see his boarding pass and walked him to first class. Showing good old American airline hospitality, she asked if he wanted a drink. He requested a double scotch. She returned quickly and put two Johnnie Walker miniatures onto the fold-down tray, along with a glass half-filled with ice. The cabin's wall telephone rang for the flight attendant. It reminded him to make a call, but he couldn't take a chance. He knew authorities can legally obtain cell phone calls.

***

The Iberia jet roared off the runway and elevated rapidly. Remmich noticed the setting sun's crown on the port side. He waited, thinking the jet's direction would change to eastward, which would put the sun in the rear. It didn't. The plane continued north-northeast. The captain's voice came over the loudspeakers. He spoke Spanish, then English, announcing arrival time to Havana was in fifteen minutes. They'd have a forty-minute stopover, then depart for Madrid.

That explained the plane's direction!

The smooth landing was a welcome change from his earlier flight. He followed the last passenger to the door but stood at the top instead of walking down the stairs. He had an urge to smoke. No one was there, so he stood at the open door. He watched the people head to the terminal and noticed a policeman walking toward the jet.

He lit the cigarette. The smoke blew out the doorway from the air conditioning escaping. He heard voices speaking English down at the tarmac. He moved backward and, leaning toward the door, he looked out. A Cuban policeman spoke in broken English to two US Marine military police. He peeked out the doorway.

It's odd these people are here—unless they're after me!

His cigarette smoke blew away in the air. One of the MP sergeants noticed it but couldn't see him. She didn't think anyone was still on the plane. Remmich could barely hear her voice. When she put her hand on the stairway railing, he got nervous. He dropped the cigarette over the side of the stairway. They didn't see it fall to the ground.

When the MPs changed their stance, they faced the jet. Their voices became more audible, and he heard his name mentioned. They each held a clipboard with what looked like his photo. They showed it to the policeman and explained why they needed to compare all the male passengers for the man in the photograph.

Remmich's fear increased when the MP took a step onto the stairway.

She's going to inspect the jet.

He hurried across the aisle to the doorway to the first class section to grab his smaller luggage out of the overhead storage. The first class bathroom faced the plane's open door. He entered and closed the toilet lid, placing the case on it. He quickly changed his shirt and put on makeup.

The stair ramp rattled. Remmich heard sounds of more than one person walking up the metal stairs. He flushed the toilet to make them know someone was inside. He pasted a mustache onto his upper lip area and added color to his blond hair, so it looked grayer at the temples. He used makeup to fill in the crow's feet next to his eyes. He smiled, thinking he looked somewhat like a movie star getting ready for the camera.

He unlocked and opened the door. First, he looked to the left toward the sound of voices. The female sergeant looked at him as he walked out of the bathroom. The other MP looked in the coach bathroom, then closed the door. Remmich approached the second row of the coach section. He sat next to the window and picked out a magazine. He wanted to hide the fact that he had first class seats.

As they walked by him into the first class section, he remembered: he left the carry-on and cosmetic kit in the bathroom. One of the MPs passed him while walking back from the first class section. The other MP started to open the door to the bathroom Remmich had used. The mole's anxiety level soared.

The Cuban policeman stood on the stair landing, looking in. For some unfathomable reason, the man's presence at the door changed the MP's mind, and he didn't open the bathroom door fully. Instead, he turned and joined the other two. They walked down the stairs.

Remmich's pulse rate slowed. He felt sweat on his forehead, behind his neck, and on his upper lip. The mustache loosened, and he held it in place, just in case. When the officers walked off, he rushed into the bathroom. After removing the disguise, he returned and put the case into the overhead compartment. He sat down, relieved. He needed a scotch.

***

It was nearing 11:30 p.m. Delta Flight 607 circled Miami for twenty minutes, their landing delayed due to heavy air traffic. When they landed, the plane got caught in traffic again. The captain announced they had to wait for other aircraft to leave the space before they could move to their assigned gate.

While the captain spoke, Elliott looked at his watch. It was close to midnight.

"Jesus," he mumbled, "a two-and-a-half-hour flight turns into a three-hour one just because the airport's busy."

He wanted to call his daughter's number, but it was too late. It could wait until morning. He still carried the fake passport, which he didn't need. He did need the Iraqi American Express credit card in his pocket. He took a shuttle to the airport hotel.

Voices outside the room woke Elliott the next morning. His Atlanta flight wasn't early, so there was no need to rush. Fully awake, he sat on the side of the bed and was about to use the room's telephone when a fleeting thought came to him: the Caller ID would be displayed on the phone he called. If the FBI ever found out about him, they'd trace his travels. It was a sure thing they'd find out where he roomed. Calling his daughter could pinpoint his location in

Miami, not Washington, DC. He checked his cell phone, but it had a dead battery. When he plugged it in, the screen indicated a message. His wife sounded worried. She said since he hadn't called her, she decided to call the Pentagon.

"Jesus Christ," he said to himself. "That's all I need."

He thought of excuses to give her as to why she couldn't reach him. He'd wait to hear who she talked to and what she said and mold his explanation around it.

***

Remmich regretted leaving the lovely Cuban weather. An attendant interrupted him, offering coffee and a snack. Relieving his hunger relaxed him, and he fell asleep. He woke up at the announcement of their arrival at Barajas Airport in fifteen minutes. Remmich looked at his watch and saw it was 1:15 p.m. An hour-and-a-half later, the jet flew out of Madrid, headed for Amsterdam's Schiphol Airport.

***

Elliott felt the colder temperature as he walked through the jetway ramp to the terminal. He wore a short-sleeved shirt, but his coat was in the suitcase. He was hungry but debated whether to wait to eat at his daughter's house or get something at the airport. The thought of getting his ass reamed for not calling his wife made him decide to eat at a restaurant. Besides, he had the credit card.

It was early afternoon when Elliott rented a four-door Chevy at the airport. He arrived at his daughter's house and heard his grandkids playing out back with friends. He was thankful for their presence, knowing there wouldn't be a big scene.

His son-in-law opened the front door, and they shook hands. The general carried his bag inside. Diane walked to the doorway, happy to see him. He tried not to look aggravated. After she embraced him, they all went into the kitchen. The younger man knew what was brewing and joined his wife outside.

"You're wondering why I called, right?" she said. "When I didn't hear from you and couldn't reach you, I called the Pentagon. They transferred me to General Morris's office. He was your assistant when you worked at Fort Carson INSCOM."

"Yes, Diane, I remember him."

"He wasn't very helpful."

"What do you mean?"

"I think he was more interested in making sure I hadn't mistaken where you were going for your meeting. I mean, where else would you go for a security meeting in Washington, DC? He asked if you might have gone to NSA at Fort Meade or INSCOM."

"Well, I'm here now. What else did you two discuss?"

"Aaron told me he was going to call Stuttgart to find out more," she explained. "He never called back, but Ed Sutherland did leave a message. I went out with Mary Ann, David, and the boys, so we weren't here. I haven't called him back."

Then she said something her husband didn't expect. "But he called again, Jerry. He said he didn't know about a Pentagon meeting with you."

Elliott became alarmed, then angry, thinking, *You bitch!* She'd gotten his commanding officer involved. *How in the hell am I going to explain this?*

With a disgruntled look, he got off the chair and walked to the back door. Looking out the window, he saw the kids playing. He wasn't paying attention to them. Instead, he was thinking of how he should handle the problem.

"I'll be right back, Diane. Don't go anywhere."

"I'll be here." She felt terrible because she knew she'd caused her husband's bad mood.

He walked to his suitcase and got the coat and cigar pouch. He saw something else that made him pause: his pistol case had a 9mm without a bullet in the chamber. The loaded magazine was beside it. He'd proved who he was to the airline before leaving Germany. They permitted him to have it, but only packed in the suitcase, where it stayed in the jet's luggage compartment. As he tried to calm himself, his anger gradually subsided. Killing his wife would be personal suicide and not really solve anything.

No. There has to be another way to handle this, he thought.

He returned to the kitchen and snipped off the tip of the cigar into the trash can.

"Care to join me for a walk? I want to have a talk before I greet the grandkids."

Her worried look changed to a smile. She felt better. They put on their coats, and he followed her out the door.

Once they got past a few houses, he said, "I don't want to cause a scene, Diane, but I'm really irritated you decided to take the ball in your court. You got me in trouble with my commanding officer. Damn it, woman, how stupid are you?"

His manner startled and embarrassed her. "I didn't think Ed Sutherland would call me again."

"Calling twice tells me he's concerned."

"Then maybe you need to call him back."

"What do you mean? Doesn't he want you to call him back?"

"Yes. But I didn't want to pay the phone bill to Germany."

"Don't bother. I'll talk to Ed. If he calls back while we're here, don't answer your telephone."

"You seem to be avoiding him, Jerry. Is anything wrong?"

Why in the hell is she so persistent?

He took a puff and blew the smoke into the air. An idea came to him.

"It doesn't look good for Ed Sutherland, Diane." She started to say something, but he waved his hand to stop her. "I can't go into detail, but it's why I went to the special meeting at the Pentagon." He decided to lie more. "We discussed his possible dismissal from V Corps. And don't tell anybody I told you."

"I understand, Jerry, but Aaron didn't talk about the special meeting. He told me you weren't there."

"Aaron Morris didn't know I was there. As a matter of fact, he's not an Army military intelligence officer anymore," he lied. He stopped to puff again, waiting for her to talk more.

"Oh, I see. Well, it goes to show you how little I know about what you really do." She hesitated for a moment, then asked, "Mind if I put my arm in yours?"

10
Istanbul

Remmich was jet lagged but dismissed it as an annoyance. It was late afternoon Thursday when he drove into the hotel parking lot. He left the keys in the ignition, got his bags, and walked in the side door. Instead of going to the condo, he walked to the front desk and asked for Lilly. The attendant said she was meeting with the kitchen staff. He wrote a note for her and handed it to the attendant. As guests walked out of an elevator, he rushed to get on. In the condo, he dropped the suitcase on the bed and took out everything. He took it to the walk-in closet and put his dirty clothes in the hamper. He needed to check emails but treated himself to a glass of Chardonnay first.

He logged into the computer. There were 23 emails. Thirteen were from unknown senders. One was Eric Miller's. All of a sudden, he felt a buzz in his rear molar. He dialed 020-632-1239 robotically.

"Hello?" said Alzuhari.

"This is PSR. I'm returning the call as instructed."

"I am calling to tell you Colonel Yildiz has made travel arrangements for you, Tara, and me. We're flying to Istanbul tomorrow. I'll call you back with the departure time. Do you understand?"

"Tomorrow, Friday, October thirty-first, you'll tell me the departure time."

"I want you to tell your wife you'll accept the transfer to Havana. Tell her you want her to go with you."

"I told her before I left to go to Havana."

"Goodbye, Paul."

Remmich's veiled subconscious gradually returned to its altered hypnotized level. He waited a few moments before sipping the wine. The ring of the condo telephone got his attention.

"Hello, my love. I missed you," Lilly said. His hesitation to respond made her wonder if something was wrong, and she asked, "Are you okay, Paul?"

He yawned and said, "It's been a busy day. I just walked into the condo ten minutes ago. Right now, I'm looking at email messages. Where are you now?"

"In the lobby office. I got your message, and I'm surprised you got back so soon."

He decided not to tell her why he got home earlier than planned. "Ah, yes. There was a change in the plans."

She didn't think to ask why and said, "I don't have to work for the rest of the day. Let's have dinner here."

"Yes, let's do it. Is there a good menu this evening?"

"One of today's specials is veal cutlets with gravy and noodles." Before he said something, she asked, "Do you want me to come up for a while?"

"The veal sounds wonderful. And yes, I'd love for you to come. Do you want to bring champagne and we can bathe together?"

"It sounds like you have ulterior motives."

They laughed. Lilly agreed to get the champagne and added, "Can you start running the water in the tub? Oh, and make sure it's hot."

***

Yury Nikulin wasn't in his flat when the voice-activated tape recorder clicked on from the hidden receiver-transmitter in Alzuhari's apartment. It recorded the conversation, and since he spoke in English, it was evident who he spoke with.

A few minutes later, the recorder started again, but this time he heard only Arabic.

***

"Hello."

"Good afternoon, sir," said Alzuhari. "Paul Remmich returned. I told him he's coming with Tara and me tomorrow. He also knows his wife will go to Cuba with him. As soon as your office calls me with the flight time, I'll call him back."

"Luma will call you with the information."

"What's our meeting going to cover, sir?"

"Paul Remmich is going to do something special before moving to Cuba. He'll have to sign a legal agreement protecting him to work for Iraq as an independent diplomat."

***

A waiter took a serving cart to their condo, including Brie and crackers, two crystal flute glasses, and chilled champagne in an ice bucket.

Remmich looked very surprised. "Oh, I didn't expect hors d'oeuvres, too!" The man smiled and left.

He checked out the champagne label and commented, "A two thousand twelve G.H. Mumm." He looked at Lilly. "Nice selection."

"I thought you'd say that. It's one you bought for Schiller when we were on our trip. Remember?"

With British humor, he said, "I do indeed. I'm surprised it arrived so soon. Is your good father aware you've chosen one of the best?"

She laughed. "Yes, he knows. I told him we planned to relax when you returned. You deserve it."

He put the bottle back into the bucket, looked at her, and said, "However, it's a good time to discuss our future plans."

Lilly remembered the talk she'd had with her father. "Yes, I want to discuss something with you, too."

He took the ice bucket into the bathroom. She followed, carrying the food platter.

He twisted the wire tie around the cork, which popped out of his grip and flew into the air. It bounced off the ceiling and landed in the sudsy tub water. The bottle started to overflow, and he poured the sparkling liquid into each glass. He sipped, and his expression showed his pleasure at its taste. They smiled at each other as he handed the glass to her, followed by a gentle kiss. They toasted and sipped.

They both undressed, and Lilly got into the tub first. The water was hot. She smiled and said how wonderful it felt while lowering herself into the sudsy water. It took him longer to submerge. When fully immersed, he removed the floating cork, and they toasted again. Each bit into a Brie-topped cracker.

She asked, "What is it you wanted to tell me?"

He swallowed, then said, "I have wonderful news." Instead of asking her, as Alzuhari had suggested, Remmich decided to say, "I've accepted a job to transfer to Cuba for a half-year or so. I'll be on a good salary and won't have to pay for living accommodations. I want you to go with me."

She didn't expect to move away, but she said, "I do want to be with you. But my father is worried you're going to become too occupied with your Army duties and be unable to help here. He's not going to be happy if I leave, too."

"Well, my new work isn't going to be with the United States government or the Army. I'm being employed as a consultant by an Iraqi company. We'll come back here to live after this work is complete."

Her countenance changed. "Are you going to have to transfer often?"

"I don't believe so. But tomorrow I'm scheduled to travel to the office in Istanbul. I'll be there for a couple days."

"But you just got back, Paul!"

In a melodic tone, he lied and said, "This trip is a final interview, so to speak. It's business, my dear."

"Why there? Why aren't you going to Baghdad, the capital?"

"I don't know." She looked at him in a puzzled way. He added, "Perhaps it's because the Iraqi government prefers to run operations in a Western Hemisphere city. I'm going to be a liaison for them with Cuban officials. Iraq considers the Caribbean country a Third World nation."

He refilled their glasses, and they ate more of the Brie and crackers.

Lilly said, "I think it's wonderful you're going to be helping countries that have poor economic conditions. I remember you talking about it."

He poured the last of the champagne and turned the bottle upside down in the bucket. They looked at each other in silence. She caught his vibe and put her glass in the corner against the wall. He put his glass to the side. In the soapy water, their hands slid over each other's body. They moved closer. The afternoon was exciting, the dinner delicious, and the evening relaxing.

***

Late Thursday afternoon, Yildiz called his cohorts.

"I'm calling for two reasons. First, Tariq'Allah wants us to drug and hypnotize the man they wanted first. If you recall, it was Paul's friend, the Black man, Eric Miller. They've learned the United States is working on other scientific projects. He works at Paul's old job and decodes classified documents. General Elliott told me Major Miller is also being trained by their counterintelligence corps. He'll look for active V Corps military defectors who've sold classified information. The general told me the number of traitors is small, and a few of these men are officers. Their families don't even know where they are.

"Since they're friends, I believe Paul Remmich can influence this other man to join our cause."

An hour later, Yako and Alzuhari got texts about the flight from Amsterdam to Istanbul. Luma added, "And the colonel said he doesn't want you or Tara to discuss any of our future plans with Paul."

***

The next morning, the Turkish Airline jet flew out of Amsterdam and landed in Istanbul three hours and thirty-five minutes later.

Remmich had never visited Istanbul, the city once named Constantinople. The city had had a profound religious and political impact in shaping Western culture.

A Hilton hotel shuttle driver called out their names at the baggage area, then drove them from the European side of the city, across the Bosporus River, to the Asiatic section on the east side.

The hotel's interior design and furnishings were better than Remmich had expected. They took their individual room cards, and the desk clerk handed Alzuhari a note. It instructed him to get settled, then report back to the lobby in twenty minutes.

The taxi drove them to Yildiz's condominium office. When they arrived, Remmich watched them greet each other in Arabic. He didn't recognize Luma Samir.

"Good morning, Paul," said Yildiz, smiling. "It's good to see you again."

"It's good to see you, too, Colonel Yildiz."

The group walked into the dining room. Alzuhari walked into another room. Seconds later, Remmich's molar vibrated. He became expressionless and pulled out his phone.

The others observed his blank look while he dialed a number. It rang three times. Alzuhari answered. Remmich gave his initials' code. The trance established, Alzuhari told him to hang up.

Yildiz looked into Remmich's glazed eyes and said, "You will get information for us. Then we will discuss the special mission for you to accomplish before moving to Havana."

Remmich sat at the end of the sofa, facing Yildiz, who sat in an armed chair. Alzuhari sat across Yako. Luma Samir sat next to her and took notes.

Yildiz said, "Paul, you will only pay attention to English. When we speak in Arabic, do not hear us. Do you understand?"

"Yes, I will pay attention when you speak English, not Arabic," responded Remmich woodenly.

Yildiz reached for a manila file, opened it, and took out a photograph. He placed it on the table before Remmich. "Paul, do you know this soldier?"

"That's my friend, Eric Miller."

"He works with security intelligence at the Thirty-second. Correct?" asked Yildiz. He didn't think mentioning Miller's CIC assignment was important.

"Yes," answered Remmich.

"We want to include Eric in our work to help Third World nations. We need to help us stop their suffering. We want him to be a diplomat, too." Yildiz spoke slowly, to be sure Remmich understood everything. "Having Eric Miller work as a diplomat for Iraq is going to persuade others to work with us. They'll want to invest in Third World nations, and trade will help advance these countries. The investors will hire people in the countries to aid economic expansion."

Yildiz stopped talking to observe Remmich. Was he absorbing the information? Satisfied by the dull stare, he continued, "For example, schools will hire teachers who'll want to stay in their countries because they'll be able to make a living; new hospital jobs will influence doctors and nurses to work in Third World countries Iraq's helping. These governments are going to become independent because of you and Eric. Do you understand this idea?"

"Yes. We will help Third World countries," responded Remmich. He couldn't consciously object.

Yildiz knew repeating words and ideas would help the objectives become more ingrained in their subject's mind. He followed up with, "Our goal, Paul, is to help promote unity with poor countries. When these nations have proof of our efforts, they'll recognize Iraq as an international business partner in many countries. You and Eric will be good diplomats to help them."

Yildiz added, "The African continent has poor countries. Thousands of people are sick because there aren't enough doctors to help them. Corrupt government officials pay terrorists to steal food as well as rob and kill, so many are starving." He showed a picture of a mother holding an undernourished child to Remmich. The child's ribs showed, and flies crawled over his face.

Remmich, motionless, calmly said, "Yes, I want to help these nations."

"I want you to meet with Miller in Amsterdam for a weekend in November. Can you do this for our cause?"

"Yes. You want me to be with Eric on a weekend in November."

Yildiz took a deep breath, realizing the hard part was yet to come. "I want you to meet with him at the Blues Alley Bar and Restaurant. Sit at the bar with him. Tara and Adnaw will be there, but they will not sit near you and Eric. When you return to Amsterdam, call him."

Remmich said, "My friend Eric will not resign from the United States Army."

"You will convince him he needs to use his education and people skills to assist Third World nations. He is going to be contributing, like you."

Remmich stared at the table, motionless. Yildiz stroked his mustache, then spoke to Samir in Arabic. "Luma, please contact Dr. Mustafa in Würzburg. He needs to know we have a new prospect."

The colonel looked at Alzuhari and spoke in Arabic. "Did you apply for a part-time job at Blues Alley?" He received a nod and continued. "Maintain the part-time job until Tara hypnotizes the new man. If the opportunity fails on the night Eric Miller visits Amsterdam, we'll have to do it again after Paul returns from Havana." He hesitated, then added, "I wonder if Eric Miller will be more difficult to convince."

Yildiz looked at Yako and said, "As we all know, Tara, Paul's hypnotism was a success. You'll give Eric Miller the same drugs you gave Paul. Be careful of the dosage. Don't forget, the Russians gave overly large amounts of Rohypnol to spies. The tests failed, and they became mentally worthless. We have to use the right amounts. We want a hypnotized state, one that'll accept our post-hypnotic suggestions. He must appear to act in a natural way when he's not in a subconscious trance. For now, we don't need to cover anything else unless you or Adnaw have additional suggestions."

No one answered, and he gave further instructions. "Tara, be sure to obtain the pills at the apothecary. And get refills of the liquid marijuana and new syringes for the serum to neutralize the Rohypnol. Do you still have the hypnosis information and medical instruments I sent you?"

"Yes."

They wanted to get Remmich back into his normal hypnotic state. In English, Alzuhari said, "Paul, goodbye."

As they talked, Remmich's deeper trance receded.

"Where are we going for dinner, sir?" asked Alzuhari.

"The Hilton, where the three of you are staying. It has exceptional cuisine, and some of the Turkish waiters speak English."

It was mid-afternoon, prayer time. A single voice sang at one of the mosque's minarets. Only a male voice chants during prayers. Islam requires a Muslim to pray five times a day, but the majority don't because work makes it impossible.

While Remmich sat by quietly, the men waited as Samir handed them each a prayer rug. The women went into another room with their rugs. Under Islamic law, women don't have the privilege to pray to Allah next to a man. They removed their shoes and knelt on the rugs, then bowed toward the singing. They prayed to Allah, vocalizing in harmony.

11
Return Calls

The USAF jet transport landed at the Rhein-Main AFB in Frankfurt early on Saturday morning. Colonel Kirby, CIC chief of staff, and his team followed the sergeant through a tunnel routing to a baggage area. The foursome picked up their baggage and drove their vehicles out of the base and headed for Würzburg. As Miller drove, he wondered if the telephone call he made from Guantánamo to Amsterdam had been received.

Once home, as he emptied the suitcase and realized he was hungry. For the moment, getting dinner was more important than telephone calls. He drove up to the officers' club carryout restaurant and placed an order for a sub. He noticed two officers he knew at one of the dining tables, and he decided to join them. Their conversation was all about stateside sports, and he found himself enjoying the small talk.

When he returned to his apartment, he walked into the living room and turned on the TV. He was too tired to call Remmich. In the interest of safety, he made sure his 9mm was under the cushion. A half-hour later, he turned off the TV and went to bed.

***

The Saturday evening flight from Istanbul into Schiphol International Airport was on time. Remmich, Alzuhari, and Yako split up after they got their bags. Remmich took a shuttle bus to the parking area to get the BMW, while the others took separate cabs. He was excited about the diplomatic position in Cuba and couldn't wait to talk to Lilly. He also realized Eric Miller had to be telephoned. He called, but Miller didn't answer his phone, so Remmich left a brief message.

"Eric, I'm sorry I didn't call you back last week. And your second call came when I was on assignment. I do want to get together soon, maybe next weekend here in Amsterdam." He mentioned Blues Alley, then said, "Take care. Hope to hear from you soon." He hung up.

It was a slow, lazy morning for Miller. He slouched in the chair, put his feet on the ottoman, and pushed the TV remote buttons to see what was on the US and British channels. He dozed off several times. Finally, he decided to lie down again and get real sleep. When he woke up, the clock read half-past eleven.

Why worry? It's Sunday.

While he got cleaned up, he thought about calling Remmich.

After he finished dressing, he checked his cell phone. It was dead. He knew he'd charged it on Friday and thought the battery needed to be replaced. After plugging it in, he left to get something to eat, hoping breakfast was still being cooked at the PX. The 3-page printout about Paul Remmich was in his back pocket. Because it was the weekend, the PX was still crowded that late in the morning. He picked up a tray and ordered, pouring some coffee into a cup and sitting down at an empty table. He took a sip of coffee and bite of the egg, ham, and cheese burrito and reviewed the notes McKinsey, Sola, and he had prepared. He made a few changes and wrote a reminder to check the next day to see if Kirby had contacted V Corps.

***

It was Sunday morning in Amsterdam also, and Lilly had to work as the hostess in the main dining room. Understanding his jet lag, she kissed her sleeping spouse on the forehead and said she'd see him later.

It was close to midday when Remmich got up. It surprised him he'd slept so long. When he finished in the bathroom, he dressed and left. During breakfast, his subconscious dictated thoughts of the transfer. It also reminded him about telling his father-in-law about resigning.

Later in the day, he mused about Eric Miller. In the kitchen section for employees, he chewed on a piece of cheese. A decision had to be made; he tried to decide whether to call his friend's cell phone again or try the apartment. He decided he might have better luck with the apartment telephone. It rang three times before the recording came on to leave a message.

"Hi, Eric. Listen, I'm repeating myself, but I want you to come to Amsterdam next weekend. Call me, and we'll get all this straightened out. I have a lot to talk about, including my new job as a foreign diplomat. I prefer we do it over beer at Blues Alley one night, then another evening we can have dinner with our women. Bye."

***

Miller parked the dark blue Saab and walked to his building. Entering the apartment, he noticed the light blinking on his phone. Sure enough, the message was from Paul Remmich. He checked his cell phone, which was charged. He pressed redial and heard Paul's phone ring.

"Hello?"

"Where in the hell have you been, man? Do you realize I've been trying to get in touch with your ass for over a week?"

Smiling, Remmich answered, "I'm sorry, Eric, but it was impossible to return the first call simply because I wasn't here. What's up?"

Miller responded to the cheer in his buddy's voice and asked, "How come you're so happy?"

"You listened to my last message, didn't you?"

"Yeah, but so what? You have a new job as a diplomatic representative. Who's it for?"

"The Iraqi government." There was silence on the other end, and Remmich asked, "Eric, did you hear me?"

"Iraq! Are you kidding me, Paul? Underground ISIS military is very active in that country, and Baghdad is suspected of consciously using too little manpower to pursue these people. Not to mention the stolen military weaponry being smuggled into Syria! You already know all this, Paul, and you know damn well where the weapons are coming from!"

"Believe me, Eric, my new job is strictly diplomatic. Tariq'Allah is a separate part of the government. Its interests are international relations. Believe me, there are no direct ties to ISIS, Hezbollah, or any group like them."

"Wait a minute. What was that name you mentioned? Something about Allah?" asked Miller.

"Tariq'Allah, which means 'the Shining Star of God' in Arabic. It's the outcome of the revolutionized past government. It's rather democratic."

The translation of the group's name made Miller think it was associated with a religious cult. "This is confusing. The name sounds like they're associated with the terrorist group operating throughout the Middle East. And how can you say you're not connected with their military? If you work for this Tariq'Allah government agency, it has direct ties to the military, correct?" argued Miller. "After all, doesn't our Congress have constitutional control over *our* military?"

"Yes, but the military workers in the Pentagon aren't actively fighting military personnel. There are other sectors of the US military for administrative work, and they don't fight in battle. And neither does Tariq'Allah," countered Remmich. "Listen, Eric, I still want to get together with you."

"Yeah, okay, I want to see you, too," Eric answered, resigned. "Next weekend sounds fine. I'll call you after I get to Candice's. But before we hang up, tell me what you were doing in Havana."

Eric Miller had deliberately put that issue at the end because he wanted Remmich to agree to get together first.

Remmich answered confidently, “I was there to investigate a possible temporary transfer to represent Tariq’Allah. How did you know I was there?” The last several months of hypnotic training induced him to play along.

“I just missed seeing you at the El Toro restaurant,” answered Miller.

“I see. But again, how did you know I was there?”

Miller was reluctant to believe what he was hearing. He answered, “Oh, I found a Hotel Schiller matchbook wrapped up and bent, like your habit after using the last match.”

“Yes, I understand,” said Remmich. He chuckled. “I’ll bet you were surprised.”

“I was shocked because there’s no other nut on Earth with such a strange routine,” jibed Miller. He laughed and heard Remmich snicker.

“I haven’t changed. Like I said before, some of my habits are heading me to the funny farm.”

“I’m in agreement with that,” replied Miller. He was somewhat gratified Remmich's sense of humor was intact, even though he was disappointed in his friend’s new position.

Paul Remmich’s subconscious mind linked the discussion held in Istanbul with being informative with his friend. He explained more about his diplomatic role, because he wanted Miller to work with Tariq’Allah, too.

“My new job is outstanding.” He went on to outline the bi-monthly salary going to his bank.

Miller's jaw was set as he listened to Remmich's obvious excitement about being transferred to Havana, where their living expenses and food were free.

“And to top it off, I’ll have a chauffeur to drive me around.”

Miller wasn't jealous. This conversation was just plucking at his nerves. He realized he needed to calm down and play along to learn more.

Taking a deep breath, he said, "I'm envious, Paul. You really hit home on that one. Your role sounds very interesting and challenging." Even as he said this, thoughts of losing his friend to a Middle Eastern country made his stomach churn. He said, "Well, how about if I give you a call this coming Thursday during the day or early evening about getting together?"

The conversation ended cordially. Six months earlier, Miller never would have dreamed Paul would do anything like this. He felt caught between a rock and a hard place.

His conversation with Kirby popped into his head, and he again considered reporting Remmich to V Corps' MI. Caution, however, persuaded him to wait until Kirby spoke with Sutherland.

Miller left a message on Kirby's cell phone. He didn't go into detail, only mentioning he'd talked with Paul. The wall clock showed almost 1300. Agitated, he reread the paperwork about his incidents with Remmich since earlier in the year. A couple hours later, Jim Kirby called back.

"Hi, Eric, I'm returning your call. Glad to hear you sound rested. How did it go with Remmich?"

"I have some more bad news. I spoke with him earlier, for fifteen minutes." He explained how Remmich reported he was now employed by Tariq'Allah, an Iraqi government agency. "I really don't know what to do, but I set up a get-together with him next weekend in Amsterdam."

"Keep the appointment. We need to get him back into Germany to work at decrypting. It's a delaying tactic, but at least we'll have him at Patch Barracks. By the way, Tom McKinsey emailed your notes. The case looks good enough to present to Sutherland. Tomorrow is Monday, so let me call you back after I talk with the general about a meeting, and I'll also call your CO, Joe

Collins. Believe me, Eric, I'm just as anxious to get to the bottom of this as you are."

Later in the day, Miller returned a call to General Sutherland, who'd left a message about the meeting. Mrs. Sutherland answered the telephone. When the general took the phone, he apologized that he didn't have more time to talk, because they were getting ready for a dinner party. He told Miller to call his secretary to make an appointment for Wednesday morning. They hung up.

Eric then called Candice's cell phone and left a message for her. He fell short of explaining why he'd been gone longer than expected. He hoped she wasn't upset because he hadn't called her while on assignment.

Before hanging up, he said, "I look forward to hearing from you. I miss you."

He went out to get the mail. He kept the military magazine and the bills and trashed the rest. He went back in and got a beer before turning on the computer. There were dozens of junk emails.

Unbelievable, he thought.

Halfway down was one from Candice. She wrote she wasn't going to be in Amsterdam that weekend and to please call her. He erased the rest.

The issues with Remmich wouldn't leave his thoughts. He put on a jacket, grabbed a cigarette and another beer, picked up the magazine, and went out to the small deck. He tried to blot out the thought of conferring with General Sutherland about Paul. He remembered McKinsey's statement about Remmich being reported and interrogated. He needed to contact McKinsey.

12
Confrontations

The Elliotts returned to Stuttgart late Sunday afternoon. During the taxi ride to their condominium, they exchanged few words. Fleeting thoughts passed through each of their minds. She was worried about the repercussions of the call she'd made to the Pentagon and speaking with General Morris. He was concerned about the call from Sutherland to his wife. Plus, he wondered if V Corps knew about him not being stateside.

She looked at him and broke the silence. "Again, I'm sorry about the call, Jerry. I guess I could have waited another day or so."

She watched him, hoping to get a forgiving response. Her husband merely looked toward the window and squeezed his lips together. He fought off the desire to scream at her.

Instead, he said, "We'll talk about it later. Right now, I'm still too aggravated."

The cab driver carried the suitcases up to the front door. Diane paid him and included a tip. Smiling, the driver thanked her and walked back to the cab.

When they got inside, she looked at the clock. It was almost 6:00 p.m. "Let's go out to a restaurant or to the officers' club, Jerry."

Visions of running into Sutherland at the officers' club and getting into an argument came into his mind. He knew Sutherland didn't frequent the place too much, but it would just be his luck the general would be there that night. He realized he was letting his emotions get the better of him. A confrontation was inevitable, but right now he was going to try to enjoy himself. They emptied their suitcases.

"Do you want to go to the officers' club?" she asked again.

"Oh, I'm sorry. I forgot. Yes. Let's drive over there."

It was a pleasant evening. Diane mingled with other officers' wives, talking about social events and vacations. He and other officers discussed various spy operations in the Western Hemisphere, as well as the Pentagon's directive about reducing civilian hiring. The evening helped reduce their stress, and Sutherland never showed up.

On Monday morning, the maid called early and said she was sick. Diane decided to do the laundry and a little house cleaning. It helped to pass the time. While she was dusting, the telephone rang.

She thought, or hoped, it was Jerry, but the voice said, "Good morning, Mrs. Elliott. This is Master Sergeant Rita Jones in Lieutenant General Sutherland's office. He wants to speak to you. Do you have a few minutes?"

Diane was caught off guard because she never had spoken to Sutherland one-on-one. They'd had brief verbal exchanges at social events, but nothing special. Elliott didn't like his commanding officer, and he told her the feeling was mutual. There was never any closeness between Diane and the general's wife as a result.

"Good morning, Diane. I know it's been a few months since we've had a chance to get together. How are you today?"

"I'm fine. Thank you, General."

"Oh please, Diane, we've known each other for over a decade. Call me, Ed." He hesitated for a moment to collect his thoughts, then said, "Would it be possible for you to have lunch with me, say on Friday?"

She paused. This guy hadn't invited her or Jerry to anything since their first introduction twelve years ago, especially not since Elliott got passed over for promotion because of him. She didn't know how to respond.

Finally, she said, "What did you have in mind, Ed?"

"Can you meet me at the officers' club for lunch on Friday, say at eleven-thiry?"

"Friday? Let me check my schedule. Hold on, please." She didn't have a daily reminder book, but she needed a minute or two to think. Suddenly, an answer came to her. She picked up the phone. "I can't seem to find my datebook, but when I do, I'll call you back. Give me your number, Ed."

Knowing she was going to talk with her husband about the call, he gave her the number reluctantly. They hung up.

***

Sutherland called the 32nd security office following his talk with Diane. He briefly exchanged words with Colonel Collins, who said not having Eric Miller there for over a week had caused chaos. Sutherland said the request for an assistant to Miller was in the works and he'd look into it.

He added, "I'm making a notation to call them again, Joe, and I'll get in touch as soon as I know something."

***

"Good morning, this is Master Sergeant Jones speaking. How may I help you?"

"This is Colonel Jim Kirby, with CIC. Can I speak with General Sutherland?"

She contacted the general, who told her to put him through.

"Good morning, Ed. How are you doing?"

"Things are hectic for a Monday. Other than that, I'm breathing."

Kirby chuckled. "When are you available to give me some time? I have a problem, and I consider it an emergency."

Sutherland quickly glanced at the wall clock. "Well, it's not even midmorning yet, so tell me what's so important."

"As you know, my men were assigned to begin an investigation into soldiers who have gone AWOL. While they were in Cuba, we also discovered Iraqis working on a project."

The general had just been confronted with the Elliott matter, and now this. "Ah, yeah, we found out from our head office at Fort Belvoir the Iraqis are setting up diplomatic relations with Cuba. They're not breaking any laws, but we wanted to shadow them, if possible. I was going to give you a couple of days to prepare before discussing the trip. I didn't think you'd be ready this soon."

"Well, here's the shocker," said Kirby. "Majors Miller and McKinsey believe our former Captain Paul Remmich is acting as a spy for the Iraqi government."

Sutherland was stunned. "Are you sure?"

"Yes, I am. We need to go over the events from the past few months to help us determine what to do about Remmich. Major Miller has an account."

"What day do you have in mind?"

"Can you give us a couple hours on Wednesday?" asked Kirby. "I think we need to do this as soon as possible. We're ready on our end. Miller has prepared an overview of what's happened since he was transferred to the Thirty-second. We can be at your office whenever you want."

"Okay, let me call a doctor I know about an idea I have. I'll get back with you later today." They said their goodbyes and hung up.

Sutherland contacted his secretary. "Rita, please get the chief hospital surgeon here on base, General Phil Thomson, on the line."

He got up to get a cup of coffee as Jones said, "I have Dr. Thomson on the line, General."

He returned to his desk and picked up the phone. "Good morning, Phil." They exchanged pleasantries before Sutherland said, "I need you to come to my office for a meeting tomorrow morning."

Dr. Thomson said, "Let me check my schedule, Ed." Moments later, he said, "I don't have any surgery scheduled Wednesday morning. What's a good time?"

Sutherland considered the time it would take for the others to get from Würzburg to Stuttgart. "How about oh-nine-thirty?"

"That's good for me, Ed. What's this about, if you don't mind me asking?"

"We have suspicions of an Army officer in security intelligence defecting to and spying for an enemy. Before we make any judgments regarding breaches he might have made, I want you to listen to the officer who's been most directly involved with this guy. As the chief of staff for the medical division, I may need you to order a series of exams on the man, including psychiatric evaluations. It's a complicated matter, and I'd like you to hear what the officer who knows and has worked with this man has to say."

"I also think our psychiatrist should attend. He's had a lot of experience in such matters."

"Who is that?" asked Sutherland.

"Victor Hatch, a full bird colonel who's been diagnosing post-traumatic stress syndrome in GIs returning from active combat. He's also worked with soldiers who went AWOL. His psychiatric experience let him communicate in personal ways. It persuaded them to speak openly and honestly to the military court. He currently deals only with the medical side of those issues but can recognize certain behavioral deficiencies. Is the meeting in your office?"

"Yes, and please see if you can get Dr. Hatch."

***

Gerald Elliott's office telephone rang and rang. It was a contest between Diane Elliott and General Sutherland to see who was going to reach him first. No one answered his line.

Elliott walked into his home at 5 o'clock on Monday evening. He changed his clothes, while his wife prepared his favorite double Johnnie Walker Black and poured a glass of wine for herself.

When he walked into the kitchen, he sipped the scotch, then said, "I've made plans for us to take a three-day trip to Garmisch this weekend."

"What weekday are we using, Friday or next Monday?" she asked, sipping her wine.

"Friday will be the first day, but we'll leave here Thursday afternoon. I'll take off a couple hours early. Make sure we're packed." He sipped the scotch again and asked, "Are our skis in the basement?"

"Yes. They're on top of the wooden storage units. Enthusiastically, she asked, "We're going skiing, too?"

"Yes. It's early in the season, but there's been lots of snowfall in the Alps. Anyway, I thought we needed to work off some stress."

As dinner ended, the telephone rang. There was no Caller ID. Elliott answered and was surprised when he heard, "Good evening, Jerry. Sorry to call you at home, but I've been trying to reach you all day." Before Elliott could say anything, Sutherland added, "No one answered your office line either. Did your sergeant secretary take the afternoon off?"

Elliott ignored the question, knowing Sutherland would barrel on ahead anyway. Sure enough, the general only waited briefly for a response, then continued, "Well anyway, I need to speak with you in person tomorrow. Can you be in my office at eight hundred hours?"

Elliott's insides hardened at Sutherland's directness. "Sure, Ed, I'll be there. Can you tell me what it's about?"

"We'll talk tomorrow. Have a good evening, and say hello to Diane. Thank you."

"I wonder what in the hell he wants," mumbled Elliott as he replaced the cordless phone in its base unit. He laughed mirthlessly, looked at his wife, and said, "As if I didn't know."

"What are you talking about?" She'd listened to his end of the phone conversation and remembered the general had called her earlier. Elliott didn't know about that yet.

"It was Ed Sutherland. He wants to meet with me in the morning."

"I think I know why," she responded. "He telephoned me here this morning."

"He did?"

"Yes. He invited me out to lunch at the officers' club."

Gerald Elliott thought, *That son of a bitch.* Narrowing his eyes, he looked at her sternly and said, "Well, tell me what he wanted."

"I don't know, Jerry, but he was too nice to be trusted." She picked up her glass of wine, sipped, and added, "Look, again for the umpteenth time, I'm sorry about calling the Pentagon and speaking with Aaron. I promise I won't do it again, but please tell me what this is all about."

"I told you in Atlanta, Diane." He sipped his drink to give himself time to think. "Sutherland is in trouble, and he's looking for a scapegoat to divert attention from himself." He thought for a moment more and added, "He wants to speak nicely to us and hopes we'll reciprocate if he's ever indicted. Just be sure to be ready to leave by fourteen-hundred on Thursday afternoon. The sooner we get out of here, the better. It's going to take four-and-a-half hours to get there, maybe longer if there's a lot of traffic."

"What kind of trouble is he in? Is it something to open a door for a promotion?"

He smiled. "Thanks for the advocacy." He took her hand and kissed it. His charming demeanor diverted her thoughts from what Sutherland was supposedly faced with, and she forgot her question.

Elliott knew Sutherland wanted to ask her questions because he knew she was weaker than her husband. Diane would cave under any type of unexpected questioning, and Sutherland wouldn't hesitate to intimidate and humiliate. It was a rotten psychological approach, but it usually worked.

***

On Tuesday morning, the crew welcomed Miller back into the office at the 32nd with smiles and pleasantries. He hung up his cap and walked to the desk. Still paying attention to the NCOs' jabber, his hand accidentally hit the stack of paperwork on top of his desk. He looked down and stopped talking.

"Good God! What in the hell is all this?" he remarked.

No one spoke a word. Miller sat down resignedly and rummaged through the pile. The first thing he noticed was how organized the paperwork looked; he mumbled curse words about the quantity and needing another officer assigned to the office. Other security clearance papers lay stacked perpendicular to each together. Another stack came from other offices on base. Separating the piles, he heard chairs scraping and looked up. The clock showed it was nearing 0900, coffee break time.

Colonel Collins walked in and said, "Care to have coffee with me, Eric?"

They got in line at the snack bar, and Collins asked, "How are you doing on the first day back?"

"Lots of paperwork, sir."

"This is the reason I wanted to chat with you. I got a call from Ed Sutherland earlier. He's contacted the Fort Belvoir INSCOM office and discussed getting a junior-grade officer to assist us."

Miller almost rolled his eyes. That was the same promise he'd heard before.

Collins finished by telling him, "I think the clincher was your recent assignments with CIC. Now they know your time is strained between two responsibilities."

They moved ahead in line. Miller's skepticism made him ask, "When is this officer going to be assigned to V Corps?"

"We should know something soon, because the person is coming from Fort Belvoir and fully trained in what we're doing," said Collins.

They walked up to the cashier, and Miller said, smiling, "This is on me, sir. You got the last one." He also mumbled cynically, "I'll believe it when the officer shows up."

The colonel chuckled.

***

It was almost 1600 on Tuesday. Sutherland had been up to his neck with conference calls and paperwork and was now trying to finish up reports so they'd go out on time.

Jones knocked on the open door. "Sir, General Thomson is on the line."

Sutherland looked up and realized he'd forgotten about tomorrow's meeting. "Hello, Phil. Thanks for calling back. Did you contact Colonel Hatch?"

"I did, and we'll attend the oh-nine-thirty meeting in the morning." They hung up.

Sutherland's office put in a call to Kirby to confirm. Kirby called the airfield at Leighton Barracks to authorize a UH-60 Blackhawk troop carrier helicopter to take the four of them to INSCOM at Patch Barracks Wednesday morning.

13

Rapid Decisions

Elliott made it to his office the next morning at 0700.

He conferred with his secretary about the daily schedule, and she said, "Sir, I have you signed up to see General Sutherland at eight-hundred hours. His secretary called here late yesterday and told me not to plan anything else for your morning."

He walked into his office to place his mail on the desk and asked, "What time did he call?"

She looked at her datebook's incoming call list. "To be exact, sir, four-eighteen."

Walking toward her desk, he handed her five dollars. "Will you go to the snack bar and get us a couple coffees? Get a doughnut for yourself, also." She thanked him and left.

He walked into his office and looked at the mail. He suddenly remembered to telephone the General Patton Hotel in Garmisch-Partenkirchen to make a weekend reservation. He made it for a 3-night stay and told them their Thursday arrival might be late because of traffic in the Munich area. While the secretary placed the coffee on his desk, he telephoned Diane with the information.

He was too nervous to sit, so he toured the newly renovated conference rooms. When he returned to the office, it was only 7:45. For the next ten minutes, he leaned against the desk with one hand in a pocket and the other one holding the cup of coffee.

Elliott's office was on the other end of the building from Sutherland's. It was better that way, because they didn't cross paths too much. Dozens of ideas went through his head about what Sutherland wanted to talk about. It sure as hell wasn't going to be pleasant. He had a plan, though, the same one he'd used with Diane.

Elliott walked into Sutherland's office at the appointed time. The secretary exchanged greetings with him. A minute later, he and his commanding officer sat across from each other. Elliott was determined to answer only after being asked, and not offer any information.

Sutherland leaned on his desk, with folded hands. "I'll be frank, Jerry. Aaron Morris telephoned here a week ago and wanted to know your whereabouts. I told him you were on leave. He said your wife called him about your whereabouts." Sutherland took a sip of coffee, put down the cup, and asked, "I want to know the same thing. Where were you?"

"In Atlanta."

"Come on, Jerry. Your answer doesn't make sense. A man with your security level is a prime target for aggressive espionage hunters. You know that. Why did your wife call the Pentagon and want to know where you were?"

He looked down at the table, repositioned himself in the chair, then looked up and said, "I'll tell you, but it must remain between you and me."

"Okay, shoot. Tell me."

"I'm having an affair," said Elliott furtively, as if he was confessing something. "She's German, and she didn't want to be away from me for over a week. I thought about it and decided to let Petra fly to Atlanta on the same flight with Diane. She got a hotel room I reserved for us downtown. I had a flight later in the morning and met with her secretly, and we toured the city."

"How long has this been going on?" asked Sutherland.

"I believe your question is rather personal, and I refuse to answer. I can understand asking your first question, but this one is invading my privacy."

Sutherland just looked at him. After a few seconds, he said, "Weren't you afraid of being seen?"

"Like I said, Ed, I have nothing more to say about it."

"I hope you're telling the truth, Jerry," said Sutherland defensively. Elliott started to say something, but Sutherland waved his hand and added, "You know how much information is lost from

V Corps security intelligence. Although you and I may not see eye-to-eye on personal issues, I want to trust you with military matters."

Elliott was about to tell him to go to hell because he so strongly disliked the man, but instead he said, "I don't think my actions are harmful to you or the military. In V Corps' security intelligence, it's your command. I respect your rank." He hoped the retaliatory remarks insulted Sutherland enough to stop the meeting. "Is there anything else you want to talk about, Ed?"

Sutherland wasn't satisfied. He still wanted to talk to Diane. He didn't like his executive officer that much either, but he didn't have a complaint about his work or military leadership.

Instead of having the conversation evolve into an outright argument, Sutherland said, "I don't see any reason to continue, Jerry. You're dismissed. Thank you for your time. And leave the door open."

He watched him walk out of the office and heard him tell Master Sergeant Jones to have a good day. When he left, Sutherland called his secretary and told her to get Diane Elliott on the phone.

Jones contacted him and said she had Diane Elliott waiting on the line. Sutherland didn't waste any time.

"Good morning, Diane. Listen, how about—"

She cut him off. "I can't meet with you for lunch on Friday."

He hesitated, then said, "Okay, then let's have lunch on Monday…or would Tuesday be better?"

She knew he wasn't going to give up. The stubborn tenacity of higher-ranked officers was a trait she'd disliked for most for the past twenty years. They always felt they could get whatever they wanted because of their rank.

"Are you still there, Diane?" he asked.

"Yes. I'm here." She hesitated. Like a sly fox, he kept quiet and waited. Finally, she said, "I guess this coming Monday would be good. What time did you mention yesterday, eleven o'clock?"

"No, eleven-thirty."

What can he possibly want from me? she thought.

Her aggravation was mounting to the point of being stressful. She couldn't wait to get away for the weekend with her husband.

14
Wednesday

It was a little past 0900 hours on Wednesday when the officers arrived at Sutherland's office.

Jones told them, "We're going to have the meeting here because the renovated offices and conference rooms are being inspected by the Army Corps of Engineers." She added, "Please follow me."

They walked into the adjoining room and stood at a large round table. Sutherland walked in and greeted everyone.

"Let's take a seat and begin," he said, looking at Jim Kirby.

Colonel Kirby didn't bother with introductions. He felt everyone was familiar with everyone, so he said, "Eric, I think the floor is yours."

Miller sat between Collins and McKinsey. The two doctors sat across from them, while Sutherland sat at the head. Miller used a chronological approach, starting with his arrival at the 32nd and finding out Paul Remmich was stationed there. He talked about how well they knew each other from West Point and graduate school, then related how Remmich's personality had changed beginning Memorial Day weekend. He outlined the character shift. The man vehemently rejected the United States backing the UN to reduce assistance to Third World countries.

"He more or less supports Iraq for helping them."

He went on about Remmich's resignation, his employment with the Hotel Schiller organization, and getting married. Eric related how his friend occasionally stopped in the middle of a discussion to make a telephone call. When it was over, he'd act as if nothing had interrupted the conversation before making the call.

"Anyway, this past week I found out he was also in Cuba. We saw him at a construction site in Havana. The week before, he told me he was scheduled to visit vineyards in the Baden-Baden area." Miller ended with, "I realized he was on the island when I found this matchbook." He showed them the matchbook cover and explained where it came from. He opened it and passed it around. "I knew it was him because of the Amsterdam hotel name on the cover. He and I just made arrangements to get together this coming weekend, and I need to know what to do."

All eyes switched from him to Sutherland. The general was thinking.

He looked at Miller and said, "You should go ahead and get together with Remmich this weekend. You need to find out as much from him about the new job as you can. We'll select two to three days the following week for Remmich to come in and translate encrypted messages here at V Corps. During that time, we'll inform him he must have an up-to-date medical examination for his new position with us." He looked at General Thomson. "Phil, why don't you take over and explain what that exam entails."

Dr. Thomson leaned forward in his chair. "We'll give him some physical tests, including vision, hearing, blood, a gastrointestinal exam, dental examination, and an MRI to view his skull and spinal column, bones, and muscles. We'll also perform a psychiatric evaluation. I'll let Colonel Hatch here talk about that." He looked at Hatch.

"Good morning, gentlemen," said Dr. Hatch. "I will conduct a ninety-minute session with Mr. Remmich. I have a series of prepared questions I've developed over the years based on what I've learned from patients, as well as data from other professional sources. My conversation works to help the patient to open up. I'm referring to solving problems with patients from combat, losing a limb, being a POW, spying, going AWOL, and things like that.

"During this question-and-answer period, I'm hoping to find a subconscious condition. For example, why did Paul Remmich begin to work for the Iraqi government? It's difficult for me to believe money was the primary impetus, especially for a person like him. It's unlikely a person with an excellent career history with the Army would defect. How he reacts to these questions will help to form a diagnosis."

He looked at Sutherland. "Ed, I'll turn it back to you."

"Thank you, Vic," said Sutherland. "We need to question his wife." He looked at Miller. "I'd like to know if his wife has noticed a difference in him. While Remmich is here, I want you to drive to Amsterdam and visit with her."

"I can do that, General. My girlfriend, Candice, is an airline pilot who travels from New York to Amsterdam, where she has a small flat. I can stay there. Are there any specific questions I need to ask?"

"Yes, and you might think of some of your own questions, as well as those I suggest. Lilly Remmich is going to wonder why this is happening, so I think you need to explain we're concerned about his future. Find out if she's noticed him acting differently. For example, has she noticed a change in his disposition? Does she know if he's met with anyone in Amsterdam other than her and the family? Does he go places and not tell her? If she asks where he went, what does he say?"

Sutherland looked at the doctors. "You need to set up a date for next week. How long will it take to do the tests and get results?"

General Thomson said, "Ed, it'll take a good day, maybe a day-and-a-half, for a physical, and the time for the psychiatric exam isn't included in that estimate."

"So, we're talking two days at the most," said Sutherland,

Hatch said, "I can perform the examination and write up an evaluation in a few hours. I'd like to begin the morning after the physical tests are complete. But I like to wait a day to review and revise if necessary."

Sutherland sat forward, with his hands folded. "After listening to Major Miller, I also have a gut feeling something's happened to Remmich." He looked at Collins. "Joe, I know you're concerned, and I, too, can't help thinking there's an as-yet-undetermined reason he resigned."

Squeezing his hands together Miller added, "I also think something or someone influenced Paul to resign." The night at the Blues Alley when he went missing flashed in his memory, but the thought was interrupted when Collins spoke.

"Paul Remmich is approaching the six-month time limit and will be outside of our legal reach. We can keep him on as a civilian, but there are too many circumstances that have developed. We can't let him slip out of the grasp of military justice. Until we get him to go through the physical, I think we need to be prepared to arrest him on suspicion of espionage to keep him within our reach."

"I'll have my office send out an email to all of you and Mr. Remmich about a security intelligence meeting next week," said Sutherland. "When Remmich attends the seminar, I want you, Phil, to get him off to the side and tell him we forgot to put him through a physical before he started the new position. If he refuses, we'll have to arrest him. I hope that doesn't happen, but I don't want to lose him either."

Sutherland looked at Kirby and McKinsey. "I'm not going to involve you two in the investigation. Instead, I'll notify the unit in Wiesbaden."

Kirby said, "I agree. We can't get involved, because Paul Remmich knows who we are. It would be awkward at best for him to see us in Amsterdam during working hours."

The meeting ended, and everyone walked into the reception area. Two civilians approached Sutherland in the reception area. One of them said, "General, I'm Corps of Engineers Bob Mathews, and this is my associate, Rick Campbell." They shook hands with Sutherland. "We finished inspecting the renovation work throughout the building. I have some bad news."

Campbell opened a box with two electronic wireless receiver-transmitters wrapped in a cloth. Sutherland stared.

"Sir, this transmitter was found behind the chair rail in conference room two-oh-five." He pulled out another one. "This was found in the conference room two-oh-seven. Have any conferences been held in these rooms since the renovation work was finished?"

"No. We were waiting for your inspection."

Mathews said, "Good. Thank you, General. I'll take these to the MP office and have some tests done to find fingerprints or chemicals for DNA identification."

"How did you find the transmitters?" asked Sutherland.

Campbell held one up with the cloth to make sure he didn't touch it directly. "I found this wire below the chair rail. Somehow it got loose and hung down a little bit from the underside of the rail in room two-oh-five. We investigated the other room and found the same aerial under the chair rail, but this one was glued to the underside. The wood rails were pulled away from the wall. They'll have to be returned and repainted."

"Please let me know the results, Mr. Mathews," said Sutherland. The engineers left the room.

Sutherland decided an investigation into the transmitters would have to wait, especially since they were no longer a threat.

He walked over to Miller, Collins, McKinsey, and Kirby. "Gentlemen, I want you to wait in my office." He looked at Thomson and Hatch and asked, "Gentlemen, what are good days for you?"

General Thomson said, "Ed, midweek is good, Tuesday through Thursday."

"It's good for us, too," responded Sutherland. "You two can leave now. I don't want to hold you up any longer. Thanks for coming."

Sutherland sat down at his desk and wrote down names on a piece of paper. "Rita, I want you to send an email to these people." He looked up at the group of men and said, "My so-called meetings will be held next week on Tuesday, Wednesday, and Thursday. At least that's what I'm going to tell Mr. Remmich." He wondered how that would go.

15
Strategies

Miller's mind jumped from thought to thought while he drove to work.

Is Paul going to be prosecuted? Why was he in Havana? How did he really get involved with the Iraqi government, or Tariq'Allah, as he labeled it? And finally, how can I forgive him if he's a traitor?

Miller had a gut feeling Remmich wasn't sharing all he knew.

The 32nd MP guard waved him through the gate and saluted, but Miller was distracted and didn't return the salute. He drove into his designated parking spot and walked into the building.

Master Sergeant McClain was on leave for a few days, and all security intelligence paperwork was being temporarily received by the first sergeant's office. McClain usually accepted and organized the incoming mail. Without his preparation, the work became even more time-consuming.

Miller had a few more forms to review, but he'd decided to leave for a coffee break when the office door opened. First Sergeant Randolph placed another armful of paperwork on his desk.

"Good morning, sir, I received these yesterday and just finished organizing them for you to review, sign or reject, and send back with our daily mail."

Miller's eyes bulged, and he laughed maniacally. "Where does all this stuff come from?"

Randolph chuckled. "It's Army security paperwork from posts in Europe, Northern Africa, and Western Asia." He straightened up and added, "I'm sure this'll keep you busy for a few days, sir. It took one of my men over a day just to get them organized."

"I think I'll have a coffee first."

Randolph picked up the paperwork in the outgoing box and left.

When Miller returned to the office, the first thing he saw was the paper stack. He took several deep, calming breaths before separating sections of the pile. The other soldiers were busy; one was helping a soldier fill out a security clearance form. Others keyed handwritten forms into the computer. Miller and an assigned sergeant used their computers to review those documents. It felt like a Monday, but thankfully it was already Thursday. It seemed the office routine just didn't stop. Miller's cell phone rang.

"Hello."

"Hello, Eric. I'm calling because—"

Miller jumped in anxiously before Remmich could say anything else. "Excuse me for interrupting, Paul, but we're still getting together this weekend, aren't we?"

"Yes. Give me a ring when you get into town."

"I'm leaving later today and will arrive in the early evening. Candice is going to be there tonight, too. She had her flight plans changed, which will let us have a weekend here. I'll call you tomorrow."

"Good."

He dutifully returned to reading one section at a time. Military intelligence paperwork had to be carefully reviewed before signing or initialing. Concentrating helped reduce his stress. He placed the categorized piles on Paul Remmich's empty desk.

I have only two hands and one brain, he thought, *I'll just do the best I can.*

Halfway through reading over the second pile, he realized he needed to get permission to leave for the weekend.

He walked into the administration office, and Randolph asked earnestly, "Sir, did you finish already?" Miller shook his head, making a sour face. Randolph pressed his lips together to avert a laugh and said, "How can I help you, sir?"

"I need a three-day pass for this weekend."

"Right away, sir." Randolph saved the computer information he was working on, then pulled up the pass and leave forms on the computer. "And where are you going this weekend, sir?" Travel locations had to be listed on the three-day pass form.

He typed in the necessities, saved it in Miller's file, printed it, and took it to Collins to sign.

He returned and said, "Here you are, sir. Have a nice time."

***

Miller didn't get away from the office until 4:30. He was exhausted from putting his nose to the grindstone. He'd examined over sixty security clearance requests during the week after his return. When he got home, his phone's message light was blinking.

One message was from V Corps about the upcoming meeting and indicated he should also expect an email. The last of the messages showed Paul Remmich's name and number.

He was tired and didn't want to change plans, so he blurted out, "Ah shit, man, don't tell me you've canceled!"

He pushed the play button and realized the call had been made earlier than the one he'd received from Remmich in the office. Relieved, he erased it.

There wasn't time to change clothes. GIs weren't supposed to wear Army fatigues into cities where they weren't stationed, but he was sure the darkness would hide his uniform. He zipped up his satchel after placing personals into the kit. Hanging the bag over his left shoulder, he grabbed a couple beers and added them to the sack.

He drove fast on the Autobahn until he reached Holland. He'd promised Candice he'd be there Thursday night but had never given her a definite time. Frowning as he approached her apartment, he remembered how hard it was to find parking in Amsterdam's Rembrandtplein sector. Finding free parking in the area was uncertain, and parking garages were expensive.

When he spotted a space, he pulled into it quickly and whispered, "I'll be damned!" He checked his watch. It was 8:10. He hid the empty beer bottles under the seat and got out.

Candice entered her apartment and placed two foam containers in the refrigerator. She wasn't sure when Eric would arrive and wanted to eat dinner with him. She took the wine bottle out of the bag and set it on the counter. He surprised her when he walked in shortly after her with his satchel strap hanging from his shoulder. Her face lit up, and she grabbed him into a hug. He kissed her, immediately forgetting how exhausted he was.

She closed the door, and they walked arm-in-arm to the kitchenette. Regretfully disengaging her arm, Miller continued down the hall to the bedroom, where he hung the satchel on the closet door and put his shaving kit in the bathroom.

She got the food out of the refrigerator and put it into the toaster oven to heat. Sniffing as he walked to the doorway, Eric said, "Smells like we're having dinner at home tonight."

He picked up the bottle of red wine. "Ah, Bordeaux from the St. Emilion region of France." He looked up and asked, "When did you have time to do all this?"

"Actually, I ordered it from the airport before getting a cab."

"Where did you buy it?"

"They have a carryout at the Schiller," she answered.

"I didn't know they did that. How convenient. Paul never mentioned it."

While he uncorked the bottle, Candice said, "Bessie Martin, who works with me fifty percent of the time as my co-pilot, was at the airport from another flight, and I saw her talking to Rita Chalmers. Do you remember either of them?"

"Vaguely. Were they at the table the night you and I met?"

"Yes. Anyway, Rita works for Delta here in Amsterdam, and I heard them talking about this service from the Schiller. That's how I found out."

She placed napkins on the table and said, "I thought you might be too tired to go out and didn't think you'd mind me choosing the menu. The wine came from the Schiller, too. Of course, it was a few more euros."

Eric placed the wine bottle on the table. Candice took his hand, looked into his eyes suggestively, and said, "We'll let it air while we tend to other matters."

He laughed, his eyes taking on the same meaningful glow. "Are you suggesting what I think you're suggesting?"

She checked to be sure the toaster oven was on low and said, "Come on, Wolfman."

***

The late morning sun shone over the peaks and down onto the snowy mountain valleys. Just standing around in its warmth felt good. Some women skied in their bikini tops to maintain their tans. The beautiful weather and early fall snows had brought out a mass of people.

The Elliotts had finished skiing, and Jerry asked his wife, "You hungry?"

Diane finished strapping her end of the skis onto the car roof rack and replied, "Very." She was thankful Jerry acted as if he'd forgiven her. They got into the car, and she asked, "Are we going back to the hotel or into Garmisch for lunch?"

"I thought we'd go up to the Zugspitze, actually. It's a beautiful day, and they have good food. Sound good to you?"

"Yes. I've always enjoyed going up there," she answered, smiling. The highest German Alp, "Die Zugspitze," was calculated to be 3,999 meters high, or around ten thousand feet. There was no skiing within the immediate vicinity because of the steep, rocky terrain. However, clear weather gave visitors a view of the lower altitude areas where everyone had been skiing.

Jerry briefly mused about the benefits of being a general, like being able to approve his own 3-day pass. The only person who commanded him was Sutherland.

He parked the car at the lot, and they walked toward the villa. It included a restaurant and cable car station. A cable car was filling with people, and he grabbed her hand and rushed her toward the building.

Trying to talk as she ran, she panted, "What's the hurry, Jerry?"

"The cable car is here. Maybe we can make it." He hustled up to the counter for two tickets.

The cable car door closed after they entered and lifted off with a slight jerk. The ascension was slow at first, then the car gradually picked up to a slow, steady speed. The scenery was gorgeous. Trees at the lower elevation still had some brown leaves, but as they rose, they saw that snow covered the pines. Winds swayed the cable car the higher they got, and the conductor slowed down nearly to a complete stop to reduce the swaying. As the lift resumed normal speed, another descending cable car passed them.

"It's amazing to think about the engineering that went into erecting and positioning these support towers," Elliott said to his wife.

"Yes," answered Diane. "And I noticed the higher we get, there are fewer trees."

The cable car slowed as it neared the top. They felt something like a change of gears as the cabin moved into a boxed-in garage. It stopped, then locked into the steel pier. Once secure, the sliding door opened. People stepped off, many with camera straps around their necks. The Elliotts passed a novelty store and headed for the restaurant, which was behind the next set of doors. Straight ahead was a double door exit to the outside observation area. He opened the restaurant door for his wife, and the aroma of warm food filled their nostrils. There was no host, so they selected their own table.

"Guten Tag. Trinken Sie Bier?" the waitress said while she looked at him and gave them menus.

"You in the mood for beer or wine?" asked Elliott.

"What are you going to have?"

"I want beer with lunch."

"I think I'll have the same," said Diane.

The waitress obviously understood English, because she smiled, and within a few minutes two one-liter glasses of cold beer were brought to the table and placed on round coasters.

"Are you ready to order?" asked the Fräulein in broken English.

Diane didn't read German and only understood a little. She looked at her husband, who was still eyeing the menu.

He said, "Yes, give us the schnitzel with some potato salad and a green salad."

"Ve have varm rolls also, mein Herr. Can I include two?"

"Yes," answered Elliott. She wrote down the order and left.

"Sound good to you?"

"Sounds wonderful, Jerry. I'm practically starving," she said, smiling at him. Fifteen minutes passed quickly because there was so much to see through the glass windows around the entire perimeter of the restaurant. "Every time we've come up here, Jerry, I've always marveled at this scenery."

Waiting for their meal, both were captivated by the sight of ravens riding the winds whipping around the summit.

The sound of pantry doors opening caught their attention, and they turned to see their meals being carried out on a large oval tray and placed on a stand. Another waitress helped serve, then their Fräulein asked if all was in order.

After receiving a favorable response, she told them, "Guten Appetit."

While they ate, Diane chattered on about all the places they'd visited in Germany. Even so, she still managed to finish her meal a few bites before him.

Placing her knife and fork on the plate, she said, "That tasted wonderful. It was just enough."

Elliott was only half-listening to his wife's prattle. Some other thoughts were forming. He was about to take his last bite of salad and merely replied, "I'm glad you liked it."

The waitress cleared their table, and he asked for the bill. They put their ski jackets back on and walked outside to the promenade area. It was fenced around the perimeter with double black iron pipes, approximately two inches wide, at knee and waist height. It was sturdy enough to lean on, but no one ever did. Parents were instructed to hold their children's hands or go back into a corridor to look at the view through the windows. The promenade could be dangerous if one of the sudden snow showers turned especially windy. When that happened, visitors were restricted from walking outside.

It was the middle of the fall, but freezing weather always arrived early in the Alps, especially at this altitude. Elliott placed his arm in Diane's, and they walked over to the railing. Fog began to roll over the mountaintop, so visibility rapidly decreased. Diane seemed to be moving slowly, and Elliott didn't know whether it was from the cold or she was a little tipsy.

He considered taking advantage of the fog and Diane's condition. Pushing her over the railing would be easy. Her death would at least solve one problem by getting Sunderland off his back. It would have to be done quickly, but since he was bigger, he could block most of her from view. As the fog continued to blanket the promenade, he got ready to lift her up. He glanced around to see if anyone was watching and they could still be seen. The glass windows of the dining room framed a family with two children enjoying their lunch. As he looked over toward them, the boy waved to him. He sighed heavily, knowing his opportunity was gone. He waved back before cupping his hand in Diane's.

"Want to go back inside?"

"If *you* do," she said.

They walked back in and sat down at the same table. He ordered two more beers. They didn't speak for a few moments; Elliott was now pondering alternatives to his situation with Sutherland. The waitress brought the beers.

Diane felt something was bothering him. "You're quiet, Jerry. Is something wrong?"

"Yes and no," he said, sipping and putting the beer down. His eyes narrowed. "I want to talk about the lunch meeting you're going to have with Ed Sutherland on Monday."

"Okay. What do you want to talk about?"

"As I told you, Sutherland is in some trouble. He's trying any way he can to find an excuse to move attention from him to someone else. This happened once before between him and me. He directly said I wasn't as fit as him, because he served an extra tour at Patch Barracks, and the judgment was made. He'd spent more time in Stuttgart than me, and he got the extra star." He took a sip and continued. "He wants to find out what I was doing while you were in Atlanta. He didn't know about my whereabouts because I wasn't supposed to tell anyone. He didn't even know I was on leave. When Aaron Morris called him from the Pentagon to inquire about my whereabouts, Sutherland saw a chance to put the fear of God in you so you'd agree with him."

She cleared her throat while repositioning herself. "Well, Aaron didn't know where you were. I had no idea he'd call Ed Sutherland."

"It's not your fault, Diane," he said, only partly believing his own words. He took a sip of beer and looked at her worried face. He decided if he wasn't going to kill her, he might as well give in. "I should have told you where I was going."

"And where did you go? Aaron said he didn't know where you were, and it's why he called Sutherland. It's why Ed told me."

"Yes, Diane, I know." He squirmed deliberately and said, "I really shouldn't tell you, but I was at Fort Belvoir. There were INSCOM meetings at the beginning of the week. I had a lot to do."

"INSCOM meetings? What are they?"

He tried not to roll his eyes. "Diane, I've been going to these conferences for years."

"Yes, Jerry, but you don't tell me everything. I forgot. What does INSCOM mean?"

He unfolded the paper napkin and wrote down the abbreviated lettering, then leaned over, placed the pen tip under the lettering, and in a low tone said, "It's the Army's 'Intelligence and Security Command.'"

"Okay, but why did they want you to attend, and not Ed?"

He smiled because she was falling for the argument he wanted her to give to Sutherland.

"Let's just say I'm better trained than he is."

"Jerry, let's get back to my upcoming meeting with him. I don't even know what he's going to say to me."

"Diane, I want you to be friendly, but let him ask the questions. Just pay attention to his inquiries and answer positively. For example, if he asks you if you knew where I was, tell him you'd forgotten where I was going, meaning the Pentagon or Fort Belvoir. Say I could have even spent a couple days at NSA at Fort Meade. Make it sound like it didn't matter where I was. It was just the fact that I didn't call you to check in."

"I understand," she said. "Talking with you about this helps me feel better. At least I know I can be deliberate with Ed Sutherland. I won't let him intimidate me."

"Good. If you let him humiliate you, he'll get his way. Trust me. This tactic is very similar to the ones we learn in classes on counterterrorism strategies. He'll try to beat you down mentally until you agree with him."

"I won't let him do that to me, Jerry." She straightened and said with a stern face, "It'll never happen to me."

People stood in the corridor, waiting for a cable car to arrive to take them down. The Elliotts got in line just as the cable car was moving into the parking position. The temperature had dropped considerably. Without the sun, people knew to be alert for an unexpected storm.

"Get ready for a blizzard," Jerry said.

***

The officers' club was crowded on Monday. Sutherland arrived early. Others recognized him immediately. Higher-ranked officers greeted him as he waited by the bar. At 11:45, Diane Elliott walked through the open doors and into the reception area. She saw Sutherland and felt brave enough to go right up and greet him. The two officers he was speaking with looked at them curiously.

"Good morning, Ed. It's good to see you again."

"It's good to see you, Diane." He lightly shook her hand and added, "These two gentlemen are with the V Corps administration division." He introduced them, and they shook hands with her.

Sutherland led her to a table. He helped her get seated and waved for the waiter to bring menus. Neither ordered alcohol. The waiter returned with Diet Cokes and took their orders.

"Before you begin to ask me questions, Ed, I want you to know I made a mistake when I telephoned Aaron Morris at the Pentagon. It was my fault, because I didn't remember where Jerry was going. I was just concerned because he didn't call me."

Sutherland recognized her determined attitude. He couldn't tell her her husband had lied to her. She thought a mistake had been made. Nothing was going to change this woman's mind without an argument; the restaurant was not the place. He decided to let it ride. The Remmich situation was more critical, and he wanted to get back to that issue. When lunch ended, he explained he needed to return to work. She let out a sigh of relief; their conversation had been cordial with no argument or interrogation.

16
Chain of Events

Paul Remmich arrived on time. Just as he entered Yako's building at 247 Westerstraat, he felt the vibrating buzz in his rear molar, and his face went blank. The deeper trance state was now dominant. He took out his cell phone and made the usual call. Alzuhari told him to come to the apartment on the 2nd floor, and Remmich hung up.

Yako, knowing he was in his trance state, opened the door to her flat and ushered him in.

"Paul, sit down on the sofa," she ordered.

Alzuhari came into the room and placed a chair in front of Remmich. He sat down and put a small bottle, plastic drink stirrer, and glass filled with beer on the side table.

"I want to talk about your friend Eric. We have a plan to make him a member of Tariq'Allah, and like you, he can help Third World countries. Do you understand, Paul?"

"Yes. Eric's going to become a member of the Tariq'Allah team, like me."

"Do you like the idea?"

"Yes. I want us to work together again." The smirk on Alzuhari's face indicated this was the answer he wanted.

"Good," he said enthusiastically. "I'm going to show you how to do something, Paul." He pulled the side table closer and picked up the small bottle, which contained aspirin tablets. "We're going to pretend this is Eric's glass of beer. I want you to put two pills into Eric's glass." He flipped open the plastic cap and jiggled two pills into the palm of his hand. He dropped them into the beer and asked, "Do you see the pills dissolving?"

"Yes."

"Then you take this plastic stirrer and mix them in like this." He told Remmich to look at him. "This is a calming medicine, and after he drinks it, he'll become sleepy. He won't be able to sit up straight. Eric will need your help, or he may fall on the floor. We don't want that to happen. We don't want him to get hurt. You need to hold on to him like this." Alzuhari moved closer and held on to Remmich's arm.

Remmich nodded.

Alzuhari continued. "We want to bring Eric here. We want to show him how good it is to want to work for Tariq'Allah like you do."

Remmich didn't say anything. It made Alzuhari wonder if he'd mentally registered what was just said to him. He moved the table closer to Remmich.

"I want you to do just what I did, Paul."

Yako took the bottle of aspirin and transferred 6 tablets into a small plastic pillbox.

Alzuhari picked it up and said, "Paul, look at this container I'm holding."

Remmich's eyes focused on the box, and Alzuhari said, "Take it." He waited until Remmich had a firm grip, then added, "Get two pills out of it, Paul."

He watched their mole follow the instructions.

"Now I want you to drop them into the beer."

He dropped them into the beer.

"Now pick up the stirrer and mix the pills in the beer until you can't see them anymore."

Paul stirred the beer and watched the aspirin dissolve.

Tara Yako sat down next to him and said, "Paul, look at me."

He made eye contact, and she said, "Paul, Adnaw is going to be a bartender at the Blues Alley Bar and Restaurant. He will be there this evening." She paused. "He will be able to help if we have a problem with Eric tonight." She stopped talking because Remmich looked straight ahead, as if seeing through her. She placed her hand on his face, and he blinked. "You do have a meeting with Eric tonight, don't you, Paul?"

"Yes. I'm meeting Eric at the Blues Alley Bar for beer and dinner."

"Good," she replied.

Alzuhari got close to his face and added, "Your friend is not to be told about this, because it's going to be a surprise. Do you understand?"

"I won't tell him."

Alzuhari turned toward Yako as if he was going to say something, but instead he got up and motioned for her to follow him.

"Paul, don't listen to us."

Remmich looked down and stared at the floor.

Alzuhari said in a low tone, "I'm not sure he can do this when he's out of the trance if he's had just one practice. Let's have him rehearse in front of us a few more times."

She suggested they take a break and sent Remmich out onto the balcony to smoke a cigarette.

After Paul was outside and the patio door was closed, they talked about how many times he'd have to repeat the steps to secure the process in his mind. Ten minutes later, they brought him back into the room and had him sit down on the same cushion.

Yako handed the pillbox to him and said, "Take this and put it in your shirt pocket."

Remmich obeyed.

She added, "Now take the pillbox out of your shirt pocket, open it, and remove two pills." He did. "Now close the pillbox and put it back into your shirt pocket. Now use the stirrer to mix the pills around in the beer." He did. Each successive attempt improved the smoothness of the steps enough for Yako to say finally, "Good work, Paul. I think you're ready."

Alzuhari told Remmich to give him the pillbox. He took it from him, replaced the aspirin with Rohypnol pills, and handed it back to Remmich.

He said, “There are two tablets in this pillbox. Wait until Eric goes to the men’s room, then drop them into his beer. When you’ve done that and they’re dissolved, put the pillbox back into your shirt pocket. Do you understand?”

Paul looked into Alzuhari’s eyes. “Yes. I will wait for Eric to go to the bathroom, so he does not see me drop the pills into the beer and then stir the beer to dissolve the pills.”

“Tara will be sitting across the bar, watching you. As soon as Eric is sedated, she will get a taxi and come back in to get both of you. You will recognize her.”

Remmich maintained eye contact with him, and he repeated, “You will know who she is and follow her directions. Do you understand me, Paul?”

After a few seconds, he answered, “Yes.”

“What time are you meeting Eric, Paul?” asked Yako.

He didn’t answer, and Alzuhari asked, “Did you set up a time with him, Paul?”

The lack of an answer suggested he hadn’t chosen a time, and Alzuhari said, “When you get home, call Eric and set the meeting for five. Is that clear?”

“I will call him when I get home,” answered Remmich.

“I have some photographs for you, Paul,” said Alzuhari.

He retrieved a brown envelope from his bag and pulled out six photographs. Yildiz had used a couple of them when he explained to Remmich what he and Miller were going to do.

He aligned them on the coffee table and proceeded to explain the people in the photos were very poor, hungry, and sick. Some were Muslim, and some were Christian. Remmich listened while he was told to show the pictures to Miller. He needed to explain the conditions in which these people suffered. They wanted to appeal to Miller’s emotions. They wanted him to understand the good he could do.

“Yes,” answered Remmich.

Alzuhari gave a pencil to Remmich. "Copy down the names of the countries on the back sides of the photographs. I want you to be as factual as possible when you talk to Eric."

He took the pencil and wrote down the names of the countries the people lived in and some details about each picture as Alzuhari spoke. Remmich listened but didn't show any emotion while writing.

Alzuhari raised his voice and said, "Paul, you can leave now."

Remmich blinked a couple of times, and his deeper subliminal state of mind began to lift. Minutes later, Yako opened the door, and he left.

By the time Remmich returned to his condo, he'd wholly returned to his then-normal state of hypnosis. When he walked into his office, the phone blinked.

There was no message, but the Caller ID number was from the Amsterdam area. He dialed it anyway, thinking maybe it was Candice's new number. Sure enough, Miller answered. They chatted for a few minutes and set up a 5 o'clock rendezvous.

***

Ambassador Linkov's secretary interrupted to say he had a call.

There was a click on the line. Nikulin said, "Hello, Mr. Ambassador. I just finished listening to an important conversation. The Iraqis had a meeting with Paul Remmich at Yako's flat."

"You are referring to the two Iraqis in Amsterdam?"

"Yes."

"Go on."

"I just emailed a recording of the conversation to you. They're going after his friend, the Black man."

Linkov looked at his folder of notes. "You must be talking about Eric Miller, the Army officer."

"That's him. When you listen to the recording, you'll be surprised to hear they're going to get Remmich to drug his friend."

"You mean the Iraqis want Miller in addition to Remmich?"

"Yes."

"Humph. Well, I look forward to listening to it." He swiveled the chair to the right a little and opened the email on his computer. "Your message has arrived, Yury. Let me listen to this recording, and I'll get back to you."

17

Blues Alley Rendezvous

Miller took out a twenty-euro bill from his wallet.

"This is all I have for taxi fare. I didn't have time to go to the bank."

"I have some cash," said Candice. She pulled out a euro twenty. "Is this enough?"

"Oh, sure. I just didn't know how much I'd need for the taxi. I'll use my credit card for dinner."

When he went to open the door to leave, her eyebrows raised as she asked, "Aren't you forgetting something?"

She pursed her lips, and he gave her a big kiss goodbye.

Candice Harper and Lilly Remmich planned to get together, also. Candice took a taxi to the Schiller Hotel. Lilly wanted to give Candice a tour of their condo, then show off the rest of the hotel. They'd finish by relaxing in the restaurant-bar.

Miller got out of the taxi at the corner just down from the restaurant. Walking along Bourbon Street, he noticed the diversity of the individuals he passed, along with their distinct style of clothes. Music resonated from bars and entertained him as he walked. The Blues Alley bar-restaurant was beginning to get busy. A group followed the maître d' to a table, and Miller walked ahead to avoid him; he didn't want a table. His eyes searched those sitting along the horseshoe curve, and he spotted his buddy on the other side. Remmich smoked while talking to a bartender.

He arrived and took off his jacket, hanging it on the back of the empty swivel chair next to Remmich. They shook hands.

The bartender approached, ready to take an order.

"Adnaw, please bring my friend a beer." He swallowed some of his and said, "You got here on time. Did you drive?"

"No. I was fortunate to get a parking space last night. You know the drama of trying to find parking around here, so I took a taxi."

"You did the right thing. Parking is scarce here, and people are protective of their spaces. I guess it's understandable since there are so many vehicles."

Miller watched his buddy open a small, flat-looking square cigarette box. "I've never seen this brand before."

"I bought several in Istanbul. Would you care to smoke one?"

"You mean Istanbul, Turkey?"

"Yes. I had a business engagement there after my Cuban excursion." He motioned for his friend to take a cigarette. Remmich lit the match.

Miller hoped Remmich would tell him why he was in Cuba. And why did he go to Istanbul? He was very concerned about his friend's employment status with a country bullied by ISIS. Iraq couldn't win any battle without aid from the United States. His embrace of the country seemed to happen so fast and was difficult to accept. Was it possible Paul was being used to acquire classified information because of his security clearance?

His face was grim as he exhaled the smoke and wondered, *Man, where in the hell is this leading?*

"You look concerned, Eric. Is everything all right with you and Candice? Or is there something else you need to talk about?"

He shrugged but didn't answer. He wanted Remmich to explain what was going on. He stared at the flat, colorful box again. The cover had an unusual yellow border, a filigree with continuous white flower designs. The middle area showed clouds in a blue sky and the name "Taksim" in the center.

The bartender placed a coaster down before putting an overflowing beer on it. Alzuhari used a damp towel and quickly wiped up the wet spots. He smiled and went to a customer, waving his hand.

Out of the corner of his eye, Remmich noticed a waiter walk by and stop at the couple to his left. Turning, he saw the waiter place two round dishes of raw oysters in the half-shell sitting on a bed of rock salt.

His mouth watering, Remmich waved and tried to get his attention, but the waiter turned away. Alzuhari noticed Remmich's attempt and approached.

"Excuse me, sir. He doesn't understand English. Can I help you?"

Paul gestured from himself to his buddy and said, "We want some raw oysters, please." The barman left.

Now Miller was salivating. "I was hoping we'd get some. I like the slightly briny ones that have a real fresh taste. It's been quite a while since we ate them here."

"Since I moved here, I don't order them much. Do you remember at my wedding party, Lilly ate some and Candice tried one for the first time? Miller grinned and nodded before sipping.

"Do you two go out to dine a lot since you moved?"

"Occasionally, but I haven't had too much free time with traveling, so we've eaten at the hotel a lot. The food is free, of course, and good."

Miller took a puff and thought for a moment while exhaling. He kept coming back to Remmich's irrational behavior. *How did he get employment with a Middle Eastern organization?* It was taxing for him not to bring up the subject.

"How do you like the Turkish cigarette?" asked Remmich.

"Stronger than ours. Different, but good."

He flicked the ash into the tray. "I heard you call the bartender by name. Adnaw. Do you know him?" Miller was curious because the man looked Middle Eastern and seemed to know Remmich.

The mole thought about it but found he couldn't recall the answer. Instead, he said, "I guess it's because I come here a lot and speak to him occasionally. I think he works part-time."

The response seemed reasonable, so Miller backed off. They exchanged small talk for a few minutes before the waiter brought a tray with their oysters.

"They have excellent service in this place. It's why I enjoy coming here."

They both speared their first one, savoring the sea taste, along with the spicy sauce. Miller inhaled a mouth of air to reduce the sting. A sip of cold beer followed. His friend did the same thing. They finished their remaining five, leaving the bowl of crackers untouched.

"What do you think?"

"I put too much spicy cocktail sauce on one. Otherwise, they're very good."

Paul wiped his mouth with the napkin. "This should hold us over for a little while. We can order dinner later."

Miller reached for the Turkish box again and noticed the matchbook. The black and red colors and symbol were familiar.

"I see you have matches from the El Toro in Cuba."

Remmich glanced at the label and picked up the matchbook. "I collected quite a few packs of them. Every day, the cleaning attendants left a couple in my hotel room's ashtrays."

His patience gone, Miller determinedly asked, "We haven't had a chance to talk for over a week. But I want to know something. What influenced you to want a job with the Iraqi government? I mean, why them? Why didn't you apply to the US Embassy in Germany or here in Holland?"

Remmich straightened, his face rigid. "First, I am employed by the Tariq'Allah as a representative for their foreign affairs. Second, I saw this job offer in the newspaper and applied."

He knew Paul was lying, because his friend couldn't read or speak Dutch. It was true. Most of the city's natives were fluent in English, but that was irrelevant in this case.

"And they offered me a decent position. It pays me much more than the Army and the Schiller Hotel. Lilly will be traveling

with me. For my sake, I'm building a foundation as a professional diplomat. My father enjoyed doing it, and I have fond memories of my younger years. I want to give it a try. Besides, I'll only have to spend six months, maybe a little longer, in Cuba, and then we'll return to Amsterdam."

"I didn't know you could read the Dutch newspaper."

The mole cleared his throat while readjusting himself in the seat to buy time to think. He picked up his glass and countered with, "Oh, of course. Well, actually, Lilly found it. She realized my enthusiasm to represent her father's wine buying was beginning to dwindle." He sipped.

Miller knew that was bullshit, too, but instead of saying so, he asked, "So, you're returning here. Are you two going to keep the condo here in Amsterdam?"

"Oh, yes. Lilly's parents won't ask us to leave."

"Yeah, okay, but I want to talk about Iraq. Baghdad had such a terrible reputation because their war efforts against the enemy relied on extremist help. You do remember ISIS used chlorine gas to murder people in Syria and Iraq? What's developed in Baghdad, or thereabouts, says there's a problem with their government. A big problem!"

Remmich frowned at that statement. "The world's opinion about them needs to change. The things they did in the seventies, eighties, and nineties stopped in the last decade. You must understand it was over a decade ago when Saddam Hussein was their leader. Granted, he governed with a group of killers and tyrants. Today, they realize their former leader was wrong. Iraq fights day and night to regain their lost cities from ISIS. It's more important to note what's going on presently. They're working toward a way to advance economically."

He waved his hand to stop Miller from interrupting. "They told me what I'm doing isn't illegal. Believe me. I signed a United Nations document promising not to do any unlawful acts against any nation." He straightened up and lied. "They sent copies to the

Department of State." He smiled and added, "And I'm still a faithful United States citizen."

"You mean you didn't sign a document from the State Department agreeing not to disclose unauthorized information? I'm surprised."

"No. All I signed was the approved UN agreement," lied Remmich. "It had nothing to do with my debriefing promise with the Army and the security jobs. In other words, the classified information I've been exposed to is off-limits to them."

Miller knew his buddy liked to lay it on thick, but this was unbelievable. He made an effort to hide his skepticism.

"I'm aware the US Army is worried about Middle Eastern spies." He sipped and belched. "But since I've agreed to the new position, nobody asked what I did in the Army. No, Eric, you'll have to look at other countries in that part of the world for spy determination endeavors."

The last part of the comment regarding espionage challenged Miller's opinion. "Well, what about the Hezbollah or ISIS? Do you blame the West's suspicion for not trusting them? They began in Iraq and spread to Syria."

"I thought the answer was clear when I pointed out they don't practice the behaviors of the past decades anymore. The government has had well over ten years to reform. Their interests are to improve internally and internationally. So, yes, I do find fault with the West. It isn't right to ignore the good things a country has to offer.

"For example, the first President Bush instituted the idea to increase involvement by foreign powers to settle international disputes. This is why the NATO Stockholm security pact expanded into a major subdivision of the UN. Since my resignation, I'm more aware of the positive elements of Iraq."

"But do you trust them enough to go after international money-making schemes with underdeveloped Third World nations?"

"They're not going after these countries. A nation coming into contact with Iraq made an effort on their own, not vice versa."

"That won't stop Iraq from a military takeover of a poor nation," argued Miller. "It's why the UN restrains them from having an armed force, except to protect their own country."

"I'm not part of a military command anymore. My attitude as an independent is simple. I'm employed by a nonmilitary organization. My income is legally earned. Iraq follows a UN pact permitting them to associate with other nations, but without military intervention. Look, I'm just repeating myself."

It was an effort for Miller to keep his mouth shut. He decided he had to go for the jugular. He straightened and stared directly into Remmich's eyes.

"What influenced you to work for them?"

With composure, Remmich answered, "I told you. Lilly found the job in the Amsterdam newspaper."

Remmich took a sip of beer. It didn't bother him that he was making up fabrications. *The hypnosis programmed him to do it.* He truly didn't remember how the Iraqi relationship began.

Trying to regain the peace, he said, "Well, all I can tell you is what you've already heard from me. I wasn't comfortable toiling in sales and marketing for the rest of my life. Today, my employment is an opportunity for eventual recognition from other nations, an international position. Something I want. After my decade-long tour with the Army, spending six years in Germany with V Corps, being a diplomat is more in my nature, I guess. I'm being employed to do something good by assisting a wealthy country to relieve poorer people from their woes."

Alzuhari appeared and held up an empty glass. The gesture prompted them to say yes.

Remmich continued. "You probably don't know they're free to explore diplomatic relations with any country, as long as weaponry isn't a factor. Cuba isn't interested in military aggression, and fortunately for them, they have potential as a resort haven. They have an excellent agricultural market in sugar and tobacco, and they'll expand in their farming efforts because they'll be trained by a division of Tariq'Allah.

"The plan is to advance them into a non-petroleum energy-producing country. The country won't need oil in the same way anymore. And there are electric cars. Pollution will reduce. Iraq has a new system, a scientific one dealing with solar energy. They believe they can help poor nations."

"That paints a rosy picture, but consider what Generals Sutherland and Elliott told us at the Thirty-second meeting. Iraq is trying to fool the world. Their intentions are two-sided; make a promise to improve the economy, then get the country to work and let Iraq decide how to divide the profit. They'll use the farmlands and industries if there are any, the way the Soviet Union used Eastern European nations. Simply put, they were a physical shield to protect Russia. But who made the most profit? Russia, of course. Are you really saying you believe a Middle Eastern country will form a partnership to help underdeveloped nations? Is that it?"

Alzuhari placed glasses onto new coasters. His eyes scanned the mole's face to see if he was ready to act. Miller's attention was on lighting a cigarette. Remmich wondered how much longer the carefully chosen one could hold off going to the men's room. He had to go himself.

Miller stopped speaking, while Alzuhari stood in front of them. He glanced at the man, wondering if he'd been listening to their conversation. Finally, the guy went to another customer, and he continued.

"Believe me, I understand where you're coming from, Paul. I agree with you in many ways, but Iraq has too many negatives in their political folder. Now, for some unknown reason, you've accepted them as pure and lily-white in the world. They're sneaks, pure and simple. They'll try anything to get out of their international restrictions."

Remmich's bladder was about to burst, so he held up his hand to interrupt Miller, excused himself, and quickly headed to the men's room.

While he sat alone, Miller breathed deeply to lessen his exasperation as best as he could. When his buddy returned, he said, "I just hope you don't get your ass into trouble." He took a sip and asked, "By the way, did you get an email about the security meeting next week?"

"I haven't had the time to look at them yet. What day next week?"

"Tuesday, at nine hundred hours."

Remmich reached into the inner lining pocket of his jacket and took out a brown envelope.

"Yes, I'll be at the meeting." He removed the photographs. Lining them up in front of Miller, he slowly pointed in silence to each tragic picture. "I want to show you some examples of the desperate conditions we're trying to change. Look at them."

Miller touched the photos. "What countries are these kids from?"

Remmich turned each over and read his handwritten notes; Sudan and Sierra Leone. "These boys are ten, twelve, and fourteen years of age. The West African Revolutionary United Front trains them to kill and maim anyone they want. Then, the Front bosses proclaim victory to show superiority and take what they want in food and women."

Miller studied them, one at a time, then said, "Okay. I agree the pictures are horrific. What in the hell are you trying to say?"

"This is the sort of Third World support I plan to do."

"Wait a minute, damn it! You're going to Cuba. There's a big difference between Cuba and where these people come from."

"Culturally, yes, but the needs are the same. We can help raise the level of a poor nation by a country with solid financial support. Don't forget, Iraq is petroleum-rich. The key element is its personal, on-the-job help, Eric. There are thousands of people in

Sudan, Africa's largest nation, and Sierra Leone, Chad, Somalia, the Democratic Republic of the Congo, and so on who need a helping hand. We'll show them how to improve. It's sad to think otherwise, isn't it?"

"It's very depressing. But the United States pledges millions of dollars to help these people, notwithstanding the UN agreement."

"Yes, but the US's intentions aren't implemented. Those in poorer homelands, whether Islamic or Christian, suffer because of illegal efforts, like the West African Revolutionaries. Are you aware that half of the world's population lives on less than two dollars a day, Eric? People aren't receiving enough food supplies, and medical aid is scarce. These photographs prove it."

Miller took a small sip of his beer, then stood up and said it was his turn to use the men's room.

Immediately after he left, the mole moved his friend's glass closer to him. He reached under his V-neck sweater to his shirt pocket and pulled out the pillbox. Two Rohypnol tablets dropped into the beer. He closed the box and looked around the bar to see if anyone was watching him. No one seemed interested, except Alzuhari. He agitated the dissolving pills with the plastic stirrer and moved the glass back to its former location. Sliding the pillbox back into his pocket, he sat waiting nervously for his friend to get back.

When Miller returned, he half-sat with one foot on the chair rung and the other foot still on the floor. Before turning to face the bar, he glanced at the customers sitting around the horseshoe and was stunned when he focused on a particular one.

"This is unreal." He nudged Remmich's arm. "It's her."

"What's bothering you?"

"If you look beyond the barman in the center, you'll see what's bothering me. It's that woman."

"What woman? There are dozens of women here."

"In the middle of the bar, damn it. The beautiful, olive-skinned female with jet-black hair pulled back. The one showing plenty of cleavage in her low-cut green blouse."

Remmich chuckled at his friend's comment. But he also spotted the woman, Tara Yako. She sat among others at the crowded bar. He couldn't deny seeing her, because she was the only olive-skinned person.

"Okay, I see her. So what?"

"Don't you remember? She sat next to you at this bar the same night we were here earlier in the year. The same night you disappeared for a couple hours." He felt Paul wasn't grasping what he said and added, "You lit her cigarette. Then we saw those American women sitting at a round table by the dance floor. Candice was with them. Remember?"

The mole recognized her from his recent hypnotic order but couldn't recall her role the night he came to the bar with Eric.

"Okay, that was the night you met Candice."

Remmich's seeming lack of recollection of the woman frustrated Miller. He sipped, confused about his friend's apparent memory gap. He tried to think of another approach as he took a filtered smoke from the box. Remmich lit his own and held the match.

Miller chuckled lightly to hide his growing annoyance, then said, "You have a way of getting around answering questions, Paul. I'm suspicious of her. Shortly after you began talking with her that night, both of you disappeared."

Because he couldn't answer his friend's inquiry, he abruptly changed the subject. "Have you given any thought to what we discussed about you resigning and working with me?"

Miller grimaced. He'd never known his friend to be so persistent. He took a sip and reached for another smoke before he realized he already had one lit. He put it back into the box and decided to play Remmich's game of not answering right away.

His buddy didn't relent. "So, tell me what you think. Would you be a diplomat, instead of continuing as an Army officer? Remember, the salary is excellent, and we could possibly work together."

"I think you're a better candidate for that kind of service. I remember you saying it's in your blood. Your father is still serving as a diplomat. I don't have the patience for a Peace Corps type of position. I attended West Point for a specific reason. It wasn't to volunteer to help poor countries."

Remmich continued to press him to get an agreement. He stopped his rant only long enough to drink more of his beer.

Miller's jaw was set in irritation. Eying Remmich, he asked, "Where in the hell did you pick up this sales pitch?" He took a puff, blew the smoke upward, and took a big gulp. "With all due respect to Islam and the millions of Muslims in the Middle East and in our own country, this Tariq'Allah is a farce!"

"You are totally wrong, Eric. Since my association with them, I haven't encountered any type of chicanery. The Tariq'Allah group is attempting to do good things. What's wrong with that?"

"I don't know if there is anything wrong. But history tends to repeat itself." He drank more and added, "It's good some people are willing to give their time to assist the needy. However, I believe most of those countries are untrustworthy, especially Syria, Iran, and Iraq. They have ulterior motives. Syria is prime for ISIS to force political and religious control on people. They want jurisdiction. Their motives are to return to old-style religious and social ways of life. Iran wants nuclear recognition, which could evolve into a trade business."

"I find your remark rather insulting. I guess you're saying you don't trust me either?"

Miller gave him a piercing stare. "Look, I can't pledge allegiance to this country because of the ISIS matter. They secretly acquired weaponry, and possibly nuclear arms." He stopped momentarily because he wanted to see a reaction. *None.* "Let's face it, Paul, we know they use these weapons. So all of a sudden, this Tariq'Allah group wants everyone to accept they're on a goodwill mission? Come on, man. That is pure horse shit."

Hoping his words would sink in if he left it at that for a while, he announced, "I'll be right back. I have to take another leak."

***

Yury Nikulin found an empty seat at the horseshoe-shaped bar. During the weeks he'd been in Amsterdam, he'd let his beard grow out, which camouflaged his face. He found the current bar scenario very entertaining. He got the attention of the Iraqi and ordered a beer.

Alzuhari placed a glass in front of him and wiped away the suds running down the side. He couldn't identify the bearded man but felt he'd seen him somewhere before, somewhere other than at this bar. The man's Siberian slanted eyes and thick black eyebrows seemed familiar.

Nikulin's attention focused on what seemed to be an argument between the Americans. Although he couldn't hear anything, the facial expressions they exchanged appeared to confirm his guess.

18
Beyond the Stars

Alzuhari saw Remmich leaning in the chair, trying to see past the people sitting at the bar. Miller wasn't next to him, so he walked over to find out what was going on.

"What were you looking at?"

"I wanted to make sure Eric went into the men's room."

The Iraqi realized the opportunity to get their new mole was close. "You really want this man to work with us, don't you?"

"I definitely do. I believe my friend will help us advance Third World nations." It was sweet music to Alzuhari's ears. He left to serve a patron.

Miller came out of the bathroom, moving awkwardly through the crowd. Trying to sit on the barstool, he lost his balance, grabbing the edge of the bar to hold on. "Paul, I'm hungry." He smiled and giggled. "I feel tipsy, too." In spite of his words, he sipped beer and mishandled getting another Turkish cigarette.

He couldn't light the match; his dexterity was terrible. Remmich lit it for him. "Yes, we'll get to eat soon. But first let's finish our beers, then we'll go over to a table."

Gazing across the room while waiting for his friend to drink more, Remmich saw Tara Yako looking at them.

Miller's beer was only one-quarter full. He belched and slurred, "Excuse me."

He fumbled, trying to open the cigarette box. Remmich said, "Eric, you already have a smoke in the ashtray." He took the box from Miller and handed the lit butt to him.

He puffed and mumbled. "We ready to eat yet?"

His hands wobbled holding the cigarette. Holding his forehead with his other hand, he muttered, "W'as wrong with me?"

His balance faltered, and his arm slid, nearly tipping over his beer glass. "Oh, sshhhittt," he slurred while blinking.

"Take it easy, my friend," said Remmich while he stopped Miller from bending over and hitting his head on the wood. He removed the butt from between the fingers of the mole-to-be.

The more Miller spoke, the more incoherent he became. His body leaned toward Remmich and slouched into his buddy's arms. His body wobbled, which didn't help.

Yako pushed herself through the bystanders until she reached them. Remmich followed her order to carry him out of the entrance door.

He turned his buddy's swivel stool until they were facing each other. He slowly moved him off the seat, but Miller was too limp and started to fall to the floor. Remmich grabbed onto his shirt. The weight made him grunt, but he pressed his body against the bar. He had to swing Miller's arm up around his neck and put his other one around the waist, struggling to get the dead weight to the door. People watched.

Yako stayed ahead of them while waving to her accomplice behind the bar. He rushed to assist Remmich. Together, they lifted him off his feet and out the front door.

Yury Nikulin followed them outside, staying two people behind.

Yako got into a cab and slid over. Alzuhari strained to sit Miller into the rear seat on the passenger side, making sure he didn't hit the rim of the cab's roof. Remmich sat on the other side to support him. Before he walked away, Yako told Alzuhari not to forget she'd activate Remmich's deeper trance once they got to the apartment and he'd get a telephone call.

The cab driver overheard her speaking English and asked, "Where do you want to go?"

The taxi drove off, and Nikulin signaled for a cab, telling the driver to follow the yellow one up ahead.

Miller swayed with every turn the car made. The drive to her flat took less than twenty minutes. They arrived, and she paid while Remmich maneuvered his future partner out of the cab. He leaned in and swung Miller's right arm around his neck, grabbing his belt on the other side. The three of them waddled to the entrance. Yako held the entrance door open, and they got on the elevator. Going up, Remmich leaned him against the handrail for support. It helped only a little. When they got off, she rushed to open the door to her flat.

Remmich practically dragged him; the deadweight was interfering with his hold. He tightened the grips on him but couldn't get through the flat's doorway. He turned sideways and moved into the apartment. Yako directed him to the recliner sofa. He lowered Miller into the seat. Standing up, he massaged his lower back.

"My God, he is heavy," Remmich complained. There was no recollection of when they brought him there the first time, drugged, then hypnotized. He couldn't remember attending meetings there; the hypnosis blocked all of it from his mind.

Yako closed the curtains before maneuvering a dimmer switch to reduce the brightness of the kitchen counter lights. She'd never thought about what to do with Paul Remmich while hypnotizing the mole-to-be. Random movements might interrupt Miller's concentration. She worried he wouldn't succumb to being hypnotized. She was concerned her subject's mind might reject the mesmerizing. What if he got up and attacked her? She couldn't figure out why Alzuhari had confidence in her to do this by herself. Maybe Remmich was to be her bodyguard.

"Paul, sit in a chair at the dining table."

She pointed to the one farthest away and waited for him to sit down, then went into the bedroom and punched in a numerical code on a device that messaged the Iraqi satellite. Seconds later, Remmich's tooth buzzed, and he became solemn, going into a deeper subliminal trance. It made him unaware of his environment. He reached for his cell phone and pressed the autodial. Four rings later, Alzuhari answered.

Remmich said, "This is agent PSR."

The loud noises from music and people talking kept the Iraqi from hearing Remmich. It didn't matter. The call was only to trigger his control. Remmich sat motionless.

She disconnected the line and said, "Do not move from this seat until I tell you to get up, and do not talk." He remained silent.

She returned to Miller and pushed the control button on the recliner, lowering him backward. Street light from outside peeked in-between the window curtains. She closed the gap, but one side wouldn't stay in place. Frustrated, she braced a chair against the draperies. All the while, her intended mole remained dizzy. He didn't know where he was.

Dimming the lighting, she waited a few moments to let her vision adjust. As she did with Remmich, she turned on the air conditioner. She rolled the projector stand past Remmich and placed it in front of the recliner. She put the stand far enough away to prevent Miller's foot from kicking it over.

He began to move awkwardly and rubbed his face. It dawned on her to be ready for him getting up. Shifting again, he opened his eyelids. She saw him staring into space.

Relieved, she said, "Close your eyes, and keep them closed."

She waited for him to follow her command before turning on the projector and adjusting the lens. Then she moved the table, so the projector's beam centered on the oval ceiling. The video began. A carousel of tiny lights circled the dome.

"Eric, open your eyes."

He did and saw the three-dimensional mass of stars and interstellar spirals move above him. He shivered because the temperature had dropped. She placed a blanket over him. She had other plans.

He reached up slowly with his arm and tried to touch the stars; the clusters seemed within reach.

She returned with a small, rectangular, stainless-steel tray with a syringe and vial of tranquilizing liquid; the one to decrease the effect of the Rohypnol. She also included a squeeze bottle containing potent liquid marijuana.

As with Remmich, the needle containing the liquid marijuana saturated the cigarette tobacco. Unlike truth serum drugs and barbiturates, which prevent a person from remembering emotional feelings and related thoughts, inhaling the smoke made a person cooperative. As with Paul Remmich, she needed his cooperation to hypnotize him but didn't intend to put him into an intense subliminal condition. She studied him while he watched the entire elliptical galaxy rotate in slow motion. It appeared as if the objects hovered in the air. The groups of stars formed intricate circles, ovals, and triangles, some very faint in appearance, in pale whites, blues, purples, yellows, reds, and orange.

Miller was compliant, but Yako didn't want to take any chances. She inserted the needle into the vial and filled the syringe with the required 10 cc's of liquid. He felt the cool of the wet alcohol wipe. Unlike Remmich's needle stab by her, Miller accepted the syringe puncture in his skin without a flinch.

"Do not move, Eric."

Seconds later, she pulled on the plunger to make sure it hadn't nicked a vein or artery. When blood didn't enter the barrel, she pressed the thumb rest to force the fluid into his muscle. He yelped and flinched. It stung, but she held on to his shoulder with her other hand. She removed the needle and used gauze to wipe away the blood that leaked out of the puncture. She put on a small bandage.

Her objective was to ask repetitive questions and make similar and repeated statements to Miller. It was part of the psychological process to achieve hypnosis.

Eric began to feel different. He became aware of his surroundings and what Yako was doing. He didn't think he was in control enough to stop her yet from whatever she was doing. He remembered anti-terrorist tactics from West Point training, but he decided not to rebel. He felt his heart flutter once, then again.

Focusing on his heart, he forgot what he'd been thinking. He didn't feel pain; just peculiar. He breathed slowly and began to sober up. The slow breathing brought his heart rate back to normal. He stared at the movement of the 3-dimensional galaxy. The moving images relaxed him, but he was still unsure about his situation and safety.

Her vision adjusted to the low glow of the projector. The darkness didn't faze Remmich, who remained in a hunched position.

The saturated cigarette was dry, and she put it between the future spy's lips. Using a lighter, she lit it. He puffed instinctively and inhaled the smoke.

"Look at the ceiling, Eric. Isn't it beautiful?"

She kept quiet for a moment and watched him take a long drag. As it had for Paul, inhaling the drug-filled tobacco relaxed him enough for him to agree robotically. The picture of the galaxy also provided a hypnotic effect. His cooperation was a blessing from Allah, she thought, because this man wasn't as obstinate as Paul had been. He'd become obnoxious and forcefully tried to stand up from his reclined position. Thankfully, Alzuhari was there to assist her that time.

She pulled out a piece of paper from the end table and read the prepared outline. "Eric, you are watching the stars pass through the galaxy. They are objects like you, but they have a particular path to follow. You also have a path. It's filled with your desire to do good things for others. This is personal power." She waved her hand in a semicircle and said, "You are like these stars, because you can move in a path also. But you are freer than the stars. Their cosmic energy only lets them travel within their bounds. You do not have to do what they do. You will travel on a path to help countries in need."

He continued to relax and puff.

"Eric, you will become smarter. You want to help Third World countries because you want to become a leader. I want you to believe you will be an ambassador for Tariq'Allah. They are from my country, helping the unfortunate nations. Tell yourself that you want to do the same."

Realizing her suggestion could backfire, she then said, "If you don't believe you can be a diplomat and a leader for Iraq in the world, you may get up and leave. You will not be forced to stay." He felt too languid to answer and stayed motionless, except to take the last drag. She took it from him and crushed it out in the ashtray. "Eric, close your eyes." She waited to let him adjust to the darkness. "Tell yourself that you can make this decision. Tell yourself that you can be worth more for all of God's creatures by helping poor countries. You need to become a member of our group and be a friend. Tell yourself you want to give your time to poor nations, Eric. We want to do good, not hurt them. The United Nations ignores them. Can you work with us to help Third World countries?"

She kept quiet while he remained silent, trying to think.

"You are trapped as a military intelligence officer and not able to advance the world's poor people. Your Army does not care for the poor nations. You will please God by becoming a member of what we call the Shining Star of God, our Tariq'Allah. Join your friend Paul. Do you understand, Eric?"

He didn't respond because he still felt some soothing effect from the cigarette, but his mind was clearing. He found himself able to think about what she'd do if he did start to leave. She could attack him with a weapon, but she couldn't stop him by herself. He was strong enough to overpower her. Remmich was here, but would Paul defend her or help him? Regardless, Eric realized if he did get up, he might never know what they planned to do with him.

They must have done this to Paul.

He realized she was trying to hypnotize him. What was she trying to explain, talking about poor nations, Iraq, and that other name that seemed familiar?

"Did you hear me, Eric?"

He modulated his voice, talking slower to make her think he was obeying her commands. Appearing to be alert wasn't good; another person might be in the apartment who could help her kill him. He would follow her orders for now.

Again she asked, "Do you understand me, Eric?"

Calmly, he answered, while moving his eyes to the revolving galaxy, "Yes. I understand."

She repeated, "You are imprisoned as a member of the Army because you are not able to help humanity, especially Third World nations. Does your work in the military make you want to work for the Army, or be like Paul, who works for Tariq'Allah? He is helping Third World nations. Do you want to be like him?"

Ah, that's the word he used. Remmich had talked about Tariq'Allah at Blues Alley.

It was tough to feign calmness and obedience, because he truly wanted to kill her. But keeping his cool was essential to staying alive, both for himself and his buddy.

He spoke slowly. "Yes, I want to be like him."

She began a repetition of words to embed the thoughts as his own. "Stare at the galaxy, Eric, and say, 'I want to be a member of Tariq'Allah.'" Almost whispering, she repeated the words. She waited and then said, "Say it, Eric."

It was difficult, but he kept a leash on his emotions, even though he was irritated. He imagined if Yako were successful, he'd become her tool, a possible mole.

In a low tone, he answered, "Yes, I want to become a member of Tariq'Allah."

"Good. Now say, 'I want to resign from the Army and become a member of Tariq'Allah.' Say it, Eric."

While he repeated those words, he mentally wanted to choke her. *He wasn't going to be her damn mole!* He once again wished he had a weapon but consciously controlled his face movements so she wouldn't notice his awareness.

"Eric, say you don't want to be with the Army anymore."

He pretended to let her think he was submitting to her. Calmly, he said, “I don’t want to be with the Army anymore.”

“Say, ‘I want to be a member of Tariq’Allah.’ Say it, Eric.”

He reduced the tight grip he had on the cushion. If he lost control, his cover would be blown wide open. She’d surely recognize he wasn’t getting hypnotized.

“I want to be a member of Tariq’Allah.”

“Keep saying it, Eric.” She paused to watch him. “Look at the heavens and keep saying those words.” She stepped away, then tiptoed to the kitchen so as not to distract him.

He continued to repeat, “I want to be a member of Tariq’Allah,” while seeing the galaxy circulating on the ceiling. His peripheral vision picked up movement to his right. He heard soft footsteps. Turning his head slightly sideways, he saw a woman’s torso. Satisfied, he looked at the ceiling while continuing to repeat the words.

He thought, *What the hell am I going to do?*

She moved a chair next to him and sat down. After handing him another dried marijuana smoke, she lit it. In less than a minute, he began to feel numbing, calming sensations. She wanted him more relaxed to let the hypnotized mind take control. She needed to be assured his conscious mind shifted into a subconscious trance. His cooperation was essential.

The pot again calmed and relaxed him while he watched the light show above his head. The stars stretched across outer space. He still wondered if this is what had happened to Paul.

I’ll never intentionally become a spy.

He thought back to the snack bar discussion when Remmich talked about resigning.

I’ll bet this is why he wanted to leave. No wonder he’s been so pro-Iraq and negative-West.

Yako heard him repeat he wanted to become a member of Tariq’Allah. The long ash fell on the chair’s arm after the second inhale. She noticed and grabbed the butt and put it out. She blew the ash off the chair arm.

She worked with him for more than an hour. He wasn't high and was still in control of his thoughts. He listened to sentences, repeating them back to her. It assured her she'd hypnotized him. Her mole said the sentences on his own now. Each time she closed her eyes and thanked Allah, it was because Miller would only do this on his own if he were hypnotized.

Paul Remmich didn't have a clue about what was happening. Suddenly, he heard her tell him, "Goodbye, Paul."

He blinked, and the deep trance began to subside. He even moved around to position himself better in the chair. She then left him alone and tended to Miller. She wasn't worried about anything terrible occurring while Remmich came out of his stupor.

Miller wondered about Paul's state of mind. He was determined to free himself and Remmich from this mess.

Her words were boring him now, saying how he was to follow a life of obedience. He just stared at the oval ceiling, while she spoke to him. The marijuana effects had worn off. He was angry with her efforts to make him betray the United States. The temptation to kill her returned.

She got up and turned off the projector. It took several seconds for their eyesight to adjust to the dim kitchen light. She went into the kitchen to turn up the lighting and returned carrying a pad and pencil.

She gave them to him and ordered, "Give me your telephone number."

His mind objected at first because this was a new order, but he knew he had to obey to keep up the pretense.

"I will call with instructions to contact a man by the name of Dr. Mustafa, an Army dentist. You need to let him examine your teeth. Do you understand?"

He stared at her as if he saw nothing. He had to repeat her words to hide his condition. Slowly, he answered, "Yes. I will wait for a telephone call from you with instructions to contact Dr. Mustafa."

"Good," she said. "We are going back to the Blues Alley nightclub, Eric. You are to only remember my call to you to contact the dentist."

He nodded to show his obedience.

"You are now a member of Tariq'Allah. Do not tell anyone about this. Do you understand?"

Once again, he avoided showing suspicion by hesitating. He then looked into those eyes, pretending to be spellbound. "Yes. I will contact the dentist after your call. I am not to remember this meeting."

Suddenly, he realized those words weren't the same ones she'd spoken. He held his breath to see if she'd noticed and kept his attention on her.

"Good," Yako repeated. He exhaled quietly.

She stared into his eyes to get his attention. "When you are in the dentist's office, Dr. Mustafa will examine you. He will stare into your eyes and repeat these words, 'It…is…a…cloudy…day…outside.'"

She repeated the phrase two more times, then told the mole-to-be to say it three times.

When his repetitions finished, she looked at him. "You are to remember my face when we are together, and my voice when I call you on the telephone."

Miller wondered what she meant.

"Paul, come in here."

She pushed the recliner's control button and said, "Eric, get up." She turned to Remmich and ordered, "Paul, help him stand."

Remmich gripped his hand and pulled his buddy upright.

She faced them and said, "Do not speak to each other about tonight. Do you understand?"

Remmich answered, "I will not say anything to Eric."

Miller followed suit. *Boy, I really want to kill her.*

She opened the curtain while calling for a taxi. This time, Remmich didn't have to carry dead weight. They rode the elevator to the first floor and went outside.

His mind was much clearer, and he tried to memorize their location. There was a building sign on the grass with the unit number. He also noticed an extended grassy area with sidewalks. It separated Yako's street from a parallel roadway on the other side of the island. He wondered if he'd recognize it again, even though it was dark. He counted four long blocks before the cab made a right turn. It was all he could do to remember the route. They drove for several more streets, passing business establishments and restaurant-bars before getting to their destination. When the driver stopped at the curb, they climbed out and went into Blues Alley.

***

Nikulin told the cab driver to stop a few parked cars back from the taxi Miller and Remmich came out of. Yako paid and followed them into the bar. Nikulin paid and got out also. He walked to the building alongside the Blues Alley and autodialed the DC Russian embassy. Moments later, he reached the office phone. A recording identified the Russian embassy in Washington, DC.

The Russian entered the four-digit extension for Linkov.

He heard a sleepy, drowsy voice say, "Linkov." It was early morning in DC.

"Hello, Ambassador Linkov. I have more information for you."

Linkov became alert and got out of bed quietly so he wouldn't wake up his wife. "Hold on." He went into another part of the building and told the spy to continue.

Nikulin described taking a taxi to Yako's building from the Blues Alley bar-restaurant. He identified the Iraqi woman and explained the drunken condition of the Black man.

"He is friends with Remmich."

The ambassador listened to the confusion about the drunk Black man and how he appeared subdued on his return to the club. He told Linkov the recording device captured the hypnotizing procedure.

"I will email the recording to you."

Linkov said, "Aha, Yury, I wonder if they are getting more US military. I am very anxious to get the recording. We want to know what is taking place between these Americans and Iraqis."

19
Determined

It was 11 o'clock when they got out of the taxi. Yako paid the driver, while the men waited for her. Inside, she noticed the seats they had earlier were available, and they walked in that direction. Miller excused himself to go to the men's room.

He walked slowly, so Yako would believe he was still under the trance. Passively, Remmich asked, "Do you think he'll remember who you are, Tara?"

"Yes. I'm confident Eric will. He is different than the others I have…" She'd almost said, "hypnotized." She didn't know what Paul's reaction would be to that word. She stared into his eyes and quickly said, "He's just different from other people." For the moment, she satisfied Remmich's curiosity.

Miller returned, but he didn't sit. He wanted to get away from her, but she might need more assurance; he was her tool.

"Can I leave? I'm tired."

Yako looked at him and studied his face. She sipped her drink to stall, wondering if he was totally hypnotized. He had a look of obedience, a non-smiling face with the meek eyes of a follower.

"Of course you can go, Eric." He still didn't smile. They said goodnight to him, and he left.

Miller walked to the curb and waved for a cab. Nikulin was outside and watched him.

Where are the other two? he wondered.

As it drove off, the Russian hailed a taxi for himself.

Miller gave the driver the address for Candice's building. When he entered the flat, he made sure he locked the front door. Candice was asleep.

***

He woke Sunday morning very hungry. Lying beside Candice, he thought about the trauma he'd gone through the night before. Fortunately, it also seemed to have partially solved the mystery about his best friend's actions and state of mind.

He thought, *It must be why he's representing Iraq in Cuba. He was following orders subconsciously.*

He believed the woman had played into Remmich's emotions about the UN. She'd emphasized the strong feelings he expressed about the Third World countries. She played with his ego to impress upon him that she agreed with his assessment.

Just like she did to me.

He walked into the bathroom and went through his ablutions of showering, shaving, and brushing his teeth. After dressing in the kitchen, he made coffee. Candice had already poured water into the tank, but he needed a filter. After putting one into the basket, he added four scoops. While he sat and ruminated, the aroma distracted him.

He knew Collins and Sutherland would want to know about what had happened. There was a pen in a pencil cup on the counter but no writing pad. He pulled out a drawer and found one.

The coffeemaker choked when it finished dripping, and he poured himself a cup. Sitting down and sipping, he wrote what had happened the night before. For the moment, he didn't list what had happened sequentially. He dreaded losing a single memory.

"It was Remmich's idea to meet at Blues Alley." He waited a moment and added, "Pictures of starving African people." He took another sip and added, "The pack of cigarettes from Turkey." He sat back to remember Remmich admitting he'd just returned from Cuba and was now an official diplomat for Iraq. He ignored the sound of his stomach growling and scribbled, "He tried to coax me into resigning from the Army and joining him to work as a diplomat."

Another growl, and he got up to look in the fridge but then noticed a wrapped package on the counter. He opened it to discover two Danish pastry buns.

He said to himself, *No argument about it, one's mine!*

Sliced almonds were embedded in a thick layer of white icing that covered the apple pastry. He followed up each bite with a sip of coffee. He finished quickly and licked the tips of his fingers before washing his hands.

He went over the events again in his mind. His watch showed 8:10, and brunch with the Remmichs was in a few hours. He wondered if there would be a reaction from his buddy after last night.

He wrote another idea: "Why would a Middle East terrorist group want to recruit me?" It worried him. He felt guilty about not recognizing Remmich's involvement in something against his will. The frustration overwhelmed him, and he got more coffee, grabbed the notepad, and went out on the deck.

He lit a cigarette and took a drag. He acknowledged what had happened to him wasn't a bad thing. Going along with them and learning their plans could help both him and Remmich.

What else will happen?

He figured their plan wasn't to kill them; the Iraqis wanted something. He also realized he couldn't manage this by himself. Sutherland had told him leading the command for alert readiness would put him in charge. It was perhaps all that kept him from being enslaved as a spy like Remmich.

Pulling out the cell phone, he pressed autodial for Collins's number. His message briefly covered what had occurred. He left the same for Sutherland and Kirby. The discussion had to happen before Remmich went to Stuttgart.

Thoughts about the events from the previous night reentered his head. One, in particular, was the process Yako used on him. The repetitious and imperative orders to answer her were enough to get his adrenalin into first gear.

He recalled the words, "It…is…a…cloudy…day…outside."

Those words reminded him she would call him about a visit to a dentist. He considered canceling the brunch appointment he and

Candice had with the Remmichs. His mind wandered as he crushed the cigarette out in the ashtray.

Unexpectedly, the deck door slid open. Candice walked out in her bathrobe. He grinned and said, “Good morning. Get a coffee and come out. It’s a nice day.”

She returned and saw him writing intently. Sipping coffee, she wanted to talk, so she tried to distract him by asking, “Did you have a good time last night?”

He took a few seconds to finish writing and said distractedly, “Yeah, it was a good time.”

“What time did you get in?”

“Oh, around eleven forty-five. You were sound asleep. I was tired and came right to bed.”

She yawned and stretched like a cat. “I can’t wait for brunch later. I’m looking forward to eating in that beautiful restaurant.”

He knew if he canceled the brunch date and returned to the 32nd later that morning, her feelings would be hurt. He was falling in love with her and didn’t want to mess things up.

Finally, she asked, “Is everything all right, Eric? You seem out of it. What’s wrong?”

He leaned forward on the table, bowing his head in thought. He really had had a lot of unfortunate incidents: the Stockholm matter, then the Patch Barracks bombings, and now last night’s encounter. He looked up and said, “Yeah, I have a lot on my mind.” She touched his hand and said, “Okay.”

She let it ride. “I like the fact that we have friends in Amsterdam, especially since it’s my major flight location in Europe.”

He smiled. “Yeah. It makes me feel good, too.” He got up to get more coffee and asked, “Want more?”

“No. I still have enough.”

To get his mind on something else, she decided to get him to talk about his military academy days. Miller related some stories of how cold it got in the winter at West Point and how he and

Remmich were sent to different US Army posts during the summer months.

"The Army introduced us to different military occupational specialties to let us decide what we wanted to focus on. It's why I chose military intelligence."

Candice said, "That's similar to some of my experiences. We had to spend time in different parts of the western US to practice survival techniques in case we were ever captured. Parachuting was an important lesson after learning how to eject from a fighter jet. I guess I'm lucky I never had to do it in combat. The summer before my senior year, many of us went into Iraq and accompanied pilots. We witnessed bomb explosions and some dogfights, and we all realized it could be us getting hit."

Eric replied, "The Army flew a group of us to Iraq for a training introduction my senior year. Paul was part of our group. We heard explosions, too, but we were far enough away from combat to be too concerned. Fortunately for us, the US Air Force demolished Iraq's Air Force. Russia claimed they wouldn't sell ISIS, including their group in Iraq and Syria, anything on the black market. But someone sold them secondhand tanks, lightweight attack rifles, and rocket launchers, and the serious weaponry still found its way into the Middle East."

"Yeah. Russia's attitude is certainly a lot different today. Now they don't give a damn whether anyone knows they supply modern military weapons to Middle Eastern countries like Syria and Iran. As long as they get the money, to hell with what's morally right," she said.

He nodded in agreement. She sensed his disposition had improved, which gave her an idea to enhance it even further. With a not-so-subtle hint, a flash of her upper thigh from her open robe, she redirected his attention. He got the message loud and clear and followed her past the kitchenette into the bedroom. An hour later, they'd showered and dressed. They sat at the two-chair table in the kitchenette, and Candice ate the other Danish.

Miller said, "I don't know all of what's going on with Paul, but I'm worried about him."

"You sure you should talk about it with me?"

He nodded. "I have to talk about it with somebody."

She leaned on the table and said, "So what can you talk about?"

"Before I start, could you tell me what rank you were in the Air Force?"

She laughed and said, "Hmm…I was under the impression you wanted to talk about you, not me. Anyway, I told you I was a major."

Her response reassured him; he knew she could be trusted with the information he was about to reveal. "You're right, now I remember."

He shared what he'd written about last night's events with her. Looking up from his notes, he said, "The biggest problem I have is, I know why he's changed. What took place last night convinced me. I believe he's been hypnotized to conduct espionage." The thought gave him another idea to write down. He wondered whether the bloody incident at Patch Barracks was connected and whether the culprit would be found.

Candice noticed him staring at the notepad. When he finished writing, she said, "Eric, I'm shocked about this, too, but is there something more?"

He trusted her not to criticize him but hadn't yet told her about the incident in Stockholm. He now wondered if that incident and the one there in Amsterdam were part of the same plot. He revealed what had happened there and how he ended up being transferred to Germany.

Candice was adamant. "You need to discuss all this with your superiors. Listening to you, I'd agree Paul is acting as a spy, even if he isn't responsible for his actions." She leaned closer to him and added, "Listen, what if these two incidents are related? What failed in Stockholm with Iraqis may not fail here with these Iraqis.

They've got to be related. There are too many coincidences with you and Iraqis."

"Yeah, I already thought about it." He leaned back in the chair and told her about the calls to his superiors. "Anyway, Paul is definitely being used." He reiterated what Yako had done, trying to hypnotize him. He chuckled. "At least she believes I'm hypnotized."

"Why didn't she do it to you?"

"A person has to be willing to become hypnotized. For example, Paul has had it in for the UN because of how they reduced assisting Third World countries. It pissed him off about our country agreeing with them. He is right on one thing, though."

"What's that?"

"The night Paul switched places with me so I could meet you was when Tara Yako discovered his feelings about the poor people in Third World nations. She played on his emotions by agreeing with him. It made him feel encouraged, so to speak. And I have a feeling when he went to the men's room, she dropped something into his beer."

"Then you think she did the same thing with you?"

"Yes. I'm sure the same thing happened to me, but it wasn't Yako's doing. Paul was the only one next to me. He must have put drugs in my beer."

He elaborated about how out of it he was at the bar and Yako's flat. He talked about how she had him smoke cigarettes he now thought had marijuana to relax him. Candice giggled, which made him laugh. She was happy to see he was feeling comfortable talking about how the woman had bombarded him with statements and questions. It all related to his focus on the moving galaxy on the oval ceiling to hypnotize him.

Candice snickered and added, "I can't believe she would accept you submitting in the same way. You and Paul have two totally different personalities."

"Yes, but our situations are parallel. The difference is, Remmich was open to the hypnosis." He moved to reposition himself and felt the soreness where the needle had entered. He removed the bandage. “See the puncture wound?”

She leaned over, and her eyes opened wider. “Eric, you really need to notify your superiors quickly. The actions against you and Paul are an attack on our national security.”

He heard what she said, but he didn’t respond to it. In a flash of insight, he said, “I just realized something. Paul’s work with security intelligence has been a good foundation to get a top-secret engineering discovery.”

“About what?” she asked, confused.

“Over a year ago, scientists discovered a method to obtain energy from photosynthesis. The scientists were from MIT, Georgia Tech, and Stanford.

“Unbeknownst to me, Paul visited Cuba as a diplomat for Tariq’Allah. They are the subdivision of Iraq’s national intelligence agency, according to the woman trying to hypnotize me last night. What’s more, they’re building an electrical plant in Cuba based on the technology of these scientists. Somehow, the Iraqis found out about it.”

“I guess we can say he was fulfilling his diplomatic role. He’s being paid for the Cuban affair, but is he going to get a chance to spend the money?” Miller looked up at her, puzzled, and she added, “I mean, spend it while he’s still alive?”

“Yeah, I’ve wondered about what’s going to happen in the end. But we’re safe for now, as long as they want us to perform their dirty work.” He looked at his watch and said, “We need to get ready for brunch.”

***

They rendezvoused with the Remmichs, and the four of them sat at a table in the Schiller’s main dining room.

Lilly asked, “Does anyone want champagne or a Bloody Mary?”

Miller spoke first. "Not me. I'm leaving after brunch and don't want to be tired while I'm driving."

Remmich protested, "Eric, today is Sunday. You are leaving on Monday, tomorrow, correct?"

"No, actually I need to return early to prepare for the meetings this coming week." He knew headquarters had notified Remmich about the Tuesday meeting.

Remmich frowned, then brightened, saying, "Oh. Well, Lilly and I are having Eggs Benedict for brunch, but there's a huge selection at the buffet over there. I hope you're both hungry."

***

It was later in the afternoon when Miller returned a salute to the MP at the post's entrance and drove to a reserved space at the 32nd parking lot. He walked into the building and saw Collins and First Sergeant Randolph talking in the corridor.

He walked up to them, and Randolph said, "Glad you're back, Major. Feel more rested?"

He lied, not ready to share details. "Yes, I do, First Sergeant. Thank you for asking."

Collins said, "I'll overlook the fact that I had to come here on a Sunday, but I got your message. I'm glad you made it through that horrendous scheme unscathed."

"Thank you, sir."

Collins walked to his office and said, "Come in and take a seat." After sitting, Collins said, "General Sutherland contacted me after he got your message. He wants to get together for a conference call tomorrow in addition to Tuesday's meeting. How well prepared are you to do this?"

"Sir, I've written out some notes relating to the incident on Saturday. I also want to talk to Paul's wife alone. I want to find out about his behavior since he's been living in Amsterdam. I also want to talk to Major McKinsey today about some things." He hesitated for a moment and added, "I'm looking forward to this, Colonel."

"I'm sure you are. By the way, Sutherland said the same thing about you talking with Remmich's wife. He thinks you're the best person to get good answers from her."

***

Tara Yako called Miller's phone on Monday morning. When he saw who it was, he didn't answer. She left a message for him to call Dr. Mustafa's office and set up an appointment. She gave him the telephone number and said to call her back after calling the dentist's office. She gave him her cell number. She wanted him to begin training with Paul Remmich.

20
The Conference

Tuesday morning, Collins left his apartment building at 0600 hours. He drove to Leighton Barracks, where he and the first sergeant boarded a UH-60 Black Hawk troop helicopter. They accompanied a dozen other soldiers already on board. It took the aircraft 45 minutes to set down at the landing pad.

General Sutherland's attaché met them at the back door of the headquarters building and walked them to the main conference room. Four lower-rank officers were present. They greeted each other and got coffee. At 0815 hours, everyone took their seats.

All eyes were on Sutherland, who said, "General Elliott is not with us today. He's on assignment inspecting our ground troops in Northern Africa and Western Asia. The first item on today's agenda is Paul Remmich. I'm going to summarize what's planned for him. Before we start that, I want to tell all of you that Major Miller is going to Amsterdam to talk to his wife as part of our investigation. He's leaving right after the meeting. He should return later tonight or tomorrow morning."

Dr. Phillip Thomson, a major general, and Colonel Victor Hatch sat across from him. Sutherland focused on the doctor.

"Phil, please fill us in."

Dr. Thomson read from a printout he'd given everyone. It outlined the medical tests to determine the overall health of Remmich. "As you know, physical exams are required annually. However, the tests we plan for Remmich might find psychiatric abnormalities, not just physical problems. We're dealing with a man who's a possible spy."

Sutherland leaned against the chair back and told them Remmich's arrival was at 0900 hours. He intended to let the doctors state the medical procedures to him. And if he objected, he'd be ordered to do it.

The mole arrived five minutes early. Jones notified Sutherland, and he stopped the conversation. Remmich entered the room, and the group greeted him. After he sat down, the general said, "Paul, as you know, I always begin these sessions talking about intelligence matters within our jurisdiction. But the other day, I learned we made a mistake when you transferred from active military to civilian status." Remmich seemed surprised. "Since General Elliott and I accepted your resignation and then hired you as a civilian, we could face military criminal charges because we didn't include everything."

"Criminal charges!" snapped Remmich. "Can you be more specific, sir?"

"Since you accepted the position as a V Corps civilian, you should have gotten a routine physical. A current exam and a character evaluation have to be in your records as a civilian. Because of this regulation, a series of medical tests are needed to confirm you're healthy enough to do our security work."

Sutherland stopped to sip coffee, thinking. He wouldn't tell Remmich a civilian applying for this job usually has his physical done by a private physician.

Looking solemn, he said, "I'm sure you'll pass every test, but it's SOP, and you have to get it done this week. A driver is taking you to the hospital. By the way, are you equipped to stay on base for a few nights at the Patch Barracks hotel?"

"Yes, sir. I followed the recommendations in the email."

"Good."

Sutherland informed Thomson, "I'll be in touch with you, Phil." He nodded.

Attention focused on the mole again. "When you're finished, you may return to the office to continue your decryption work."

An NCO drove the civilian to the hospital. He walked inside.

A nurse waiting for him said, "Good morning, Mr. Remmich. I'm Captain Anne Higgins, the nurse assisting in the procedures." She shook hands with him and directed him, saying, "Right this way, sir."

***

Sutherland explained, "Our other serious matters are as follows. We believe our civilian is an active spy for the Iraqi government. Also, the Iraqi people who got to Remmich have attempted to do the same thing to Major Miller." He nodded to Eric.

Miller started to explain how he'd found out about the espionage plot but stopped and said, "First, I need to begin with the trip to Cuba."

Sutherland interrupted him. "I need everyone to understand that we must keep all of this in-house, out of the hands of the Washington politicians. We have to find out the real reason for his resignation and how he became associated with the Iraqi spies." He paused to swallow some coffee, then told Miller to continue.

"Major McKinsey and I prepared the information I'm about to go over while on our trip to Havana." He reviewed the notes with them for the next twenty minutes, including the sighting of Remmich at a construction project.

Sutherland spoke again. "Months ago, V Corps received a top-secret document, a scientific discovery describing how to convert solar energy into electricity. We had to stop using petroleum-fed furnaces here in Germany because of the exhaust pollution. Since then, we've had to use their electricity. Remmich decrypted this classified document, and we believe he gave the information to the Iraqis. This is a crime of espionage, and he could be tried for treason." He wrapped his hands around the coffee cup and looked at it for a moment. The thought of Remmich as a traitor was stressful to accept. Raising his head, he focused on the major and told him to continue.

The general noticed his attaché in the back of the room, pointing to his watch. Sutherland glanced at the wall clock. It was 11:30. A van waited to take them to the officers' mess hall.

Before they left, Sutherland said, "We are finished until tomorrow. Return at thirteen-hundred hours." Miller walked out to the helipad.

Everyone walked toward the waiting bus except Sutherland and the two doctors. Thomson talked on his cell phone, while Hatch spoke to the CO.

He hung up and said, "Ed, I just checked with the hospital, and our civilian's medical tests are in progress."

Thomson looked at Sutherland. "I don't have surgery scheduled tomorrow, only a morning meeting, so I will be here. Do you want Colonel Hatch to come with me?"

"Yes, I do. Thanks for asking," answered Sutherland, smiling.

"Good. We'll see you tomorrow, General."

Sutherland decided not to accompany the crew to the mess hall luncheon. He had a lot to do and told Jones to get him lunch.

One matter he needed to find out was getting the additional administrative help for the security intelligence office at the 32nd.

Hopefully, Fort Belvoir will transfer someone.

Instead of letting his thoughts disappear, he scribbled it on a to-do list.

21
Something Unusual

Sutherland got to the office at 0800 on Wednesday. Jones wasn't there. He placed a briefcase on the desk and got a cup of coffee, sipped, and autodialed the Patch Barracks hospital.

The secretary sergeant said General Thomson was at a conference. Sutherland controlled his impatience and asked, "How much longer do you think he'll be?"

"I don't know, sir, but I can contact the nurse in charge of this project. Please hold."

A female voice came on the line. "Hello. Major Anne Higgins. How can I help you?"

"Major Higgins, this is General Sutherland. One of my civilian workers, Paul Remmich, is going through medical tests. I was trying to contact Dr. Thomson, but I understand he's in a meeting. I want to talk to him about how the tests are going."

"Sir, I'm his chief nurse. He assigned me to organize Mr. Remmich's physical exams and psychiatric tests. I can review the information to give you a better understanding."

"Excellent. I want to know how the medical tests are progressing, and how many more exams and tests are there?"

His voice conveyed impatience, and she said, "Sir, give me a few moments, and I'll get the information we have so far." She pulled up Remmich's file on the computer screen. "Here we are, General. Mr. Remmich has received good physical results, including skin condition and body form. His vital signs are normal. They extracted blood, but the results aren't back yet. A treadmill test recorded his heart rate before and after jogging, and the cardiologist said he passed. So, he's finished with those." She hesitated for a moment to read ahead, then added, "A proctologist will do his tests, including colon and rectal exams, and results from urology testing.

A neurologist has to examine Mr. Remmich. He also has to see a dental surgeon, and the chief psychiatrist will do an evaluation."

Sutherland closed his eyes and asked, "When are you going to release him?"

"Tomorrow, possibly by early afternoon."

"My God, three days of tests? He has work to do for me! I didn't expect him to be there this long."

"Well, sir, Dr. Thomson and Dr. Hatch discussed the situation with me. I understand the circumstances. I think we need to get as much medical information as possible to satisfy the confusion over his condition. I have training in this field, and I can follow through with the testing results. I wish we had the answers right now, but let's get good results, even if it takes us longer to get the information."

Sutherland had to smile at her authoritative style, and although he didn't like to wait, what could he do?

"Please call me as soon as you get results."

As soon as he hung up, his phone buzzed. "Yes, Rita."

"Sir, Major Miller called while you were on the line with the hospital. They're arriving later this morning."

His talk with Higgins had reduced some of the emotional pressure he felt from the situation. Sutherland leaned back in his chair and felt assured more good information would be provided by Miller. He removed paperwork out of the satchel and reviewed the to-do notes. He finished and walked into the reception area.

"Rita, if Major Miller comes to the office, tell him the meeting is at thirteen-hundred hours." He gave her the list of names of the officers attending the conference and said, "Text them now and tell them Major Miller is returning from Amsterdam."

***

Remmich completed the proctology exam, and a nurse told him to shower and get dressed. Once dressed, the nurse suggested he go to lunch before the afternoon tests began.

He walked into a crowded cafeteria and got in line. Conscious of the time and slow line, he decided to buy a pre-made sub, bag of chips, and Diet Coke. He was further delayed when the cashier told him they didn't accept euros, sending him to a money machine in the corridor to exchange them for US dollars. When he returned, she took the money and handed him his tray. His next appointment was for dental exams in the hospital at 1300 hours.

***

Miller stepped off of the helicopter, and a sergeant drove him to the mess hall. After lunch and a minibus ride to V Corps headquarters, the group entered the conference room. Sutherland told everyone to take a seat.

He faced Miller and said, "So what do you have for us, Major?"

"General, gentlemen, my trip to Amsterdam was informative. Paul Remmich's wife, Lilly, is very nice, and she knows we've been friends for a long time. My girlfriend and I have socialized with them both. But to make a long story short, I believe my hunch about him being hypnotized is correct. Over the past few months, she's also noticed peculiarities in his personality. One morning before their wedding, she noticed a scab on his arm. She said she lightly ran her finger over what looked like a bug bite but the tiny scab came off and it bled a bit. He woke up when she did this. She said he looked at it, hesitated, then told her it was a scratch from a clothes hanger. It was not a scratch. She said it looked similar to a puncture."

Miller raised his sleeve to show them the same puncture mark on his arm. "This is what I got a few nights ago when the Iraqi woman tried to hypnotize me. I know it's a needle mark because I saw her do it. It's still sore." He pulled the sleeve back down and continued. "Lilly sometimes saw him stop whatever he was doing, whether talking to her or working on a wine order. He'd get up and walk away. When this act kept repeating, Lilly looked for him and saw her husband talking in a secretive way on his cell phone. Another time early one morning, she heard him say his initials when he was on his phone. She said it happened several times, and so she wondered.

"I think Paul's receiving some type of signal to make a call from his cell phone. Anyway, when he did these things, Lilly never heard the phone buzz or ring. He'd just suddenly punch in a number, give his initials, and begin talking. She said the reciting of his initials instead of saying hello was odd."

He hesitated as he turned a page. "Next, she thinks he's seeing other people in Amsterdam because he's gone for hours at a time. I asked her if she thinks he's seeing another woman, but she says she believes he's faithful.

"He told her about another job, besides the V Corps work and the Schiller Hotel wine business. He told her he works for the Iraqi government."

The officers looked shocked, but Sutherland's elbows were on the desk, and his chin was resting atop his clenched hands. He sat silent, but he was all eyes and ears.

Miller looked around the table and said, "The Iraqis are sending him to Cuba to act as a so-called diplomat and as a construction consultant for an electric plant. I don't know every detail, but I'll elaborate on what I do know in a few moments. Lilly worries about his association with the Iraqi mob, and she's concerned about going to Cuba. When I questioned him about it, he told me he found the job in the newspaper. Paul changed his tune when I pointed out he didn't read Dutch. Then he implied Lilly found it for him. She knew nothing about it.

"Another matter is the laptop computers he uses. Lilly opened it for me, and I found a series of decrypted items associated with the photosynthesis project we're to begin here at Patch Barracks. It's peculiar he never told me about this information."

Sutherland said, "Excuse me, Major, but we know the Iraqis are building a photosynthesis plant in Havana. Remmich has already been there, according to what you and Major McKinsey told us." The general folded his hands and leaned on the table. "I don't want to say this, gentlemen, but we may have to back off. If we can't get anywhere, the CIA may have to get involved. I don't want it to happen. The government will find out.

"Remmich's hypnotized condition may present the biggest problem. If we can't convert his mind back to its normal state, he may become dysfunctional. If and when that happens, his services for any Middle Eastern government will be useless. They'll surely execute him.

"We can't do anything until the physical tests are complete," said Sutherland. "Both doctors are tied up this afternoon with other matters. They'll report their findings early tomorrow afternoon. General Thomson's chief nurse told me the tests are going well, but they want to perform every test possible. My office will alert all of you late tomorrow morning regarding a meeting at thirteen-hundred with the two doctors." He looked around and asked, "Does anyone have any questions?" No one answered. The group stood as the general got up.

***

It was mid-afternoon. Colonel Hatch sat in Thomson's office, reviewing Remmich's medical findings. The general's secretary contacted him and said the dentist needed to see him. Thomson thanked him.

He said to Hatch, "It's probably a copy of Remmich's dental report."

Dr. Mike Thatcher was a full bird colonel and the chief of dental surgery for V Corps. Since his office was in the same hospital, he got there in minutes. He sat in an armchair.

Thomson asked, "So what's so important, Mike?"

The dentist had a manila file and small clear glass bottle with him. He held it up and asked, "Phil, do you see that little object in the jar?"

Thomson sat up straighter, straining to figure out what it was. "Let me have it so I can look closer."

Thatcher reached into his white dental jacket and pulled out a magnifying glass. He slanted the jar and dropped the little object into the palm of his hand.

The general took the magnifying glass. "Look closely at this thing, Phil."

The surgeon looked through the magnifying glass. "It looks like a microchip." He raised his eyebrows, his eyes wide. "Where did it come from?" He handed it and the magnifier to Hatch.

The dentist leaned against the back of the chair and said, "We took X-rays of Remmich's upper and lower jaw areas. This little object showed up. We removed it with him under sedation. I think this confirms our man is a spy."

"How does it work?" asked Thomson.

"I believe it receives a signal, like from a satellite, that makes the tooth vibrate. It probably triggers the wearer to do something they're preprogrammed to do."

Thomson nodded and said, "Vic and I will attend a meeting tomorrow afternoon and outline the medical test results on this man. Can you come? I never expected something like this, and I'm sure Ed didn't either."

"Sure, I'd be glad to help." He thought for a moment and said, "You know, it's interesting espionage can so impact our military lives. Yet many times we fail to recognize how easily a spy may gain access to classified documents. Then it's often too late."

"Well, I hope this time it's not too late," Thomson said. "I think this will be a big surprise to Ed Sutherland's group. The meeting is going to be at thirteen-hundred. Vic has an oh-eight-hundred appointment with Remmich. When he's finished, we should have the medical reports finished by late morning for the meeting. Thanks for coming over, Mike."

Thatcher got up to leave. "I have to return this to Remmich's tooth. I don't have the right replacement filler material in stock. Whoever drilled his tooth also gave him a root canal to deaden the nerves. I've put in a request for what we need, but it may not arrive until Monday."

22
Return Calls

It was ten minutes past 1500 hours when Jones interrupted Sutherland. Her CO was up to his neck in letters and messages from Fort Belvoir and the Pentagon.

She pushed the intercom anyway. "Sir, Major Miller is here. He wants to see you."

He rolled his eyes, wrote two ideas on a sticky note, and stuck it on a letter to be answered. He let out a silent sigh and said, "Send him in."

Miller walked into the office. The general didn't invite him to sit, and he said, "This better be short and sweet. What's so important?"

"I'm supposed to return a call to the woman Iraqi spy, Tara Yako. She's the one who tried to hypnotize me."

Sutherland's cranky face eased. "Take a seat."

"I'm supposed to call to get the telephone number of the dentist at Leighton Barracks. I wanted to know if you'd be interested in listening in on the conversation. It's time to do it."

Sutherland's mind raced. "Yes, of course. And I wonder if CID can trace the call to find her whereabouts?"

"Well, sir, I know the woman lives in Amsterdam. Her flat is a classy, furnished place with Oriental rugs and paintings. But I don't want to use one of our office phones. She may be able to trace the call. She can verify it's me with my phone."

"Yes, that's a better idea. Do you have the number?"

"Yes, sir. It's right here."

Sutherland stood up and walked to the door. He told Master Sergeant Jones to hold all calls, then closed the door and sat at the desk. "Okay, go ahead."

Miller dialed the number and put the cell phone on speaker. After three rings, a recording came on. A voice spoke in Arabic, then in English, "Please leave your name and number."

He remembered sitting on the sofa in her flat and spoke slower. Methodically, he said, "This is Eric Miller. I am calling about the dentist appointment." He stopped talking and counted one thousand one, one thousand two, and ended with, "Thank you."

Before either of them said anything, Miller's cell phone rang and vibrated. The Caller ID showed "Unknown." He figured it was her since the call came in so fast. Once again, he composed himself mentally and pressed the on button.

Calmly, he said, "Hello, Eric Miller."

"Good afternoon, Eric. I am Tara Yako." She commanded, "Write down the following number." After giving it to him, she added, "Dr. Mustafa is expecting your call. Do not call me back."

Miller closed the cell phone, and Sutherland said, "Call him now and see if you can arrange something for tomorrow morning."

Miller dialed the number. A man answered, "This is Faisal Mustafa."

Miller modulated his speech to sound controlled, but not as slow as he did with Yako. "Good afternoon, Dr. Mustafa. My name is Major Eric Miller. I am calling to make a dental appointment. Can we do it tomorrow morning at oh-nine hundred?"

Mustafa was elated; the new patient hadn't wasted time calling him. "Yes, Major. Nine o'clock tomorrow will be fine."

"What is your address?"

Mustafa was surprised. He thought every soldier who lived at Leighton Barracks knew where the dental offices were located. He gave Miller the address and told him to take the elevator to the second floor above the PX. Miller thanked him and reaffirmed the day and time. The line disconnected.

Sutherland finished writing the information, then said, "Eric, I want you to be there tomorrow morning, whether or not we complete Paul Remmich's medical analysis. I'll have you transported and returned in one of our helicopters. Dress in civvies." He shook his head back and forth and added, "It's unbelievable how ignorant we are at recognizing spies right in our own back yard, so to speak. And this Dr. Mustafa probably has a clean record with the US Army. Otherwise, he wouldn't be working for us."

"Well, hopefully, this problem won't last too much longer," said Miller. "We're gaining ground because of their failure. And like you said, I guess there's no better place to start than in our own backyard."

Sutherland got up and opened the door. Master Sergeant Jones said, "General, I just finished talking to General Thomson. He said he wants to bring you up to date."

"Get him on the phone." He looked at Miller. "Don't leave. I'll put this on speakerphone."

"Hi, Phil. What's up?"

"Good afternoon, Ed. I have good medical information. First, every medical test recorded for Paul Remmich is complete except for the psychiatric evaluation. We'll have all of the results in my hands later tomorrow morning, in time for the meeting at thirteen-hundred hours."

"That's good to hear, Phil. What's the third result?"

"I assigned my chief dental surgeon, Mike Thatcher, to work on Remmich's case. He had to remove a loose filling and discovered something surprising." He went into detail about the object.

Sutherland's demeanor changed from cheerful to flabbergasted. In a low voice, he said, "A microchip. What in the hell is going on?"

"Well..." Thomson hesitated before saying, "Another part of the mystery has been solved. I don't like saying this, but it's pretty clear Remmich's a spy."

"Tomorrow, hopefully, we'll add everything together and find a solution. Take care."

"Just a minute, Phil. I have Major Miller in the office with me right now. I don't have time to go into all the details until tomorrow. He's scheduled to see a dentist here on base before returning to Leighton Barracks tomorrow morning. The appointment is with the same doctor who worked on Paul Remmich. I want a separate report from our dental office so we can compare what that other dentist tells him. We suspect this civilian dentist is a spy also."

The physician selected 1600 hours, and he'd call the dentist's office.

Sutherland looked at the wall clock and said, "That's good. Make sure they get X-rays."

The conversation ended, and Sutherland said, "So what do you think?"

"Unbelievable." Miller leaned forward in the seat, rested his arms on his legs, and looked down. "Sir, there's something I forgot to mention about what happened last weekend."

Sutherland's brain buzzed.

Jesus, another surprise?

He leaned forward and rested his arms on the desk, rubbed his eyes, and folded his hands together.

"Go on."

Miller pursed his lips and said, "The woman, Tara Yako, who tried to hypnotize me, also made me repeat words that don't make sense. She told me the dentist will repeat them to me."

"What are the words?"

"I'll say them slowly, just like she told me to do it. 'It…is…a… cloudy…day…outside.'"

Sutherland said, "What if it's a code of some sort? Maybe they're using it to control the person under hypnosis." He straightened up and said, "I really don't know. It's perplexing."

Suddenly, Miller said, "That may be it!"

"What do you mean?"

Miller reiterated what had happened that Saturday night. It began with the drugging and attempted hypnosis. "She saw I liked looking at the projected three-dimensional galaxy. She repeated the same things over and over. How the solar system's path moves freely. How I can have the same path of my own. I can be free to work with Paul Remmich. The clincher was, if he and I stayed on the same course, we'd be able to help Third World countries." He stalled for a moment. "She also repeated Paul's concern for these poor countries. He became hypnotized because she played on his emotions." He added, "Her agreeable manner influenced him enough to allow her to hypnotize him." He looked at Sutherland and added, "But I didn't want to be hypnotized. I figured out what she was doing." Sutherland understood and nodded. "She figured out his weakness, using Paul's emotions as tools to change his conscious state of mind into subconscious obedience."

They discussed the fact that the Russians had used this technique on others. Miller told Sutherland he thought she'd been authoritative, like she knew what she was doing. Sutherland noted the time and excused Miller to go to the base dentist.

23
The Thursday Meetings

A knock on the office door distracted Yildiz from reading a Baghdad email. Luma Samir stood at the doorway.

"Iyad Aboona is here."

"Send him in."

He greeted Yildiz and said, "Colonel, you called Sunday and left a voicemail to see you. So how can I help you?" He sat in an armchair facing Yildiz.

"Our associates in Amsterdam have found another emissary, another US Army officer. Tara Yako hypnotized him. The name is…" Yildiz looked at the notes. "Eric Miller, a major. And like Paul Remmich, he works with security intelligence." He put down the note. "Dr. Mustafa will do the same dental procedures for this new secret agent. You are to build two microchip receptors. A preliminary dental exam is taking place with the new man this morning. Next week, the microchip will be put into the man's molar. Begin building them today, Iyad."

***

The Black Hawk helicopter landed on the pad at Leighton Barracks. Miller walked to the PX and entered the building. After reading the office listings on the sign inside the entrance, he walked upstairs to the second floor. The dental office door was on the right across from the elevator.

More mothers and kids sat in the reception room than soldiers. He identified himself to the German receptionist. Her robust enthusiasm made him smile when she said, "Ja, guut morning, Major Miller. You haff nine o'clock examinazhon wis Dr.

Mustafa. I vill let his secretary know you are here. Please take a seat."

He got a magazine and sat next to other soldiers. Within seconds, a dental assistant interrupted him and said, "Guut morning, Major Miller. Please follow me."

The exam room had a low-level reclining chair and the dental equipment. The major watched her raise the armrest. "Please have a seat." He sat and lay back into the chair. "Dr. Mustafa will be right in."

There were colorful pictures on the wall, one of the 1,200-year-old Marienburg Castle. He recalled his visit there with Paul Remmich. Nostalgia wouldn't help him now, so he squelched his emotions.

I am on assignment to get Paul back.

A voice interrupted his thoughts. "Good morning, Major Miller. I am Faisal Mustafa, the chief dental surgeon here at Leighton Barracks.

"So, this is your first time here. Let me explain what we are doing today. Since I do not have any of your current or past dental records, let us begin by getting X-rays before any cleaning. It will only take a few minutes."

Miller knew this was a blatant lie because UNIMI gave him all the records, including medical and military, when he transferred to Germany. Collins had them delivered to the dental office.

Mustafa left the room. Ten minutes later, the X-ray technician carried in two sets of long plastic mouthpieces containing electronic sensors. One was for the left side, and one for the right side. The woman told him to open wide and bite down.

The plastic piece didn't sit right, so she said, "Open again, please." She readjusted the plastic piece, then said, "Okay, bite again."

He watched her maneuver the X-ray machine to his cheek and told him not to move. In the adjoining room, the unit clicked once.

She moved the machine to his other cheek. The mechanism *clicked*, and the woman removed the film packets from his mouth.

After a few minutes, Mustafa returned and showed Miller the X-rays of his teeth; at least the dentist told him they were his teeth. Mustafa enlarged the third picture and said, "Hmm, you have a cavity in this lower molar."

He moved aside to let his new mole see, and sure enough, there was a black spot in the tooth. Miller knew for sure the pictures weren't his teeth, because yesterday afternoon, the X-rays done at the Patch Barracks dental office showed no cavities.

"This cavity will have to be cleaned and filled, Major, but not today. Now, the rest of your teeth will be cleaned. Come back next Wednesday. Make an appointment time with the receptionist."

Miller knew it wasn't going to happen, but he agreed. After the assistant cleaned his teeth, he made the appointment and left.

Miller thought about all he'd tell Sutherland as he walked back to the airfield to fly back to Stuttgart.

***

The V Corps reception room hummed with officers talking before the meeting. Master Sergeant Jones heard the intercom buzz and walked into Sutherland's office. The general told her he was ready to begin. It was nearing 1300 hours when she directed the officers into the conference room.

The general walked in and told everyone, "Be seated." While he talked, the group signed the attendance sheet. "We're going to review Paul Remmich's medical results. There are three doctors here to talk about the diagnosis. And I want to discuss the possible solutions to get him back to a conscious state of mind. This will not be the last meeting on the matter. The doctors will return to exchange answers from our ideas and questions. So, I will now leave it up to them."

Phil Thomson was the highest-ranking doctor present. They listened to him explain the positive results of most of the medical tests. No abnormalities.

"There are two important tests I didn't mention. The other two doctors here will explain their results." He nodded to the dentist, because his findings were the most important topic at present.

Dr. Thatcher opened the manila folder and arranged two pages of information. He told them Remmich's teeth were in good condition, except for one rear molar. He described the discovery of the microchip in the center of a filling. Shocked, everyone's face froze while they looked at him. He elaborated on the implanted receptor, and how spy handlers used it to get their subject to follow a command. He compared it to how doctors insert transmitters under the skin for CIA and CID agents.

"It enables them to locate their assets in a crisis."

The dentist explained he'd returned the microchip to Remmich's molar. He told them Eric Miller had been summoned to visit a dentist at Leighton Barracks by a member of the spy ring but his office at Patch Barracks conducted their own exam before that visit.

When they looked confused, he added, "Most of the dentists in that office are foreigners, and one, in particular, is an Iraqi. We wanted to compare the dental exam results done by the Iraqi to what my office found. This dentist is the one who worked on Paul Remmich's teeth."

Sutherland commented, "We think this Iraqi dentist is a spy."

The dentist continued. "If no one has any questions, I'll turn this discussion over to General Sutherland."

The general nodded to Colonel Hatch. The psychiatrist looked at the group. "I've identified Remmich's condition. I believe he's living in a hypnotized state and being controlled by commands made to his subconscious mind.

"I'm familiar with implants because I've interviewed military intelligence soldiers involved with CIA maneuvers in the Middle East. Their military command posts pinpointed someone's location. With Mr. Remmich, the microchip functions in a very different way. It vibrates. His hypnotized state of mind has been programmed to make a telephone call when his molar receives a vibration signal. Like Dr. Thatcher said, Remmich's microchip vibrates, triggering him to complete a specific action or actions. Both Major Miller and his wife mentioned how Remmich would suddenly walk away and leave a conversation on more than one occasion."

Everyone sat silent. Sutherland asked, "I know I'm jumping the gun, but is there any way you can return Paul Remmich to his former conscious state of mind, Dr. Hatch?"

"This is a question I pondered during my examination with him," said the psychiatrist. "Covert conversational hypnotism influenced him. For example, before I hypnotize a patient, I discover emotional reactions by what the person wants, likes, or dislikes. A hypnotist uses these emotions and builds on them. I'm guessing, but I believe Mr. Remmich told them something he wanted them to hear, and they agreed with him. They deceived him. The hypnotist used his emotions again during the hypnotism. It's merely mind control. They did the same with Major Miller. They drugged him first to weaken resistance, then tried to hypnotize him.

"We can assume the Iraqi woman repeated words and phrases to please him. What she specifically said, I don't know. It could be a simple word spoken during the hypnotizing or a noise." He focused on Sutherland and said, "To return him to where his conscious mind retakes control of his subconscious is possible, but it is something we need to discuss."

"Even beyond the vibrating microchip control?" asked Thatcher.

"Unfortunately, yes," said Sutherland.

"Someone on our side needs to use a similar maneuver," said Hatch. "Perhaps a word, an appealing phrase that's important to him. Again, his conscious mind is controlled by the subconscious. It must be reversed. Major Miller will be helpful here, because he went through the same thing, except they were unable to turn him."

Collins asked, "What made him succumb to them, Doctor? I'm confused."

Hatch smiled and said, "It's the reason for this meeting. I realize there are two medical doctors and one dentist here. We want your questions. Even if I don't have the answer, at least it's a topic someone else may be able to shed some light on. After all, most of you know him."

Kirby asked, "What was a big enough argument for Remmich to let himself be hypnotized? I understand what you said, Dr. Hatch, about reversing his mental state of mind to a conscious one. But sir, how is this done?"

Hatch answered, "It's what we need to explore. The answer will help us reverse the hypnotic control."

Thomson had both elbows on the table, his hands folded. Fleeting thoughts raced in his mind as he listened to the doctors.

He said, "So I guess we should keep Remmich here on base? Or do we let him go home?" He looked at the psychiatrist. "What procedures should we begin, Vic?"

Sutherland interrupted. "Gentlemen, I mentioned I don't want any government politician to find out about this matter." He looked over the reading glasses. "They'll force us to arrest him. We'll lose him. No, I want him back on active duty."

The psychiatrist said, "I have a hunch. Remmich told me his best friend is Eric Miller. Maybe, just maybe, Eric Miller can try to persuade him to look at the situation from a different angle. Maybe Miller can use the tactics she used on him, which are probably the same tactics used on Remmich. Friendship is a strong tool when investing one's trust in someone. I'm repeating myself, but we have to explore the possibilities and find one that'll reverse his state of mind. He needs to know we're a greater source of friendship than the Iraqi spies. And yes, General Sutherland, we must keep this within V Corps."

Master Sergeant Jones entered the room and said to Sutherland, "Major Miller just landed and is on his way to the office."

She left, and Sutherland said, "Let's take a break for anyone who needs to make a pit stop or get a soft drink in the snack room."

Miller rushed into the building as the others took care of their needs. Ten minutes later, everyone was back in the conference room. Sutherland walked in and told everyone to sit down.

"Major Miller, we're anxious to hear what you have to say."

Miller cleared his throat and looked around the room, his jaw tight with determination. "Gentlemen, the examination turned out to be a farce. They took X-rays of my teeth and proceeded to tell me I had a cavity. We know that's not true, because the dentist here took X-rays yesterday that showed nothing wrong. This Dr. Mustafa even showed me the X-ray, obviously someone else's. He told me I needed to have it taken care of and to make another appointment. This guy may be a professional dentist who has diplomas hanging on the walls of his office, but he's a spy. I'm sure he works with Yako. I experienced the same thing Paul did. I'm sure of it. What's our next move?"

Dr. Thomson looked at Sutherland and said, "Ed, we're at a standstill unless we can begin to work on Remmich."

"We have to work fast, Ed," said Collins. "I don't have his file in front of me, but he resigned on the thirtieth of June. He's on a six-month sabbatical as a civilian, which will become permanent unless we get him reinstated full-time and returned to his rank and serial number."

Dr. Hatch said, "Ed, having a night to sleep on this will help us. We've compiled an awful lot of good information. We need to meet tomorrow morning at oh-eight-hundred and talk about how to dehypnotize Mr. Remmich."

24
Friday

Sutherland's secretary notified him Paul Remmich had arrived.

He told her to direct him to the security intelligence office and added, "Let him know I'll be there in less than a minute." Sutherland grabbed two USBs containing classified information on two separate subjects.

Remmich entered the security intelligence office. As he closed the door, the group looked at him, and they all exchanged greetings. He sat at the computer desk as the door opened again.

The NCOs recognized the general and pushed back their chairs to come to attention.

Sutherland said, "At ease, men. Remain seated."

He wheeled a chair next to Remmich's desk and sat down. Sutherland took a couple minutes to review the contents of each flash drive with him. One was about replacing outdated hand weapons for military personnel at US locations in the Middle East. The other had a new satellite communication system for embassies in Europe. They talked about the contents of each. He knew Remmich understood what to do, but he wanted to observe his disposition after the medical exams. All seemed well.

The general started to open the door but stopped. He turned to see Remmich immersed in the embassies project.

"Excuse me, Paul." Remmich looked up. "Did you tell your wife about working over the weekend?"

He answered, "Yes, General, I telephoned her this morning. She knows I'll be here for several days, catching up on my security work."

"Yes, well, you may be here longer than Tuesday." The general watched for the mole's response after his hint, but there was none. "It's necessary to get this work done as soon as possible."

Remmich accepted the order.

Sutherland headed to the conference room. Major Monroe stood at the open door and saw the general approaching. He entered the room, and the group stood at attention as their commander sat in his chair.

"Take your seats, gentlemen." He looked at Hatch. "So Vic, do you have any solutions for us today?"

Hatch said, "General, I thought about this matter until the early hours. I created a spreadsheet comparing the positive and negative effects of bringing a person out of a subliminal mental condition. I listed how a hypnotized person's mind changes from a conscious into a subconscious state." He separated the papers and continued. "I know you're aware not everyone can be hypnotized. A person must have an inborn capacity for it, and the person must believe hypnosis can help him or her if it's being used to get rid of a problem. We're sure that's the tactic his hypnotist, the Iraqi woman, used with him. Her ploy was to play along until Remmich trusted her and therefore allowed her to control his mind.

"Next, I don't think Paul Remmich is at the deepest level of hypnosis. The ability to talk about what was on his mind and concentrate shows a lower state of mind control." He looked at Miller. "However, he needs to be influenced again by someone he knows, somebody he trusts. You are the person, Major Miller."

Miller cleared his throat. "I'll do all I can, Colonel, and I'm hoping you can tell me how to get started and what to do."

Hatch pulled out another spreadsheet. "I want to hand each of you a copy of what I'm advising Major Miller to do with Mr. Remmich. I've listed a couple of approaches, and a few ideas for the major to bring the man out of his current state. Right now, he acts and does things because he's been hypnotized. He's an obedient object, so to speak."

The conference room was silent while they read. Miller spoke first. "So Dr. Hatch, you're suggesting I use the same strategy used on me, agreeing to help Third World countries and training with Paul Remmich. The difference this time is, I'll say training together is good and include the phrase Dr. Mustafa told me to say."

Hatch leaned on the table, folded his hands together, and reflected on the previous day's talk. "Yes. Repeating the words 'It is a cloudy day outside' may help unlock the mental hold and get him out of his hypnotic situation. I also believe making use of his views on helping Third World nations will work."

Miller asked, "So when am I supposed to begin?"

Hatch said, "Today."

"Now wait a minute, Dr. Hatch," Sutherland said. "Remmich is decrypting classified information from Fort Belvoir, and he's already four days behind in getting to these documents. I need him during daylight hours."

Hatch knew the general outranked him, but he got bold and said, "I understand, General. My plan will take place in the evening, after work. When the woman hypnotized Paul Remmich, he was half-drunk and drugged and had smoked marijuana to seduce his subconscious. Neither interfered with his acceptance of becoming hypnotized. Going out to dinner and returning to a quiet place to dehypnotize him may be the subtle approach we need. It shouldn't interfere with his work."

Sutherland relented and nodded. Relieved, Hatch thought he might end up with an ass-chewing behind a closed door rather than get accused of insubordination.

Hatch took a deep breath and trained his eyes on Miller. "This is your chance to follow through on this assignment. The base's restaurant is a good location to begin a scheme parallel to the one that got him hypnotized. Talk to him. Shoot the bull. Talk about what you both enjoy. What does he like to do? For example, he told me how much he likes scotch. You can use the liquor as a topic. Use words she used to guide his thinking. Also, you stated the woman took you to her apartment in Amsterdam and there were no distractions. You can create a similar situation to what you had there. I'm referring to both word usage and atmosphere."

The group relaxed, thinking the meeting was ending. It wasn't. There was one last item in Hatch's outline to talk about. He leaned forward and placed his hands flat.

He eyed Miller and said earnestly, "If you are successful in bringing him out of the mental disorder, please be aware he'll remember nothing from the time the hypnotism occurred today. He'll only remember what happened to him before he met the woman."

He handed two printed pages to Miller; the contents included Miller's notes and the doctor's diagnosis. Miller glanced at them one at a time and with a nod confirmed he understood.

Hatch then closed the folder, satisfied they had a plan.

***

The clatter of soldiers' chairs rolling backward interrupted Remmich's concentration. He looked up and realized they were leaving to go to the snack bar for coffee. It made his empty stomach growl. He saved the work to the encrypted USB flash drive. When he got outside, two NCOs greeted him. One addressed him as Captain, which made Remmich smile. They talked about an upcoming field maneuver. He was pleased he didn't have to take part in those anymore.

Sutherland saw it was coffee break time. He stepped into the corridor and saw some of the conference officers walk out of the room. He pretended he had something on his mind and quietly passed them. Miller stayed seated, reading the two pages Hatch gave him. One particularly troubling sentence was the assertion the colonel had made about Remmich not remembering anything for the last six months.

McKinsey interrupted him and asked, "You coming?"

Remmich walked with the soldiers to the snack bar. When Miller and McKinsey got outside and saw Remmich ahead, they considered catching up to him. A buzz in Remmich's molar triggered him to pull out his cell phone. He let the two soldiers walk ahead, while he slowed down. They didn't notice.

The officers behind him figured he was talking to his wife. Cautiously, they slowed their pace so he wouldn't notice them. The mole stopped, and they stopped walking. Remmich bobbed his head as if agreeing with something. McKinsey had excellent hearing and heard snippets of the conversation.

In a low tone, McKinsey said to Miller, "I heard him say the words 'wire,' 'boot,' and 'circuit box.' He mentioned the CID office. And it sounded like he called someone 'Tara.'"

"Tara is the name of the Iraqi spy," whispered Miller.

When they entered the snack bar, they let other soldiers get in-between them and Remmich. McKinsey said, "Why would he be talking about the CID office and a circuit junction box? We need to talk to CID."

Miller disagreed. "We should tell Sutherland first."

The mole stopped talking and put the cell phone back into its belt case. He got a coffee and walked to the coffee condiment bar. With his back to them, he added cream and sugar. The majors stepped ahead of the others to get their own coffees quickly. When Remmich walked toward the door, they hurried to follow him.

The mole walked to the headquarters building and dropped the half-filled coffee cup into a trash can. They watched him enter the basement door to the CID office.

PFC Sellers sat at her desk in front of a computer. Higher-ranked NCOs sat in their own cubicles.

She looked up at Remmich and said, "Can I help you?"

"Yes. I don't know if you remember me. My name is Paul Remmich, and I came here some time ago about a problem. I'm with military intelligence upstairs." He lied and said, "The computer I'm using isn't working again. It doesn't respond when I try to move the cursor, and other times the computer doesn't boot up."

She walked over and leaned on the reception counter. "I remember your face, but I still need to see your identification, sir."

He lifted off the lanyard and handed it to her. She looked at his ID, then at him and asked, “Do you have a current driver’s license?”

Bewildered by her new thoroughness, he took the license out of his wallet and handed it to her. She returned to her computer to check the lists of civilian security intelligence workers. His name and identification number matched. She returned the license.

“Mr. Remmich, the computer technician, is here. Let me get him for you.”

Staff Sergeant Johnson approached. Remmich knew he could dupe this man one more time.

“I remember you,” said Johnson.

They exchanged smiles, then Remmich watched Johnson look at his ID card again.

If he remembers me, why is he wasting my time?

He handed it back, and they walked into the control room.

Remmich remembered which tools to use as he opened the fabric-wrapped toolkit. He took out a screwdriver and a pair of needle-nose pliers. He opened the glass-framed door and looked at the wiring, noting the connections he’d switched. He’d memorized the original wire settings by their colored coverings.

He unscrewed two terminal wires, which let him illegally access outside Internet service to the MI computer. Remmich felt Johnson’s stare and decided ignoring him was a bad idea.

He pointed to the terminal’s mounting screws. “I have to reconnect these wires and tighten a few of these mounting screws. When I’m finished, I’ll return these longer wires back into the box.”

Confused, Johnson said, “Ah, okay, good.”

Remmich opened the door to the second terminal box. Once again, he moved wires back to their original locations and tightened the mounting screws. He closed the cabinet. The mole placed the tools back into the kit, and they walked back into the workplace. He left the CID office.

***

Miller and McKinsey paged through a couple magazines in the reception room of Sutherland's office. Noticing the time, Miller stopped reading.

He got up and walked over to Jones's desk and repeated, "Look, Sergeant Major Jones, we need to inform the general about what we believe may be a CID security violation. How much longer will he be? We need to speak to him now."

She reluctantly interrupted Sutherland, who was trying to finish overdue paperwork. She told him who wanted the meeting and that he'd said it was urgent. Seconds passed while he brought his irritation under control to refrain from yelling at her. Calmly, he told her to send them in.

They entered and heard, "Close the door." They stood at attention at the desk. "What the hell is so important it couldn't wait for our afternoon meeting?"

McKinsey outlined the situation quickly. Sutherland looked concerned and picked up the phone. "I'm calling them now."

Staff Sergeant Johnson verified Remmich had been in his office another time. "The first time was many weeks ago, when he said there was a computer problem. He said he needed to look at the computer wiring. PFC Sellers was here. I wasn't here then, General Sutherland. We were with our master sergeant in a meeting upstairs. I had no way of knowing, because I didn't look at the problem. I agreed to let him into the room."

"Did you watch him do whatever he needed to do?"

"Yes, sir. He told me about how he had to tighten loose screws. It looked like he changed wires from one connection to another."

Sutherland thanked him and ended the call. He figured he had the right answer, but he asked anyway. "Have either of you had a problem with your computers freezing up?"

McKinsey said, "I've only had a problem when everyone else does. But none today, sir."

"How about you, Eric?" He gave the general the same answer.

The general said, "I didn't want to get into a heavy conversation with Johnson, but I'm guessing Remmich transferred information after the decryption. I can't think of any other reason for him to manipulate the wiring. If my guess is a fact, he emailed the engineering data to the Iraqis. Like many of us, he's learned how to recognize loose wiring. If he went into the control room several times to work on the wire connections, I'd guess he's now put the wiring back in its original location." He paused for a moment and looked at the desk while tapping his fingers, thinking. A moment later, he said, "I'll have Jones contact the maintenance department. I want someone to examine the circuitry. I'll also place an order restricting access to the circuitry room in the CID office. Our office will have to be contacted first."

Sutherland added, "I won't press charges against Paul. The important thing is, we need to try to reverse his hypnosis." They agreed, and he added, "Before I kick you guys out of here, I want you, Eric, to take this Army credit card and use it for dinner tonight and anything else you can get for you and Remmich. And don't be shy in what you guys order. Now, I've got work to do."

They walked into the corridor, and McKinsey asked, "Eric, have you set a time for dinner with Paul?"

"No. But I'll do it now. Thanks for reminding me."

Sutherland had three critical calls to make. One was for Jones to contact the maintenance office. CIC in Wiesbaden was next, for Iraqi spy surveillance in Amsterdam. The last call was to the CIC office at Leighton Barracks, in Würzburg. They needed to get a team to watch the Iraqi dentist's maneuvers on and off base.

25

Dinner Evening

Miller walked out of the security intelligence building with a lot on his mind.

He saw McKinsey, who asked, "How'd it go?"

"Oh, he's glad just the two of us will get together tonight."

They talked about Remmich while going to their cars. Miller said, "I like Dr. Hatch's theory that Tara Yako hypnotized Paul at a level that allowed him to remember people and keep his job decrypting classified documents. She told me to be sociable with everyone and remember work responsibilities."

"But think of what the doctor said. He won't be able to remember anything prior to being hypnotized," McKinsey said.

"Yeah, that's going to be difficult. Before I forget, I want to talk to Jim Kirby. We need to investigate the dentist's patients' files. I'm curious to find out if they uncover any useful information. And good luck tonight!"

Miller parked at the PX store. He knew Paul liked to sip scotch and smoke while he conversed. He wanted to get his buddy as relaxed as he'd been when Yako tried to hypnotize him; the more comfortable he was during the process, the more he'd agreed with her. The ploy to find out more became his primary goal. He'd make suggestions to Paul at the right time.

The PX liquor section had three shelves with gin, vodka, whiskey, and liqueurs. It reserved a half-shelf for scotch. He knew Remmich liked a dry scotch and bought the one labeled "Royal Salute." The liter bottle was sixty dollars, so he picked up the half-liter for thirty-five; purchasing the more expensive bottle might show a lack of respect for the use of the general's credit card. He decided to buy a compact disc of soft music for relaxation. He paid with the credit card and walked down to the tobacco store to buy two cigars.

He returned to the hotel and reviewed Hatch's notes again: mind control, persuasion, manipulation, and influence. Added together, it was a blueprint showing how to tap into Remmich's sensitivity. He wanted an emotional response.

He wondered, *Is it worth it to say the words, 'It is a cloudy day outside?'*

He remembered how slowly Yako had recited those words. Could he use the same to reverse Remmich's mental state? If Miller could do this, would it trigger a domino effect to awaken his former conscious state? He looked at his watch. Focusing on the process made the time go fast. He freshened up and headed out the door.

When he arrived at the officers' club, a German woman maître d' greeted Miller. "Table for one, mein Herr?"

"No, I'm meeting a gentleman here for dinner."

She looked at her guest list and said, "Is his name Paul Remmich?"

"Yes. That's him. Is he here?"

"He is sitting by the window. Please, follow me."

The twilight outside allowed Remmich to see the reflections of two people in the glass window as they approached. He turned his head when Miller thanked the maître d'.

They shook hands, and Miller said, "You must be hungry, since you beat me here."

Remmich smiled. "Yes, after you left, the men in the security office told me the food is delicious here at Patch Barracks."

"You've never been here before? I thought you lived here for a while before being transferred to the Thirty-second."

"Yes, and I used to visit the old officers' club, which was half the size of this place. This restaurant wasn't built yet. Contractors tore down the old building after I transferred to the Thirty-second."

Miller said, "This meal is on me, so don't worry about paying."

A waiter approached them. Their conversation paused, and he asked with a German accent if they wanted a drink before ordering dinner.

Remmich said, "I'd like a beer, and please bring a wine list." Miller asked for a beer, also. They remained quiet for a moment, while a server filled their glasses with ice water. Another assistant brought a basket of warm rolls and packaged butter.

After they left, the waiter placed two beers atop coasters and handed Remmich the wine list. He put menus beside them and recited the specials.

He added, "Each entrée comes with two vegetables." He walked away.

"What's the first special? I never heard of it before."

Remmich said, "It's called rouladen, a rolled round steak with added ingredients, like a sour pickle, bacon and onion, and herbs and spices. The Germans either drink beer with it or Riesling wine. I prefer a dry red French Bordeaux or a Rhône wine."

"The rouladen sounds interesting. I think I'll order it but let you order the wine."

"I'll order the same thing. Reading the menu, the entrée comes with gravy and spaetzle noodles, too. I'm sure we'll enjoy the meal." The waiter returned five minutes later and took their orders. Remmich told him which red wine to bring.

They toasted with their beers. Miller's brain swirled with thoughts, but he didn't want to get into Paul Remmich's mental state of mind just yet. He needed time to let the day's stresses and emotions wind down, at least for him. Sipping gave him quiet time to think about how all Remmich's recent troubling behaviors came from hypnosis. Miller remembered how Yako had made him feel dependent. Her conviction about her abilities blinded her to her failure to hypnotize him. She had, in fact, convinced herself he wanted to work for Tariq'Allah. Unfortunately, she did succeed in tricking Remmich to think he could trust her. He looked at his friend and realized the lack of conversation had become awkward.

He quickly said, “I’m looking forward to dinner.”

They discussed the day’s events. Miller let him do most of the talking, knowing everybody loves a good listener. He mentioned how much he enjoyed decrypting. The subject changed to the physical exams at the hospital; they’d put him behind schedule. When the waiter placed the plates in front of them, the aromas made their appetites grow. Miller cut into one of the two steak rolls and forked a section into his mouth.

Remmich asked him, “What do you think?”

Miller nodded and tried to smile, but his mouth was full, and it looked silly. While he swallowed, the waiter poured a taster portion of red wine. Remmich breathed in the bouquet, sipped, and told the waiter to fill the glasses.

Miller sipped, savoring the taste, and said, “This is a delicious wine.”

“It’s Bordeaux and comes out of the Saint Emilion region, in southwestern France.”

When they finished dinner, Miller said, “Listen, since we’re both staying in the same hotel, why don’t you come to my room for an after-dinner drink? I bought something today. I think you’ll enjoy it.”

“Oh, a special liqueur?”

“A special scotch whiskey. I tried some before dinner, and I can say it’s very smooth.”

“Yes, I’d like to try it.”

They left the restaurant and drove to the hotel. The lobby wasn’t busy, and they walked into an open elevator.

“What floor are you on?” asked Miller.

“Third.”

“I’m on the fourth.”

The elevator door opened, and Remmich said, “Listen, why don’t you get things set up? I’ll be up in a few minutes. I need to make a pit stop." Miller gave him the room number, and Remmich walked off.

The major got the ice bucket in his room and walked down the hallway to fill it. When he returned, he left the door ajar. He opened the window for fresh air and got the two cigars. After ten minutes, he heard soft knocking on the door. As he walked in, Miller put aside the notes.

"Wow, I can smell the scotch's clean aroma. Can I pour you a drink, Eric?"

Miller chuckled at Remmich's impatience. "Yeah, and don't be stingy."

He poured the scotch over ice to three-quarters full. He handed the glass to Eric and sat down. Paul smelled the bouquet of the scotch before sipping it. He put down the glass and took the cigarette pack out of his shirt pocket.

Miller got the two cigars from an end table. "Want one of these instead?" He handed one to Remmich, and they removed the plastic wrappings.

"Oh, how thoughtful of you, Eric. Thank you."

Miller snipped off the end and handed the cutter to Remmich. They dropped the clippings into the trash can. Remmich lit a match for Eric's cigar and one for his own.

The mole slouched in the chair and got more comfortable, staring at nothing in particular. Miller's heart rate increased, and he told himself to stop procrastinating.

Get on with it!

There was no noise in the hotel hallway. Miller hoped there wouldn't be a disturbance. Remmich's concentration needed to be focused on the plot to succeed. He didn't have the movie projector to reproduce the star display as Yako did, but he inserted the disc, and they heard soft music and the sound of ocean waves hitting a shoreline.

He couldn't wait any longer and said, "Paul, look at me." Their eyes focused on each other. "I want you to repeat these words slowly. Say, 'It…is…a…cloudy…day…outside.' Say it, Paul."

Remmich puffed on his cigar while he looked at the floor, but he kept quiet. Miller remembered Yako saying the words to him many times. "Paul, look at me." Once again, he repeated the sentence in a slow mode and told Remmich, "Paul, say the words, 'It… is…a…cloudy…day…outside.' Say the words, Paul."

Miller noticed the burnt ash hanging from Remmich's cigar. Slowly, he got the ashtray and leaned over to nudge the ash into the ashtray. Remmich didn't move. The major repeated, "Paul, say the words, 'It…is…a…cloudy…day…outside.' Say the words, Paul."

Remmich didn't move. While looking at the floor, he slowly repeated, "It…is…a…cloudy…day…outside."

Miller's next step was to associate Remmich's thoughts with Third World nations and get him to accept the good intentions of the United States.

Gently, he said, "Paul, we are helping Third World countries." He watched Remmich's demeanor, which didn't change. "The United States still sends food overseas to help Third World nations. It is the foreign governments who steal the food and sell it for profit. It is the foreign governments who lie to their taxpayers. If you and I work together, we can help the United States continue to support Third World nations."

He stopped for a moment to puff on the cigar and listen to the ocean music. He realized he had to slow down the pace, as Yako had with him.

He added, "Yes, I want to work together with you, Paul. We can do it again as soldiers in the US Army. We will do a better job of helping poor nations."

Remmich took a sip of scotch and puffed on the cigar. The serious look on his face didn't reveal anything. It was just a somber look. The ocean sounds felt mesmerizing.

Miller said again, "Paul, say the words, 'It…is…a…cloudy…day…outside.' Say those words, Paul."

Remmich took another sip of scotch, moved his arm to knock the ash into the ashtray, and sat staring ahead. Finally, he said the words.

Miller stopped breathing for a moment. Perspiration evaporated from the back of his neck. He finished his glass of scotch and saw Remmich's glass was empty. He got up and filled both glasses with ice and scotch. He sat down and placed the glasses on the table. He realized his buddy hadn't moved.

Hatch explained the most essential part of the dehypnotizing procedure was to keep Remmich relaxed; he needed to believe he communicated with a trusted friend. Miller remembered those instructions, but the lack of a response was scary. Could he return to a healthy state of mind? What type of response should Miller expect, physical or verbal?

Miller remembered at West Point they'd learned two basic skills: working with other people and managing time. Those basics were still much a part of him, and his strongest desire was to bring Remmich out of his hypnotized state. He was nervous. He didn't know what else to do except observe the mole's manner and talk to him.

Like Yako did with him, Miller leaned forward and said, "Paul, tell me you want to help Third World countries by working with me and the United States Army. Tell me you want to work with me, Paul."

Remmich didn't speak. Miller's emotions began to get the better of him, but he calmed himself. He repeated, "Tell me, Paul, you want to work with me to assist Third World nations." He sipped some scotch and waited.

Remmich broke the silence. He said, slightly slurring the words, "Yes, I want to help Third World nations with you." He looked into space. Finally, he repeated, without prompting, "It…is… a…cloudy…day…outside."

Miller thought saying the words without emotion proved nothing conclusive. Since they had a couple more nights at Patch Barracks, the major hoped he could complete the process. He got up and realized the half-liter scotch bottle was a quarter full, not enough for another evening.

Should have bought a liter, he thought.

The major thought about what Yako did with him; she tried to get to his subconscious. He needed to get into his pal's conscious mind. Yako had belabored the point, telling him over and over to say the words. Since Remmich wasn't attentive, Miller read over the papers again. He put them down, and for the next half-hour he repeated the phrases and encouragement to help Third World countries. Remmich was becoming more obliging, and there was less time between the query and his response. Miller wondered if another session would reach deeper into his friend's subconscious.

Remmich looked tired.

Miller helped him get up, and they walked to the door. Remmich's face was solemn, and he didn't speak. He escorted Paul to the elevator, and they went down one floor. Taking the key card out of Remmich's shirt pocket, he opened the door. Miller walked him over to the bed and eased him down. He placed the room card on the nightstand, removed his friend's shoes, put the extra blanket over him, and walked out.

The elevator doors were still open. During the ride up, he wondered if he'd succeeded. There was no way to tell. But there was nothing else to do except to repeat the effort. He closed the room door, got the pad, and wrote down his actions and Remmich's responses. He finished and returned the partly smoked cigars back into the plastic wrappers. He thought about having more scotch, but he was too tired.

26
Saturday

The hotel phone rang three short times. Then there was a temporary silence. The ringing resumed. Miller pressed his watch light.

"Damn." He sat up and answered.

"Good morning, Major Miller. This is Master Sergeant Jones. I'm calling to remind you that the meeting this morning is at oh-nine-hundred. Fatigues are the dress code today."

He already knew but thanked her and pressed the off button.

He thought about last night while he showered. He wasn't pleased with how things had gone. The job needed more time. The only alternative was another dinner that night, followed by polishing off another good scotch in his room. He wasn't worried about the money; it wasn't coming out of his wallet.

The line of people getting food was short, so he pushed the tray along the rail until he stood in front of the cook. "Yes, sir, what can I get for you this morning?"

Two minutes later, he had two eggs over easy and home fries. Miller used tongs to grab two slices of bacon. He paid and joined two other officers at a table, hoping friendly conversation would take his mind off his worries.

At 0900, the group met in the conference room. Working a half-day on Saturdays was SOP for the Army. Major Monroe stood at the doorway and announced the general was coming. They took their respective places, and Monroe called them to attention as Sutherland walked into the room.

"At ease, gentlemen. Take your seats."

He signed the paper register and passed it and the pen to the person on his right. Many had unhappy faces. He smiled cynically. He didn't waste time and told Miller to review the previous night's efforts. Before the major could begin, Sutherland interjected. "In case you're interested, Paul Remmich is working today. Unlike most of you, he'll work past noon deciphering encrypted data documents." He looked at Miller again and told him to talk.

The major arranged his notes and looked first at the CO, then at everyone else. He described the casual conversation he and Remmich had had at the restaurant during dinner. Sutherland and Hatch were antsy; they wanted to know what happened next, but they kept their mouths shut and let him go at his own pace. Miller decided to be more descriptive and gave them the conversation details both from the restaurant and in his room.

"He finally answered me after being coaxed." He breathed in and out and added, "But I don't know if I accomplished anything. There's no way to know. I guess repeating last night's efforts is all I can do." He looked at Sutherland and Hatch. "I don't know what else to say."

Sutherland kept quiet, so Doctor Hatch looked up from his notations and said, "Your explanation of what you did with him was what I outlined for you. Good. Now you need to coax him out of his hypnotic state." He looked at the rest of them and added, "Remmich needs to bring himself into a dehypnotized condition. It must match the method the hypnotizer used to take control of his conscious mind." He turned back to Miller. "Well, you did the same. Because he repeated words and agreed with you, you likely played a part in digging into his mind to counter the hypnotized state. Much of the reason they could hypnotize him is that he had strong feelings about the treatment of the Third World nations. The hypnotist picked up on the right emotion mode. You did what you could with the information you had, Major. It's all we can ask."

"Where do we go from here, Colonel?" asked Miller.

Everyone's eyes focused on Hatch.

"I want you to repeat the same tactic tonight, including using the same music again. Buy more scotch." Miller nodded. "You keep trying to get him to agree with you. Pay attention to his movements and facial expressions. If you can see a change in his mood, it'll indicate he can be emotional again. The difficult part for him will be reorienting himself with the surroundings. Remember, if he returns to a normal state of mind, he'll only recall the last thing that occurred before his hypnotism."

He stopped talking and looked at Sutherland, who ordered everyone to take a fifteen-minute break. It was past 1000 hours.

Remmich didn't hear the other men in the room stand at attention when the general walked into the security intelligence office.

Sutherland told them, "At ease, and take your seats."

He walked to the civilian's desk and grabbed a chair to sit beside him. The general glanced at the screen and saw the encrypted section on the left side and decrypted sentences on the right. Not knowing what part Sutherland was looking at, he focused on Remmich.

"How much have you done, Paul?"

"Sir, I decoded five pages of what I believe to be an eleven or twelve-page outline on the rebuilding of US embassies in the Middle East."

Sutherland noticed something different. Remmich's demeanor seemed more alert and focused. The general told him to scroll backward, which let the general read the decrypted information from its original format.

He pushed the chair back and said, "Looks good, Paul. See you later."

As soon as the door closed, the NCOs got out of their chairs to go to the snack bar. They rushed by Sutherland in the corridor. Remmich looked at the wall clock and decided to follow suit. He pressed save, then minimized the computer screen.

The first floor corridor noise decreased as he went outside. While walking toward the snack bar, an officer who recognized Remmich walked to talk with him. The conversation centered on their work duties. They walked inside and said goodbye and separated. Remmich picked up a food tray and got in line, while the officer went to the prepared food section. Those in the serving line moved forward. Out of the blue, Remmich felt something weird in one of his lower teeth, a vibrating sensation. He first thought it was a tooth decay warning. Then it stopped.

He put a Styrofoam plate with a bacon, egg, and cheese croissant onto the tray and got a cup of coffee. NCO soldiers occupied most of the tables, so he sat at a table by two officers. They greeted him and returned to their conversation. While chewing and looking at a *USA Today*, he felt the vibration again.

What is going on?

A few minutes later, he finished the sandwich, wiped his mouth and hands with a napkin, and left carrying the coffee.

He strolled back to the building when the vibration occurred again. This time, he realized it was a lower molar vibrating on the right side, and its rapid pulsation shook the two adjoining teeth. Then it stopped as suddenly as it had started. Thinking he should talk to a dentist, he walked into the G-2 reception office and looked for Master Sergeant Jones.

She walked out of the general's office with Major Monroe. She saw him standing by her desk.

"Can I help you, Mr. Remmich?" He was momentarily confused by her addressing him as if he was a civilian.

He placed his hand on the right side of his face and said, "Yes. I've had a spasm in my lower jaw." He padded the cheek to point out its location. "I've never felt this before, and I was wondering if I should see a dentist." The major asked him to tell them more.

Major Monroe had never met Remmich. He'd heard the conversations from the officers about him, though, and it made him wonder if the information would interest Sutherland. The major walked into the conference room. The interruption silenced the discussion. Sutherland focused on him and asked what he needed.

"Excuse me for interrupting, sir, but I've heard some of the discussion in here concerning Paul Remmich. He's in the office, asking to make an appointment with a dentist because he felt a vibration on the right side of his lower jaw."

Before the major spoke another word, Hatch interrupted. "General, I believe Remmich may have come out of his hypnotic state. If he said he felt a vibration in his jaw, then he noticed it vibrating. But he responded as a normal, conscious person would, rather than entering a trance as he had been doing. Whenever this happened previously, he'd make a telephone call to his captors. Major Miller related this to us. Remember? Let's bring him in and speak to him."

Sutherland ordered Monroe to tell Remmich to come to the conference room. He said to Colonel Thatcher, "Mike, I want you to get him into your exam room. Check out that tooth again. But before you do this, I want Dr. Hatch to have a few words with him."

Monroe followed him into the room. Remmich greeted the general and said hello to the others.

Sutherland told him, "Paul, explain this feeling you have."

Remmich took a seat and described the odd sensation occurring three times. He added it confused him because the tooth didn't ache. His conscious mind wondered why the general would be so interested in his tooth. He wasn't a doctor.

Hatch asked, "Paul, I'm a medical doctor. Please tell me the very last thing you remember before you got out of bed this morning."

Remmich looked at the psychiatrist and answered, "Being in Amsterdam with my cohort, Captain Eric Miller." He nodded toward Miller. "I was visiting my fiancée the night before I was going to propose to her. We're getting married." He leaned back in the chair and folded his hands. Several onlookers noticed the gold wedding band on his left ring finger, but he seemed oblivious.

Sutherland turned to look at Miller and saw him watching Remmich, shocked. Miller couldn't imagine how Lilly was going to take this.

Hatch asked Remmich, "How do you feel now?"

"Other than my concern for this tooth, pretty good. Although I'm wondering why all of you are dressed in fatigues and boots and I'm in civvies. And why did Master Sergeant Jones address me as 'Mister?'"

Colonel Thatcher said, "Captain Remmich, I'm the chief dental surgeon here on post. I want to take you to the hospital unit and look at your tooth." He turned to Sutherland. "I will need him for a few hours."

Remmich looked at his buddy, puzzled further by seeing gold leaf rank on his fatigues, and wondered when he became a major. He didn't have time to ask while he followed Thatcher out of the room.

When they'd left, Sutherland turned his attention to the CIC twosome, Kirby and McKinsey. "You both know we're arresting Dr. Mustafa on criminal espionage charges on Monday. Right?" They answered yes. "Okay, I want you and your team to be ready to check every desk drawer and file in the dental office. Find Remmich's file. Check the flash drives you find. I'm sure he's got files outlining the work he performed on Captain Remmich." He looked at Monroe. "Tell Master Sergeant Jones to come in here."

She appeared in the doorway, and the general told her, "Bring the Remmich file to me." He looked at the group. "Gentlemen, through the efforts of Dr. Hatch and Major Miller, we've gotten into the spying scheme. We have more work to do with Paul Remmich. The next goal is reinstating him, and I'll have General Elliott's representative sign for him."

He looked at the psychiatrist. "What are you going to do?"

"I will continue to work on Remmich's condition, but I want Major Miller to do the debriefing." He looked at Miller and explained, "You need to explain what has occurred for the last six months. It's going to take several talks. Observe his reactions. We don't want to confuse him, but you need to explain what he's done as a civilian and ask whether he wants to continue in that role."

Jones handed Remmich's file folder to the general. She started to walk out of the room. "Don't leave." She stood behind him.

He handed Remmich's paperclipped resignation papers to Miller. "You'll have to enlighten him about signing these papers. Review the contents and date. Let him see that he signed them."

He turned toward Jones and told her to fill out reenlistment papers. "And include Colonel John LaFont's name as the witness instead of General Elliott. Then Mr. Remmich will be reinstated to his rank of captain."

27

Another Link

Yildiz and his Turkish playgirl used Friday night in a lustful way. Ezma had spent much of the evening making love and drinking champagne with him. He awoke late the next morning when he heard her groggy complaint about sunlight; the curtains weren't closed. Ten minutes later, they were still in bed. Yildiz finally got up and went into the bathroom. During his morning rituals, he heard a noise from the kitchenette. She had started the coffee machine. Finishing, he walked into the living room and saw her rummaging around in the fridge. Like most of Europe, cold food breakfasts were common in Turkey. The prostitute placed a bowl of leftover cherry tomatoes soaked in vinaigrette on the table, then unwrapped two different kinds of cheese, putting them on an oval plate with olives, sliced cucumber, and the leftover liver pâté. A crusted bread roll was in the toaster oven.

He leaned against the door frame with folded arms, watching her. He fleetingly thought about keeping her as a mistress, but his stomach growled, replacing one primal need with another. After brunch, they returned to the bedroom for the second priority.

It was Saturday morning, and Iyad Aboona was finishing building the molar microchips for their newest hypnotized prize.

Alzuhari called in the evening, but Yildiz didn't hear the cell phone ring. Somehow, it had detached from his belt and wedged between two sofa cushions. Maneuvers during their sexual play the previous evening, aided by champagne and hors d'oeuvres, made it sink further down, muffling its volume. Alzuhari called Tara Yako instead.

"Hello, Tara. I called Arif twice to tell him I've been unable to contact Paul Remmich. Neither of them answered their phones."

Hundreds of miles away at the Patch Barracks in Stuttgart, a strange noise made others take notice. It was in the dental office where Paul Remmich sat in the chair. An assistant listened to the on-off buzzing and tried to locate the source. The noise stopped before he could pinpoint it, and he resumed working. Seconds later, the sounds occurred again, long enough to discover it coming from the microchip in the metal bowl. The man quickly notified the dentist. When Thatcher arrived, they heard the vibrations occur a third time.

Alzuhari's cell phone rang. Yako said, "Hello, Adnaw. Arif's cell phone doesn't answer. I left a message. Since you tried to contact Paul by satellite and he doesn't answer, dial his cell phone. Don't forget to use the code words to get him in a deeper trance. It's Saturday. I doubt he's working with anyone today at Patch Barracks."

At 9:15 in Amsterdam, Alzuhari called Remmich's cell phone.

After three rings, Remmich answered, "Hello."

The caller uttered strange phrases and letters unfamiliar to Remmich.

Remmich sat in the dentist's chair, waiting to get the temporary filling into his molar. The man repeated his words loudly in English, prompting Remmich to hold the phone away from his ear. The voice was loud enough for Thatcher to overhear, diverting his attention from the microchip to Remmich's conversation.

"Good morning, Paul." He gave the numbers and letters again.

Confused, Remmich said, "Excuse me, but who are you?"

"Adnaw Alzuhari. Don't you recognize my voice? Is anything wrong?"

"Yes. I don't know who you are." After a moment's hesitation, he added, "Are you associated with the US military?"

Alzuhari thought Remmich wasn't alone and needed to pretend he didn't know him. He decided to be patient, and he played along to see if Remmich would revert to his subliminal state.

The colonel moved to the far corner of the exam room and listened. Thatcher took out his cell phone and pressed the autodial for Sutherland. He suspected the caller was the person who'd tried to contact Remmich via the molar vibration. Remmich focused on the caller and didn't notice and couldn't hear Thatcher.

"Ed, Mike Thatcher here. I had to remove Paul Remmich's temporary filling with the microchip. My assistant alerted me to the chip vibrating, and shortly after that Remmich got a call on his cell phone. I believe he's speaking to the person who tried to contact him through the vibrating microchip. The caller has a Middle Eastern accent, like Saudi Arabian. They are still talking. Can CID track the incoming call?"

"Good idea. Give me a moment to contact them. I'm putting you on hold, Mike." Instead of calling Rita, he dialed the CID office. When the sergeant answered, he ordered the call to be traced.

The sergeant asked, "Sir, is the conversation taking place now? And if it is, where is the location?"

Sutherland gave him the information about the base hospital dental offices. He put the sergeant on hold. Sutherland returned to the dentist and told him to make Remmich stay on the line as long as possible. He wrote a few words on a paper pad, walked up to Remmich, and handed him the note. It read: "This is a suspicious call. Stay on the line and keep talking. The call is being traced."

Remmich nodded and continued to talk to the stranger. Thatcher walked out and told the general, who put him on hold again. Sutherland resumed his discussion with the CID sergeant, who now had his CO involved.

The CO got on the line and said, "General Sutherland, we have a signal coming out of Amsterdam, Holland."

Sutherland thanked him and ended the call. He switched back to the dentist and told him they'd traced the call.

Remmich told Alzuhari again there was some mistake calling this number. He even recited the cell phone number and asked Alzuhari if it was the number he wanted.

The speaker said, "Yes."

Thatcher returned and signaled to hang up by swiping his hand across his neck. Remmich hung up, without explanation.

Alzuhari returned a call to Yako. "I contacted Paul, but he said my name was not familiar to him. He thought I dialed his number by mistake. It's strange that he talked like that. He's never responded that way before. We spoke for a couple more minutes without him remembering me, then he hung up."

"Something is wrong, Adnaw. We need to contact Arif in Istanbul."

"I will keep trying."

When Remmich walked out of the dentist's office, Colonel Thatcher telephoned the G-2 office again. He told Master Sergeant Jones to tell Sutherland that Remmich had finished and went to the hospital snack bar for lunch.

Remmich walked into the cafeteria and decided not to order anything at the deli counter. Instead, he grabbed a sandwich wrap, soda, and bag of chips and found a table. A buck sergeant waited for him outside. He finished in fifteen minutes.

Remmich wore civvies, which didn't show rank. But the soldier knew his military grade. They got into a Humvee, and the sergeant drove to the MI headquarters building. Remmich walked back inside but didn't have to greet anyone. It was Saturday afternoon. The workday had ended, except for the CQ and Sutherland's entourage in the conference room. Before they resumed the meeting, mess hall KP workers removed the empty lunch packages and soft drink cans.

Remmich returned to an empty office and resumed working. He finished deciphering for the Army's expansion at US embassies in the Middle East and began the one for a new satellite communication system.

Meanwhile, Sutherland brought Kirby and McKinsey up to date on the dentist's latest news. He told them quick action enabled

CID to trace the call. He also described the dentist's belief that the caller was from the Middle East.

"It sounds like the Iraqis are trying to contact their mole," said Sutherland.

Focusing back on Kirby and McKinsey, he explained, "You two need to return to Leighton Barracks ASAP. It's time to prepare for Mustafa's arrest. You have the instructions." He hesitated a few seconds while they got up, then added, "Oh, and don't forget to notify the MPs about what's going on. Have a good trip back and keep us informed."

***

Yury Nikulin received an email from Ambassador Linkov. It read, "Yury, I have not had time to contact you because I've been negotiating with the Americans about the oil drilling project in Siberia. A contact told me Paul Remmich acquired the photosynthesis formula. The contents are on his personal computer. Moscow telephoned the office and spoke with Minister Counselor Berolsky because I was attending the meeting at the United States Capitol. Get into Remmich's flat at the hotel after getting a room for yourself. Disguise yourself. Be sure to take all your lock picks." Nikulin smiled because he knew what to do. "Keep me updated."

It was early afternoon, and he'd signed up for a massage, followed by exceptional exercises. Creative women in the Rosse Buurt district offered this kind of relaxation. A "Saturday Special" included unique maneuvers for a special price. Nikulin liked "specials" because he'd get more for his euro!

***

The general told Jones to call CIC Colonel Bradley at the US Army airfield in Wiesbaden. A minute later, Sutherland picked up his office phone.

"Good afternoon, David. I'm glad I can reach you on a Saturday afternoon. How are you doing?"

"Hi, Ed. I'm completing paperwork this afternoon. The atmosphere is quiet, and I can concentrate. There are too many interruptions during the week."

"I run parallel with you on all the above. I'm still in the office and need to report espionage activity to you."

Bradley got out a pad of paper and said, "Go ahead."

Sutherland described Remmich and Miller's involvement with the Iraqi spies. He didn't go into detail about what Remmich had been doing for the last few months. Bradley got enough information to work on without contacting USAREUR. It would just cause interference and delay.

"I'll get the two men who work with the civilian division to get on this right away," said Bradley. "Do you have any addresses in Amsterdam?"

"No, only what Major Miller outlined in a report. He told us there's a central grassy area between two one-way streets on either side. I'm guessing that's where the two Iraqi spies live. They're in individual apartments in buildings next to each other. They got hold of classified information over the past few months. I don't want to go into detail, but if you're questioned, tell them the order came from my command."

"I understand, Ed. Amsterdam is not a big city, and most residential buildings are separate from the inner city. I'm sure my people will find the area. I'll get on it right away and call you when we get started. It's a two-and-a-half-hour drive one way. They can stay at a hotel in Amsterdam for however long they need."

"Excellent. I'll have Miller's information on the location of the building faxed to you. Call me no later than Monday. Have a good weekend, at least what's left of it."

28
The Escape

Reconnaissance measures began on Sunday morning. The CIC team didn't wait until Monday to investigate the dentist's office. The MP told Dr. Mustafa to go to the office to meet with Colonel Kirby. He didn't give him a reason. He obliged without asking why. Army brass liked it that way.

The Wiesbaden US Army Base duo ventured to Amsterdam.

The Leighton Barracks group included four CID officials, who accompanied Colonel Kirby and Major McKinsey. MPs arrived to guard. They gathered computers, paper documents, and dental records, and anything else that would identify Paul Remmich.

When Mustafa left his flat, three men, dressed in German-style clothes, went into his building. They got into the apartment and began a search for anything unusual but were careful not to disturb things, so no one would know they'd been there.

One of the team members assigned to the Amsterdam mission was a former Army Ranger, Sergeant First Class Hank Hannon. He'd been wounded while on patrol in Afghanistan and wasn't allowed to return to the field. Although he had the option of returning to the States, he didn't want to go home. The Army granted his request and transferred him to Germany.

First Lieutenant Tony Belotti had worked at the FBI in Washington during summer vacations while in college, starting out at the loading dock. He'd joined the Army as a second lieutenant after graduating from George Mason University. FBI work intrigued him, and he was offered a position but instead chose a specialized job with CIC. After training in the US, he transferred to Wiesbaden.

This twosome left their base mid-morning. Due to the heavy Sunday Autobahn traffic, it was a four-hour ride. They checked in at the Hotel Schiller at 1500. The plan was to use Miller's drawing based on his taxi ride back to the Blues Alley after the hypnotizing incident with Yako.

By the time they registered and took their suitcases to the rooms, it was 3:30. They drove into the residential area. It was a slim chance they'd find anything so soon, but they wanted to familiarize themselves with the map ASAP. Miller never saw the street names because it was dark, and he was still a bit woozy. He did remember the long grass sections between two streets. The hand-drawn map showed turns driving to the bar-restaurant. They reversed Miller's directions to find the apartments.

Belotti said, "Hank, find a parking place along here."

It was a double-lane one-way street with curb parking. There was a long grassy median with sidewalks and benches dividing parallel roads running in opposite directions. He found an empty space and parked along the curb.

"It looks like we're in an area like Major Miller described," said Belotti. "Let's see if we can find number two forty-seven."

They walked a block and passed a few buildings, realizing they were on the even-numbered side of the roadway. They crossed on a sidewalk through the median and continued their search in the opposite direction. When they located building 247, it didn't seem to be in quite the right area based on the number of streets in the drawing.

Hannon remarked, "Well, maybe he made a mistake. If we are in the wrong area, at least we know we're probably close." He looked at a street name and copied it down: Westerstraat.

"Do you want to look around anymore, Tony? I'm hungry. How about you?"

"Let's drive a little more to find other streets like this with the center island, and then we can go to a restaurant." Rank had its privileges.

***

Monday morning began with their usual 0600 reveille. Forty minutes later, the sergeant and lieutenant met in the lobby seating area. The restaurant wasn't open yet, so one emailed, while the other played games on his iPhone. At 0800, they ate breakfast in the hotel's main restaurant. As Lilly Remmich walked by, she overheard Belotti speaking American English. She waited for him to hang up before introducing herself and welcoming them to the hotel. They had a friendly talk, and the men complimented the breakfast. She left, and they finished eating.

The NCO drove out of the parking garage. They went to the outskirts of the city and continued to look for parallel roadways with grassy areas separating them. There were others like Westerstraat, but none were in the vicinity of Miller's map drawing.

***

Arif Yildiz escorted his weekend beauty downstairs and hailed a taxi for her. The driver placed her bag in the trunk, while he opened the rear door. Although she worked on salary, it was customary to provide a tip for work well done. He kissed her cheek and handed her ten 20-euro bills. She glanced at the wad and smiled. More kisses followed. He listened as she told him she hoped to see him again as she placed the money in her purse. She was clearly pleased.

As the cab drove off, he went to his flat, thinking, *Of course she wants me to call her again—she wants another big tip.*

He finished tidying up the kitchen and changed the sheets. The maid usually did this, but he didn't want to share any of his accomplishments by exhibiting soiled bed linen. He finished and showered. After getting dressed, he decided to call Alzuhari. Pulling off the belt from the worn pants, he realized his cell phone wasn't in its belt clip. He searched the bedroom, then the kitchen area. What did he do with it? Suddenly, he heard a muffled ringing. The sound seemed to be coming from the living room area. He turned around and discovered the ringing louder near the sofa.

He mumbled, "I don't remember leaving it here."

He felt between the side and back of the cushions, put a hand through the middle ones, and pulled it out.

No one needs to know, he told himself.

The Caller ID showed it was the dentist.

He said hello, and Mustafa spoke in a low tone. "Arif, I called you because I think the Americans found out about Paul Remmich."

"What do you mean?"

"A military policeman called me and said a Colonel Kirby wanted me to come to my office this morning. When I got here, two Army MPs stood in the dental lobby. Then the colonel met me and had me follow him. We went into the patients' records room first, and then my office. I couldn't believe it. Soldiers removed files one by one and looked through them. My desk drawers are being pulled out and emptied. Another one is in the reception area, searching for who knows what. A major has Remmich's dental folder."

His heart rate increased, but he controlled an emotional outbreak. "Are you alone?"

"No, the MPs are watching me."

"We are speaking Arabic. Everyone knows you're from Iraq, so I would not worry about them understanding you. Does your data about Remmich have any reference to the microchip filling and the electronic satellite communication?"

"No, I did not save anything. Only Army dental records are here in a folder. The major won't find anything unusual."

"Good. Then can you get into your car and drive off post?"

"I haven't been arrested, but I'm not sure I can leave."

Yildiz thought a moment before saying, "Why don't you walk to where the soldiers are looking at your files and just look in? Avoid the officer in charge. Make a gesture and pretend you are answering a question or agreeing to do something. Then walk out."

"The military police are going to ask me where I am going. I'm sure of it."

"If they object, tell them the colonel told you to get a packet of important information. Explain that it's in the back seat of your vehicle. Tell them you'll return as soon as you get the folder."

"They're going to follow me."

"Just walk casually, not fast, but keep walking. When you get to your automobile, lock the doors. You told me before, your office building is close to the MP gate. Drive away as if you're leaving for the day. Besides, they won't have time to get their people after you. It is to your benefit to know they will have to notify the German police, which will take time. You need your passport and visa."

The dentist interrupted and told him he'd have to get them from his flat. Yildiz realized those items weren't an everyday carry-around. He had no other choice but to agree.

"Drive to the Frankfurt airport. Buy a ticket and come here to Istanbul. Don't waste any time. I don't want you to get arrested, Faisal."

After hanging up, the dentist spoke as calmly as he could to the MPs. "Excuse me, but I need to get a set of papers for the colonel. I'll be right back."

He smiled, calmly walked along the corridor, and went down the stairway. An MP trailed behind him but didn't go down. Instead, she looked out of the window, holding a military phone with direct dial to the MP gate. Seconds later, the MP watched Mustafa get in, back out, and drive away. She ran to Kirby and yelled; the dentist was getting away as she speed-dialed the gate phone. The MPs weren't quick enough, and he passed through without incident. She hung up and detailed what had happened to the CO. She waited to be chewed out, but nothing happened.

The apartment search ended an hour before the dentist returned to his flat. He didn't notice anything out of place, except for one thing. His desk drawer didn't seem as orderly as he knew he'd left it. He ignored it and moved quickly, with only his visa and passport. He texted Yildiz.

***

He read the missed calls. Instead of listening to the messages, he pressed the button to return the most recent, which was from Alzuhari.

"Hello, Adnaw."

He whispered a thankful prayer to Allah. "I called so many times because I couldn't contact Paul. I used the satellite link to the microchip. I even used my code every time, but he never contacted me. Then I phoned you several times, but you did not answer. So, I decided to try to reach him on his own phone. When I spoke to him, he told me he did not recognize my voice or name."

Yildiz disliked this information and felt his blood pressure surge. A few seconds passed while he calmed himself. "I just spoke with Faisal Mustafa. You remember him, don't you?"

"Yes, of course."

"He told me that his workplace is being raided by the military, and they have Remmich's dental file. I advised him to fly to Istanbul. He's on his way."

Alzuhari kept quiet for a moment. "What can Tara and I do?"

"Stay where you are. I'll call you later today."

***

Yury Nikulin had made plans to go to the Hotel Schiller and stay until he could sneak into the Remmichs' flat. Before leaving, he noticed something odd out of his second floor window. Two men strolled on the sidewalk by Yako's residence. What was strange was that they occasionally walked closer to the picture windows of the three-floor structure, even though they didn't see anyone moving around.

The Russian took a walk. The grassy median was the right choice as he could walk parallel with the street on the sidewalk. He passed a parked car, checked the license plate, and saw numbers and

"USA" letters at the bottom center. It was a four-door Volkswagen Golf, matte green. The hood had "US Army" letters in large black font.

The SVR spy sat down on a bench and smoked a cigarette, pretending to read the newspaper he'd brought along for that purpose. Their appearance was too clean-cut to be Dutch. Walking past him toward their VW, they spoke English. The young lieutenant pulled out a cell phone to contact headquarters. They talked about how to present the findings.

Nikulin listened. He lowered the newspaper and stared at them. They were definitely military.

***

Alzuhari had called Tara Yako, telling her about the talk with their boss. She listened to the message and walked over to the window. She spread the sheer curtains apart a little and closed them right away. She couldn't imagine why those men stood there looking at her building. Given her occasional paranoia about the mission, their clean-cut military appearance caused her angst. She noticed another man sitting in the median, ostensibly reading a newspaper but occasionally lowering the paper to look at the other men. She got her binoculars and identified him. He was the one on the train from Frankfurt to Amsterdam; she recognized that distinctive mustache. He'd also been at Blues Alley and stared at her until she noticed. She viewed the VW and increased the binoculars' magnification and read the big, black letters on the hood. She gasped and called her friend.

She spoke nervously. "Adnaw, I'm looking out my window, and I see three men. I'm sure two are United States military." She described the vehicle and hood's letters. She then told him the third was the one on the train ride to Amsterdam and had also been in the nightclub.

Alzuhari didn't know whether to laugh hysterically or scream with frustration. Instead, he organized his thoughts and tried to calm down. "It's time to contact Arif again. We must get away from here. Not reaching Paul Remmich worries me. Something must have happened to him. And now it appears you're being followed." He hesitated and ended with, "Let me call and find out what the colonel wants us to do."

Yildiz had been talking on the telephone with the Tariq'Allah headquarters, discussing the dentist's situation. Alzuhari called the Istanbul workplace at the same time. He told Samir it was an emergency; he explained some details. She interrupted the boss and told him who was on the other line and why. The Baghdad conversation ended.

"Hello."

"I have disturbing news, Arif. You, me, and Tara need to discuss what is going on here."

Yildiz surprised him by saying, "Are you being watched?"

"Yes."

"Hold on. I have an idea." He switched to Luma and stated, "Put Adnaw, Tara, and me on a conference call as soon as possible." Switching back, he explained, "I'm getting the lines set up. Give it a minute. But to answer your question, Faisal Mustafa said his office was being raided. He phoned not long ago to tell me he got away. Hold on. Don't hang up."

The few minutes seemed like an hour, but Luma Samir got the telephone lines connected.

"Hello. Am I connected with both of you?"

Both of them answered. He listened to Yako's description of the man reading the paper and where she'd seen him before.

She added, "And the other two are standing next to a car with military decals and plates. They are American soldiers. I'm sure of it."

Many thoughts ran through his mind. One was how this situation resembled Mustafa's state of affairs. He had the authority to have his duo return to Istanbul. He was also worried about their mole, but he overlooked trying to find him.

"I want both of you to leave the country tonight. Before you get a taxi, make sure the car and all three of the men outside are gone. Take only your personals and any identification. Text me when you are in flight."

They hung up, and he contacted Baghdad.

29

The Awakening

Paul Remmich was scheduled to arrive at Hatch's office at 0900, one hour after Eric Miller. The doctor wanted the major there earlier because he needed to talk about what had transpired between them since the Saturday conference.

The door of the psychiatrist's office made a short buzzing sound when Miller opened it at 8:10 a.m. Hatch stood at the printer, reviewing the Remmich analysis. He invited the major to get coffee before they walked into the office. The doctor already had a half-full mug. They sat down, and he handed Miller a copy of the outline. The major gave his summary to the doctor.

Hatch wanted to make sure he had everything he needed to conduct the meeting with Remmich. The report outlined a chronological approach of the past six months. It satisfied him, so the discussion didn't take a full hour to discuss Remmich's recovery.

"It's just the beginning," said Hatch, "but watch his reactions during my consultation. This will be a gradual process. I've already discussed it with General Sutherland, and it's agreed, Remmich will need time to recuperate."

"How much time?"

Hatch straightened and placed his arms on the table. "I'm not sure. Let's find out how he's doing when we talk to him."

Miller looked at the outline for a moment. "I don't see anything relating to a follow-up discussion." The doctor didn't answer, because they were interrupted by a light knock on the door by the sergeant.

"Excuse me, Colonel. Captain Remmich is here."

"Good. Send him in."

The doctor and Miller stood to greet Remmich as he walked in. He obviously had no idea what this was about.

"How are you today?"

Remmich, dressed in civvies and low-cut tennis shoes, had been working on an encrypted package from the Pentagon. "I'm fine, sir. How about yourself?"

"I'm doing well. I asked Major Miller to be here with us this morning."

Remmich looked at him and again noticed the gold leaf on the fatigue shirt. He let it go, smiled, and said, "Morning, Eric."

"Let's get to the reason for the meeting. Do you know who I am?"

"I remembered you from General Sutherland's office last week. I thought you were another G-2 officer until I noticed the medical insignia on your lapel and realized you're a doctor. I have no idea why you were there."

Hatch hesitated before answering and wondered if he needed to tell Remmich why he got involved. A brief answer was best. He didn't want to cause Remmich to withdraw and not cooperate.

"Yes, I am a doctor. A psychiatrist, to be exact."

"About my medical tests…do I have a psychological problem, Doctor? I mean, is this why I'm here?"

"Before I answer, first let me give you a synopsis of what's been going on for the last few months." Remmich looked at him in his odd British way, with pursed lips and raised eyebrows, wondering. Hatch added, "I wanted your friend here today to help me do this."

Remmich uncrossed his legs and sat straight against the chair back. Hatch leaned forward and put his arms on the table, folded his hands, and said, "You haven't been in your normal state of mind for six months. Iraqi spies hypnotized you. Being in your subconscious mind, they made you do illegal acts against the US Army. You're here today because the man on your right helped restore you to freedom.

"I don't want you to think you're on trial for committing illegal acts. I'm going to talk about a series of occurrences during the time of your hypnotism."

He began with Miller's arrival at the 32nd intelligence office and what had happened during the Memorial Day weekend. It included the major's introduction to Lilly before their tour of the Rosse Buurt section of Amsterdam. Remmich burst into a laugh, which made Miller follow suit. The doctor listened to a brief explanation of why they visited. Everyone laughed, and the meeting resumed.

"You took Eric to the Blues Alley bar-restaurant after that, and he met a woman, Candice Harper."

Remmich said he remembered everything so far.

"You went missing for two hours, then reappeared in the restaurant." Remmich kept quiet. "We believe you were drugged at the bar, escorted to a woman's apartment, and hypnotized."

Remmich looked shocked. "Yes. I was hypnotized. I remember now it's what Eric told me. I can't believe I allowed her to do that to me." He shifted in his chair.

Miller said, "Oh yes, it is true, Paul. A woman by the name of Tara Yako drugged you and got her spy associate, Adnaw Alzuhari, to help. I know because you got me drugged. Then the woman tried to hypnotize me, but it didn't work."

Hatch watched the expressions on Remmich's face and his body movements and concluded Remmich was accepting the facts. The doctor could tell this man was trying to remember what had happened that night.

"You resigned from the Army a few weeks later, on June thirtieth. You also agreed to act as a diplomat for V Corps in Stuttgart the same day." Remmich looked shocked but didn't say anything. The doctor told him to look at his left hand and asked, "What do you see?"

"I'm looking at a gold band, like a wedding ring. I don't understand why it's there. I didn't ask Lilly about it when I talked with her a couple days ago." He shook his head and added, "I thought she gave it to me early because she didn't want other women trying to get involved with me. We're getting married."

Miller breathed calmly, wondering what the doctor would say next. Remmich looked more confused than ever.

"Paul, you got married during the summer and vacationed in southern France."

Remmich looked at the ring while twirling it around his finger. Puzzled, he said, "I didn't know that." Hatch saw confusion on his face and thought taking a break would be helpful.

"Would you like a cup of coffee?"

Remmich nodded, and Miller said, "Good. I need a refill." They didn't talk while pouring their coffees.

While the two were in the other room, Hatch added notations to the report. He was glad Remmich seemed to accept the talk positively.

They reentered the office and took their seats. Remmich said, "This is a bit much to take in, but I want to hear more. Let's continue."

The patient's attitude pleased Hatch. "Okay, once they had you under their control, in a hypnotized state, they instructed you to get a top-secret document, one you decrypted. I'm not familiar with all the details, but it's known you emailed the information to your personal computer.

Miller added, "We've established the only way that could have been done was by you tampering with the electrical connections in the CID office for computer systems. There isn't a video camera in the control room where the wires are, but you are on videotape entering and leaving their office several times. Everyone thought you were there to resolve what you described as a computer glitch."

Remmich shook his head. Putting his coffee cup on the table, he leaned forward. "I'm ashamed of my actions, even though I wasn't aware of what I was doing."

It concerned Hatch Remmich might withdraw. He countered those words with, "Paul, your actions were without normal deliberation. You were not in control. Sure, you could carry on conversations and act normally most of the time. But you were in what we call a subliminal state of mind. This mind control made you take a back seat to a conscious way of thinking. The subconscious part of your mind was directing your actions. Hypnotizing someone limits their overall vision of the surroundings. The controlling force was your subconscious."

He leaned back in the chair and explained, "Paul, look at me. Your actions were illegal, but the real crime was hypnotizing you to steal classified information. You aren't in that state of mind anymore, which is the reason for this discussion. We hope you never get put back into it again."

Another hour passed before the meeting ended. Hatch told Remmich he could leave. Miller drove his car to the officers' club for lunch, minus Remmich.

***

Yury Nikulin signed in at the Hotel Schiller. He used the same disguise the day he and his partner visited Patch Barracks as electricians, without the company uniform. The SVR agent registered for a room on the third floor. This time, he had a small carry-on bag containing tools, a change of clothes, and toiletries for a few nights. The spy agent didn't know where to find the Remmichs' flat. But he knew Lilly managed much of the hotel. He had a plan to get the information from her.

The Russian returned to the lobby and asked the clerk about a suite for long-term rental. He told the woman he planned to spend more time in Amsterdam for business. The attendant agreed to show him a two-bedroom flat.

They took the elevator to the fourth floor and went into an empty suite. Nikulin said he wanted to look at a furnished apartment to get a good sense of the space. The clerk called her boss, Lilly Remmich, who said she would be right there. Discussion between the women about what Nikulin wanted gave Lilly an idea.

Lilly felt no reservations showing him her flat instead of another tenant's, since she couldn't do that without getting their permission in advance. When they arrived at her door, Nikulin focused on the entrance locks. She showed him several rooms. When they finished, he smiled and said although the flat was beautiful, he felt he didn't need that much space. All he wanted was a one-bedroom suite with a kitchenette. When she asked when he needed to move in, he explained he had to talk to his company about the price. They took the elevator to the lobby. The registration person gave him a spreadsheet showing costs for the type of furnished flat he wanted. It included costs per week and monthly. He thanked her and returned to the third floor room. Time was on his side.

30
The Reverse

Paul Remmich finished lunch at the PX snack bar and walked out. An NCO waited to drive him back to the V Corps building; although the building wasn't that far away, Remmich had to be watched for safety reasons. The driver called ahead to notify the office of their return. Remmich still had decryption work to do. After entering the building, he found Master Sergeant Jones waiting at the doorway. She greeted him and said to follow her.

Colonel John LaFont was in the conference room to serve as a witness and substitute for General Elliott, who was in the Middle East. Sutherland and LaFont were conversing when Jones led Remmich into the room. Sutherland took six pages from her.

He looked at Remmich and explained, "Captain, I realize you remember nothing about your resignation as a military officer and assignment as a civilian here at V Corps."

Sutherland put two resignation papers in front of Remmich. They had his signature and date. He recognized his own handwriting but didn't remember signing them. There was nothing else to ponder.

He shook his head and said, "Yes, those are my signatures."

The general didn't mince words and asked, "Do you want to return to active duty?"

Remmich straightened and said with a grin, "Yes, sir, I do."

Sutherland expected that answer, but he had to ask in front of a witness. He took the signed resignation papers and put them aside. He then placed two pages before Remmich and the same before LaFont. They signed, and Sutherland reversed them and got signatures on the copies.

He then signed all four and said, "Congratulations, Captain. I'm glad to have you back full-time." He and LaFont shook hands.

Sutherland added, "Before I forget, next week wear military attire. And get a haircut. You can go back to Amsterdam as soon as you're finished with the current decrypting work. We'll need to discuss your living arrangements since you're married." He hesitated for a moment, then asked, "You do still have your military clothes?"

Remmich smiled and answered yes.

During lunch, Eric Miller received a text to return to the doctor's office at 1400 hours. The psychiatrist wanted to review the recent diagnosis. He needed to determine if Remmich could be classified as capable of carrying out duties as a military intelligence official.

The receptionist led him into the doctor's office. He told Miller to sit down and slipped on his reading glasses. "I wanted to discuss this evaluation before I present it to the therapeutic committee. They specialize in overseeing trauma-afflicted soldiers and those with conditions like Remmich's. If you find I need to change something, please say so. I'll present the evaluation to Sutherland later."

Miller said, "I was unaware this was going up the ladder so fast. I appreciate being asked to come back to listen to your evaluation, but I'm confused. Why did you call me?"

"Because you're Paul Remmich's best friend. You can assist me. I need to provide an up-to-date evaluation of him. We're not out of the woods yet. He provided classified information to the Iraqis, and an Army court can prosecute him. I've said Remmich wasn't responsible for his actions, but I did so in therapeutic terminology." Miller nodded in agreement. "I'll explain the technical wording for you."

Doctor Hatch's evaluation explained how Remmich returned to a normal conscious condition. He then returned to the beginning of the problem, being drugged, hypnotized, and used as a mole. Occasionally the doctor asked Miller if he understood. He then outlined how Remmich performed as a spy, but his evaluation said the captain's actions weren't under his own control.

"However, Paul may have repercussions of guilt. His mind might oppose an occasional positive mental attitude and not realize why. He must regain a balanced way of thinking on his own. You can help to keep him from falling into a depression. So, I've suggested you remain stationed with him for as long as necessary."

"What about his marriage? He's living in Amsterdam. I don't think his wife even knows he's reenlisted and been brought out of his hypnotized state. Where do we go from here?"

"General Sutherland will decide. I'm a doctor, not an MI specialist."

***

Sutherland expected a telephone call from Hatch soon after lunch. He didn't know the doctor was having a discussion with Miller. He was working on being patient when Jones buzzed him and said he had a caller on hold. She told him the guy had a foreign accent. He punched the button.

"Hello, this is General Sutherland."

"Good afternoon, sir. I'm glad to be speaking with you. I guess you're wondering who I am."

"Well, sir, from your accent, I could guess and say you're from Saudi Arabia."

"You are very insulting, General Sutherland. I am Colonel Arif Yildiz from Iraq. I am calling to tell you that our loss of Paul Remmich and Major Eric Miller is an issue. For now, the loss is temporary. Our goal has not gone unnoticed by Tariq'Allah. Let me assure you that Mr. Remmich's past efforts will not go to waste. We obtained one secret formula from the United States Army, and now we will find another secret. Let me say the Iraqi leadership and I consider these two men traitors, and there is a bounty on them. As far as we are concerned, these men belong to us. We will find them."

Sutherland held back a laugh and smiled. "Yes. I think I understand. You mean while they were hypnotized, they belonged to you, Mr. Yildiz. I know you were using them as tools to get classified information. I think you are the one who faces a threat. You will not succeed, Yildiz. Iraq will pay for these illegal deeds." He waited for a moment and added, "I have the two men in question, and they will continue in active service to the United States."

Yildiz replied, "It is in our blood to not surrender until we win. We will find them. Goodbye."

The phone line went dead. Sutherland pulled a pad of paper in front of him and made notes of the call. He knew time was on his side. He dialed the HQ station in Heidelberg and spoke with his commanding officer's secretary. General Stanton wasn't in. A decision needed to be made.

***

Tony Belotti made the call to his CO in Wiesbaden. The receptionist transferred the call.

"What's the good news, Lieutenant?"

"Not good. I'm outside the buildings where the two Iraqis lived. They've moved out."

The colonel commented, "They may have moved elsewhere or out of the country."

"A moving company has trucks here now at each of their apartment buildings. The moving official told me they rented the furniture in both apartments and all of it belongs to his company. I asked if he had the names of the renters. He read the agreement papers; Adnaw Alzuhari and Tara Yako. Looking for these two spies now will be like looking for a needle in a haystack."

"Don't leave the area," commanded Bradley. "Search each apartment and look for anything that might be of use. Then call back."

Forty minutes later, the lieutenant called his boss. He told the colonel about finding a receiver-transmitter in each flat.

"Someone's been listening to them, but it's all I can tell you for now."

***

Jones alerted Sutherland, "Sir, Colonel Bradley is on the phone. I'll transfer you now."

"Hello, David, what news do you have for me?"

"It's not good, Ed." He outlined the situation in Amsterdam.

"That sonofabitch!" yelled Sutherland.

"Who?"

"An Iraqi colonel named Yildiz. I got off the phone with him right before you called. He telephoned me. Apparently, from what Miller told me, he's the CO of the two Iraqi spies your men are tracking in Amsterdam. They may have left for good, but we don't know for sure. Yildiz wants my men back, and he says he'll keep at it until he does."

Bradley chuckled and said, "Yeah, and how the hell is he going to get that done?"

"Oh, he was clever enough to get them in the first place, so I imagine he has other tricks up his espionage sleeve. Anyway, one of those men, Paul Remmich, married a Dutch woman, and her family owns the Hotel Schiller, where I had your men stay. I want them to remain there to protect her until I can figure out a plan." The general explained that since Remmich reenlisted, he would work on base in Würzburg during the week.

"I'll keep my men in Amsterdam, but do you have any idea how long it's going to be?"

"I'm hoping to have a plan later today for my men, but no later than tomorrow. In the meantime, you have to let the agents remain in Amsterdam."

Bradley explained he needed a few moments to look over the personnel and put him on hold. Sutherland read emails to pass the time.

A new message appeared. Yildiz was the sender. "General Sutherland, we will do what is necessary to bring Paul Remmich and Eric Miller back to us. Paul Remmich belongs to us because he signed an agreement with Iraq as a civilian. If he's not back in Amsterdam by Monday, there will be consequences." The last part of the email didn't mention Miller. Sutherland had no idea why.

Bradley came back online and told the general Belotti and Hannon would alternate with two others. Satisfied, the general thanked him.

He made another call to his CO in Heidelberg. Stanton still wasn't available, and Sutherland was advised to call back.

The desk phone distracted him again, and the master sergeant said, "Sir, Colonel Hatch is on the line."

Hatch told Sutherland he'd completed Remmich's evaluation. The CO told him to come to his office.

The general acted quickly; keeping two men alive was paramount. First, they needed to get Remmich and Miller away from the area. The Iraqi might get lucky. He called Miller and told him to come to the office as quickly as he could.

The major drove to the headquarters building and walked rapidly to the general's reception area. He found Hatch sitting and reading the evaluation.

Sutherland walked out of his office and said, "Gentlemen, let's talk."

The psychiatrist handed a copy of the evaluation to the general, and the doctor reviewed the psychiatric assessment.

Hatch finished the evaluation report and added, "I'm under obligation to send a copy of this to the medical chain of command in Heidelberg."

Sutherland knew he had to speak with his CO before Remmich's evaluation got into the hands of the Heidelberg team. He thanked Hatch and said he'd contact the doctor at a later date. The psychiatrist left the office, but Miller sat quietly, waiting for dismissal. The general spent a few moments in silence, thinking about a scheme to thwart the Iraqi threats.

As the major got up, deciding he could leave, Sutherland said to him, "Hold up." Sitting down, the general handed him a copy of the email from the Iraqi colonel. "This guy, Yildiz, the sonofabitch from Iraq, sent this after I had a phone conversation with him earlier."

"You spoke with this guy?" Sutherland nodded. "You mean he had the balls to call you in this office and then send an email?" Sutherland nodded, and Miller continued. "Sir, this guy is ruthless. We've got to protect Paul and Lilly. There's no way we're going to lose them."

The general liked it when an officer was on the same wavelength. "Don't discount yourself as a sought-after defector either. Anyhow, I tried to call the Heidelberg office about this matter a little while ago, but my contact was in a meeting. I need to do something with both of you, not just Remmich." He leaned back and rested his arm on the chair arm. "His wife will be protected. But until I talk with my CO, I'm not sure what I can do at this moment."

The intercom buzzer interrupted him. Jones informed him General Stanton was on the line.

Sutherland thanked her, but before picking up the phone, he said, "This might be our answer. I want you to listen." He put the line on speakerphone.

"Hello, John. Thanks for calling back."

Stanton said, "Ed, my secretary notified me that you called twice. Sorry, but I was on a NATO conference call for over an hour. What can I do for you?"

"I want to introduce you to Major Eric Miller." They exchanged greetings. "He and Captain Remmich are West Point grads, and friends."

Vhen you're finished, report to my office." He walked over r and told him to come along to his office when Remmich e with his work.

hey walked into the reception area a half-hour later. Jones he general.

Send them in."

utherland liked tense situations, how the adrenalin rush s heart beat faster and send more oxygen to his brain. He he captain to sit, then greeted Miller.

You're going stateside as soon as you can get your duffel cked. You can also take a suitcase of civvies if you wish. of the urgency, you will take separate helicopters to get sonal things, one to Amsterdam for you, Captain, and one to rg for you, Major."

he general looked at his watch and notified Jones. He told ontact the chief warrant officer at Patch Barracks and USAF nmander at Rhein/Main in Frankfurt. They sat patiently and vhile he fiddled with the computer. Minutes later, he was on ne discussing departure plans for the two men. The call ten minutes.

ones called again. "Sir, the Air Force commander is on the

utherland had known this man since his assignment to y, and they engaged in small talk for a few minutes. nd then explained the state of affairs.

hey saw a smile on his face and heard a friendly, "Thank ke" from Sutherland.

he call then ended.

You guys are going to fly stateside tomorrow with the Air A driver will take you to the aviation station, where your ers will be waiting."

Ie leaned on the table, folded his hands, and looked down oment. The general didn't like what he needed to say next.

the explosion. One agent took away his suitcase, and the other one handcuffed him.

Nikulin said, "You can't arrest me. I am protected by international law at the Russian embassy here in Amsterdam."

They ignored him, knowing he'd lied, and put him in the back seat of a van.

One of the CID men said, "We have authority here from the US consulate." He smiled and slammed the door shut, without securing Nikulin in the seatbelt. The driver locked the back doors and back windows.

Four hours later, they reached Patch Barracks. They accused Nikulin of espionage and murder. His credentials identified him as a Russian. They fingerprinted and photographed him. They also found the USB that had the classified information about the scientific project. Sutherland was notified, but he decided not to make the matter known outside V Corps. The higher command approved the decision.

It took two days for the Interpol records to arrive. Nikulin's identity was verified and compared to the SVR connection, fingerprints, photographs from hidden cameras in France and Germany, and the espionage connections. Unbeknownst to him, secret police teams let him lead them to other spies.

One of those caught was Vladimir Usmanov, the very man who'd trained the young Nikulin. The older Russian was one of the spies in Germany. He got caught with a remote radio receiver and compact recorder outside the German Chancellery in Berlin.

Sutherland imagined the hell Putin would raise if he found out about his spy's capture. The general snickered and thought, *Yeah, in retaliation, the sonofabitch would order another cyberattack.*

Senator Karper and Representative Martin were still irritated about the cyberattack by Putin's spy team during the elections. They also thought it was better to keep the matter quiet and let Putin find out months later one of his SVR agents was missing. The

"Lilly can't go along right now. I'll assign CID agents to watch her until we figure out how to handle the Iraqi situation."

Remmich looked at the floor, leaned on his legs, and sighed. He looked up and said, "Yes, sir, I understand." An order is an order.

Miller asked, "What about our cars, General?"

"I didn't think about that. Well, we can have the cars shipped to Fort Belvoir. It won't be soon, but you'll have transportation."

They shook hands, and he said, "I won't be in touch again until you're stateside."

They left.

***

Yury Nikulin checked out of Hotel Schiller at 5:00 p.m. The front desk clerk thanked him. The manager on duty, Lilly, asked him if he was still considering renting. Nikulin repeated he needed to discuss it with his company before a contract agreement. He walked out a happy man because the two door locks on the Remmich apartment door had been easy to pick. Inside the flat, he got into Paul's computer and copied the decrypted photosynthesis information onto his flash drive.

He got to the car and began to remove the facial disguise. He didn't quite finish cleaning his face before two undercover CID agents walked up to his car. The photograph they had confirmed his face and haircut, only the mustache was gone. It didn't matter, because he wasn't getting away. Outside cameras at Patch Barracks had recorded him and the undercover partner walking into the MP station. It was the second time they entered the post as different contractors. The murder of the two CID agents at V Corps was still a hot item at their office. His identification from the bomb attack at Patch Barracks also came from base camera surveillance. The authorities confirmed it was the Russians who devastated the post entrance. They were the only ones who left the MP building before

Sutherland spent 25 minutes giving a detailed account of Remmich and Miller.

Stanton, not a man to procrastinate, said, "Okay, you want to get them out of Germany. When? And where do you want to send them?" Miller was all ears.

"This coming weekend. I want them transferred to Fort Belvoir, but I'm not too sure about Remmich's condition. I think all of this may be too much for him to take at one time."

Stanton said, "I can assign them to Fort Belvoir, which isn't far from the Walter Reed Medical Center in Bethesda. If your captain doesn't do well, we can have him transferred to Bethesda."

The conversation continued for another ten minutes. The general put Sutherland on hold to contact the G-1 office.

Stanton came back on the line. "Major Miller, are you in agreement with being with Captain Remmich?"

"Yes, sir. As General Sutherland told you, the psychiatrist recommends I stay with him. The doctor is aware we're good friends. I believe I can help him stay in a normal state of mind. He's been through a lot, and it would be good therapy for him."

Stanton said, "I like the way you think, Major." The general then advised after they got stateside, he and Remmich would work at Fort Belvoir. "Anyway, I'll recommend a sabbatical for him not to exceed six months. You will be with him during this time." He told Sutherland to hold on and transferred the line to the G-1 personnel office for transfer approval.

Sutherland told the secretary to take care of the paperwork after it was faxed to their office. He hung up and walked into the security intelligence office, where he observed Remmich concentrating on translating an encrypted document. Miller was sitting at another desk.

Sutherland leaned his hands on the desk and looked at some of the decryption. He asked Remmich how much more time he needed.

"I'm almost finished, sir."

"When you're finished, report to my office." He walked over to Miller and told him to come along to his office when Remmich was done with his work.

They walked into the reception area a half-hour later. Jones alerted the general.

"Send them in."

Sutherland liked tense situations, how the adrenalin rush made his heart beat faster and send more oxygen to his brain. He invited the captain to sit, then greeted Miller.

"You're going stateside as soon as you can get your duffel bags packed. You can also take a suitcase of civvies if you wish. Because of the urgency, you will take separate helicopters to get your personal things, one to Amsterdam for you, Captain, and one to Würzburg for you, Major."

The general looked at his watch and notified Jones. He told her to contact the chief warrant officer at Patch Barracks and USAF base commander at Rhein/Main in Frankfurt. They sat patiently and talked, while he fiddled with the computer. Minutes later, he was on the phone discussing departure plans for the two men. The call ended in ten minutes.

Jones called again. "Sir, the Air Force commander is on the line."

Sutherland had known this man since his assignment to Germany, and they engaged in small talk for a few minutes. Sutherland then explained the state of affairs.

They saw a smile on his face and heard a friendly, "Thank you, Mike" from Sutherland.

The call then ended.

"You guys are going to fly stateside tomorrow with the Air Force. A driver will take you to the aviation station, where your helicopters will be waiting."

He leaned on the table, folded his hands, and looked down for a moment. The general didn't like what he needed to say next.

Printed in Great Britain
by Amazon

41198727R00145